The Last Wise Woman

—The Wise Woman Chronicles—

Kathleen Baldwin

WHAT CRITICS SAY ABOUT KATHLEEN BALDWIN'S BOOKS

THE STRANJE HOUSE NOVELS

"A *School for Unusual Girls* is enticing from the first sentence ...Baldwin has an ear for period dialogue as she draws us into this world of sharp, smart young ladies who are actually being trained and deployed for the British war effort by the mysterious head-mistress, Miss Stranje. It's speculative historical fiction, with a trace of steampunk inventiveness."

— ***New York Times Sunday Book Review***

"Sign me up for Kathleen Baldwin's *School for Unusual Girls*. It sucked me in from the first few pages and kept me reading until late into the night."

—**Meg Cabot**, #1 NYT-USA *Today bestselling author of The Princess Diaries*

"Spellbinding! A *School for Unusual Girls* is a beautifully written tale that will appeal to every girl who has ever felt different . . . a true page-turner!"

–**Lorraine Heath**, NYT-USA *Today* bestselling author

"I enjoyed this story immensely and I closed my kindle with a satisfied sigh." —**YA Insider** on *Exile for Dreamers*

"(Readers) seeking period romance with a twist need look no further." —**Kirkus** on *Exile for Dreamers*

"An outstanding alternative history series entry and a must-have for teen libraries."

—**School Library Journal** on *Refuge for Masterminds*

"***Refuge for Masterminds*** moves at a fast pace from the first page and doesn't stop. Although it is written with a young adult audience in mind, it is a fun and enjoyable novel and will also appeal to adult readers." —***Historical Novel Society***

"I am in love with the Stranje House novels. Seriously, in love."
—***Book Briefs***

My Notorious Aunt Series:

"Kathleen Baldwin evokes some very tender moments as Willa learns that love will find a way in this warm and charming tale."
– ***Romantic Times*** 4½ Stars on *Mistaken Kiss*

"...laughter aplenty... sparkling dialog that left me with a smile on my face. I highly recommend this engaging Traditional Regency." – Cheryl Sneed, ***Rakehell Reviews*** on *Mistaken Kiss*

"Baldwin knows how to write characters who make me laugh and make me cry. Her sweet Regency historicals are a delightful way to spend an afternoon reading."
— **Suzanne Ferrell**, USA Today Bestselling Author
on *The Persuasion of Miss Kate*

"I love these "Aunt Honore" books and this one does not fail. ... I really enjoyed this sweet story and the wonderful characters."
– **Clean Romance Reviews**

"...a charming book, with the lightness and freshness of a sunny day in the park."
– Yvonne Choi, ***Rakehell Reviews*** on *Cut from the Same Cloth*

Other Books by Kathleen Baldwin

The My Notorious Aunt series:

Humorous Regency Romps

Lady Fiasco
Mistaken Kiss
Cut from the Same Cloth
The Persuasion of Miss Kate

The Stranje House Novels:

A School for Unusual Girls
Exile for Dreamers
Refuge for Masterminds
Harbor for the nightingale
Sanctuary for Seers (Coming soon)

A Regency Novella

The Highwayman Came Waltzing

Contemporary Teen Fantasy

Diary of a Teenage Fairy Godmother

The LAST Wise Woman

Kathleen Baldwin

The Wise Woman Chronicles

INK LION BOOKS

Thank you for buying an authorized copy of this book. Your investment keeps authors writing high quality stories for readers. Copyrights protect and encourage creativity.

This story is a work of Fiction. Apart from a few well-known public figures, all other characters appearing in this book are fictitious. Any resemblance to actual persons, living or dead, is purely coincidental. The characters, entities, organizations, and events por-trayed in this novel are either products of the author's imagination or are used fictionally.

THE LAST WISE WOMAN

Published by Ink Lion Books

5100 Eldorado Pkwy Ste 102-518
McKinney TX 75070

Edited by Jason Letts of Imbue Editing

Some images for cover art by Canstock/Goodstudio

First Edition September 2022

Printed in the United States of America

0 9 8 7 6 5 4 3 2 1

To Ryder's mother,
for her devotion to this project,
her valuable insights, and support.

And to you, my brave and loyal
readers, for following me into a
completely different kind of story.

May God pour out His richest
blessings on you all.

Remember, my daughter, who you are.

Prologue
The Novice Awakens

Long before I met Ryder or the Wise Woman, I drowned.

Water splashed and clapped hands, closing above my head. Bubbles fizzed, gushing past my nose as I slid toward the bottom of the pool. I tried to climb up, reaching, clawing, grabbing at the water, only to have it slither between my fingers and toes as I slipped further and further from the shimmering surface.

Hopeless. I gave up, holding onto the last swallow of air as it swelled out my cheeks and pressed for escape. One by one, traitorous bubbles trickled out of my mouth. Wiggly pockets of lost hope drifted up toward the light. I sank to a place where babies do not splash happily in the sunshine—down into a gray cocoon where death awaited.

No!

I gasped for air and shook my head.

Not me.

The drowning child wasn't me. I wasn't even wet. And I was eleven, not a toddler. But I knew that baby.

"Jace!"

I ran to our motel door and flung it open. From the second-floor landing, I saw him—my little cousin floating in the pool. I screamed for my mother and raced down iron and concrete stairs, my footsteps echoing in the empty courtyard like gunshots. Finally, I got down to the deck and slid belly first onto the pool's edge. Reaching into the water, I caught hold of his tiny arm and yanked him up to the air he craved.

Except he didn't breathe.

Didn't move.

He hung in my arms like a broken doll. I shook him. Wild with panic, I demanded to know how he'd gotten down there. "How!"

No answer—only the soft steady drip of water from his dangling arms. Death had lulled him to sleep. I screamed louder for my mother.

Terrified, I turned him upside down, held him by his ankles and tried to shake the water out of his lungs. Tears blurred my vision. I pleaded with him—pleaded with God. "Live!" I shrieked. "Live."

Letting go of one leg, I slapped his back. Water and vomit spewed from his mouth and nose. He choked, coughed . . .

And, finally, he cried.

I held him tight, rubbing his back. Tears stung my eyes until I felt my mother's hand on my shoulder. She lifted the child out of my arms, and I crumpled to my knees on the hot pool deck, rocking and sobbing louder than the toddler.

That was the day I knew for certain I was different. I'd always suspected I wasn't quite normal, but after Jace drowned and I drowned with him, I never wondered again. Later, in college, professors hooked me up to a machine that monitored brain waves. We discovered there were times when my brainwaves dropped like a rock into the theta range even though I was wide awake. Maybe that explained some things, maybe it didn't.

This anomaly, this curse, this blessing that makes me different, has both ruined my life and made it wonderful beyond my wildest imaginings.

Jace was my cousin, sunny blonde, bright, sweet, and only two years old when we drowned. He'd been staying with us that summer while his mother struggled through a difficult pregnancy. Five months later, Jace died in an automobile accident.

I wondered endlessly if I had merely staved off the inevitable. Had I altered Jace's timeline or kept it on track?

Chapter 1
The Llama Girl Cometh

Coldwater, Minnesota, twelve years later, on the day of the Great Quake

That afternoon, when everything we thought we knew about earthquakes changed, I sat at the Coldwater Herald news desk doodling. Sun glinted off my monitor as I waited for a graphics program to update changes to a photograph.

"We need a new computer," I said to no one in particular. My complaint floated through the sunny newspaper office as if it were a soiled candy wrapper caught on the breeze. No one responded. The old printing press hummed noisily in the backroom, and my boss, Ollie, sat encased in his glass office, door shut, talking on the phone with considerable agitation.

The sluggish update spinner on my screen continued to whirl. So, I rested my chin in my palm and gazed out the front window at two centuries of architecture lining Main Street. I knew each and every building by heart. I knew the way the maple floorboards in the drugstore creaked and how the thick walls in Maggie's Emporium trapped a musty lavender smell that always made me sneeze. First National Bank had an ATM, but I liked going inside and tracing my fingers over the 1920's brass scrollwork while waiting for a teller. And, like everyone else in town, I knew exactly how many donuts Mr. Larsen baked every morning for Coldwater's only coffee shop.

Home.

I came back during my first year of college—to bury Dad.

Three years later, though, I was still there. *Yeah, I get it. Education is important.* I liked school, and I planned to go back. Or so I'd told myself. It could be that grief and guilt were just too bulky to cram into a suitcase and haul off to school. I didn't know. Anyway, there was the farm to run until my older brother could finish school, and after that I just never felt right about leaving.

Maybe it was because the people in Coldwater didn't care that I was different.

Sure, some of them might cross the street to avoid me if they had an ugly secret they wanted to hide. On the other hand, long before anyone scheduled a sonogram over in Rochester or up in the Twin Cities, they'd come running to ask me the sex of their baby. I tried to keep stuff like that to a minimum, but it had a way of slipping out.

Everyone in town took my strangeness for granted. No one wanted to run me through yet another MRI machine, make me take a bunch of pointless tests, or try to figure out why I am the way I am. It didn't seem to bother them. I was simply part of their world. As ordinary as the donuts in Mr. Larsen's bakery case every morning—two dozen jelly-filled, one dozen lemon cream, two dozen glazed, another twelve with sprinkles, and three dozen chocolate with fudge frosting.

Coldwater was home.

As much as I loved this town, for months I'd felt something tugging at me, some invisible force pulling at me. Except, I couldn't leave Coldwater, it's my home. Maybe that feeling was just my imagination.

Relax, I told myself. *Don't think about it.*

So I didn't.

The stoplight down the street blinked from red to green, and Mrs. Donovan in her faded green Chevy turned the corner. I closed my eyes, basking in the summer sun radiating through the front window.

That may have been my mistake, right there.

Drifting off.

If I could go back to that moment and force myself to stay sharp, to pay attention and concentrate, maybe everything would be different. Maybe destiny would have picked someone else for this task. Maybe the world wouldn't be tumbling into the next ice age of ignorance.

Maybe.

Then again, destiny can be strange and perplexing. It might have snared me no matter what I did. Destiny seemed pretty stubborn in that respect. Still, there was a remote possibility that if I had stayed alert and been ready all this might have turned out differently.

In my defense, earthquakes don't happen in Minnesota.

They don't.

Scratch that. *They didn't.*

There's no scary fault line running up the middle of the state. No volcano nearby. It's Minnesota. Land of 10,000 lakes. Snow and ice. Moose and milk cows.

At exactly 3:29 the floorboards shook.

I glanced down to see what was going wrong with my shoes. Then the ceiling rattled, and our lights swung crazily. The front windows shattered. Glass exploded into the room.

I clutched the edge of my desk and readied myself for armageddon.

Had I been thinking properly, I would've gotten *under* the desk. But like I said, I'd been dozing off, and this was Minnesota. They didn't teach earthquake preparedness in our schools. Tornado preparedness, *yes*. What to do in a flood, *sure*. How to survive a blizzard, *heck yeah*. Earthquake, *no*.

I couldn't look away.

The whole world shook.

When the earth split open, it sounded like we were in the bowling alley of the gods. All the other sounds, breaking glass, horns blaring, screaming, rattling, and clinking, all those other noises seemed incidental. One low gut-quivering sound reminded us we were not in control. A roaring whoosh, a thunderous roll, a series of loud bangs and fierce jolts, like gigantic bowling pins crashing down around us. And then...

A fissure ripped open Main Street.

The stoplight toppled over.

Slabs of the red-block stone walls from Maggie's Emporium plummeted to the sidewalk, splattering, sending shards of rock flying into the air.

All this happened in mere seconds. I gaped, unable to fathom the earth shaking apart. One of our overhead lights crashed to the floor. Still, I stood there, not believing any of it.

Later, Ollie told me he saw a chunk of ceiling plaster fall on my head. That could explain why everything suddenly went dark.

Night.

In this case, at 3:33 in the afternoon, it fell on me alone. The rest of Coldwater remained sunny, shaken, torn, and yet still bathed in stark unrepentant daylight.

Not me.

Night swallowed me up in one enormous gulp.

Crickets chirped. Everyone knows crickets usually tune-up in the evening. Except that afternoon I distinctly heard crickets and frogs. Before the quake, there hadn't been so much as a vapor trail in the sky. Now Prussian blue filled the horizon and charcoal black stretched overhead. The newsroom ceiling vanished. Stars twinkled back at me, and a bright full moon illuminated my surroundings.

This sudden night appeared to be coming from somewhere else, some other land. A land where storks foraged beside a meandering stream dipping their long bills among the rushes. While the back of the office remained as it was, this night someplace else arose in front of me. Our shattered front window disappeared, and a tall skinny hill jutted up where Main Street should have been.

First the earthquake, and now this.

I stumbled back, bumping into my chair. It clunked against my desk, but the clatter drowned in the growing oboe-like song of bullfrogs. Night birds trilled, and the crickets sawed louder and louder until I was sure Ollie would come charging out here and demand the racket stop. But mist shrouded his office, and vines snaked up the sides.

That was when I realized this was a vision.

No stopping it now.

I plunked down in my chair and lowered my face into my hands. When I finally gathered the courage to peek out from my fingers, a young woman holding a shepherd's staff stood in front of me. She had thick, dark, shoulder-length hair, and no way could she be from our century—not wearing those heavy fur boots and that hand-woven tunic. I couldn't tell if she was Mongolian, Peruvian, or from somewhere else entirely. Behind her stood a herd of llamas, with a few long-haired goats mixed in, or maybe they were sheep—I couldn't tell—and a handful of geese.

All of them seemed to be looking at me.

I'd never been this close to a llama before. The largest of

the herd stood protective and alert beside the small shepherdess. This guardian llama seemed extraordinarily tall. She looked a little like a camel, only she was covered in thick white hair that hung in short curly dreadlocks everywhere except for her curious face.

She blinked uncommonly long eyelashes at me. Then, as if understanding my unspoken comments about her appearance, the animal chortled—a weird mixture of a goose honking and a goat bleating. The llama's chin went up, and I thought for a minute she was going to attack me. Instead, she stretched out her long neck and snuffled the papers on the edge of my credenza.

Her floppy lips opened in a malicious grin, and that ornery creature crumpled up the Jorgensen wedding announcement for tomorrow's paper. Then, as if it tasted bad, she let the wad of paper flutter down past her furry neck to the floor. With a decisive grunt, she stomped her two-toed foot right on the middle of Mellie Jorgensen's face.

"Stop!" I lunged for it and yanked what was left of the announcement out from under her sharp, pointy toes. "Are all llamas this rude?" I muttered and tried to smooth the torn wet edges of the photo.

The llama shepherdess thumped her staff down in front of the tall fiend, who reluctantly stopped snorting around in my papers. Llama-herder girl looked to be about thirteen or fourteen. Her brown cheeks were smudged, but that didn't mar her dignity. She stood with the poise of a young queen, except instead of a crown perched atop her straight black hair she had a pointy red cap with a tiny bell. Rows of Aztec-looking symbols embroidered along the edge of her coarsely woven cloak captivated my attention.

"Sophie." She startled me. Hers was a gentle voice, musical and sweet, haunting and flute-like. Yet, when she called my name, it seemed to awaken every cell in my body, even my bones shivered with aliveness. "You must leave this place and go in search of the Wise Woman."

Now, I've watched enough TV to know that if I started taking orders from apparitions it was just a hop, skip, and a jump into the loony bin. So, I kept mum.

The herd of llamas let loose with a few disgruntled whimpers. It sounded like a room full of unhappy preschoolers. Llama girl and her pesky paper-demolishing companion exchanged meaningful glances.

Yes, meaningful. I lived on our family farm with my brother and his wife. Our sheep and goats had a wild-eyed stare that either meant "Keep away from me!" or "Hmm, I wonder if there's anything edible on you?" This big llama was different. Plain as day, the old gal's expression said, "Uh oh, Llama-herder, are you sure you've got the right girl?"

The shepherdess nodded as if she understood.

I took a deep breath. "No, your llama is right. There's been some mistake. I can't run off and hunt for your missing Wise Woman."

Thick black hair whisked the top of her shoulders as the Llama-girl shook her head in disagreement. "Not my Wise Woman. *Yours.* And she is coming to the end of her journey." The girl pointed her staff at me. "You are the novice, Sophie, chosen for this generation."

Novice?

"Oh, now, see, that proves there's been some sort of cosmic mistake. I'm not even a Catholic. There's a lovely convent over in Rochester chock full of willing novices. Thank you for dropping by, but as you can see I already have a job."

That wretched llama rippled her lips in a wicked sneer. Before I could stop her, she spit bits of paper and green goo onto the center of my screen. I cringed and grabbed a tissue. While I turned my back to wipe it off, that surly animal clamped her teeth around my brand-new blue-line pencil and cracked it in half.

I scooted the rest of my papers and equipment across the worktable away from my uninvited guest. "At least, I did have a job before that animal of yours came in here and started vandalizing everything."

"Daughter of Eve, do you not feel it?" Llama girl searched my face.

I looked away, hoping to escape her scrutiny. She couldn't have known there'd been something plaguing me. I shrugged and immediately regretted it when sadness overwhelmed her features.

She gestured with her staff, encompassing the newspaper office in back of us and her mountain and pasture in one broad stroke. "I know you feel it. All around you, wisdom is seeping out of the world. You must find the Wise Woman and preserve what is left. Time grows short."

How could a girl so young look so incredibly mournful, so long-suffering? It was as if she'd been watching civilization for a thousand years, witnessed every act of cruelty, every dying child, every bomb exploding, every killer plague and volcano, every lamb gone missing.

"The earth itself is groaning," she said.

That was when the first aftershock hit.

The newsroom rattled so hard I thought the huge stone walls would tumble down. Was this part of the vision or reality? The shepherdess and her llamas stood with their heads bowed and eyes closed until the shaking stopped.

"Was that real?" I asked.

She gave me a single nod.

"This earthquake can't have anything to do with wisdom. How can they possibly be related to one another?"

She gazed at me, gentle and kind but bright with expectation. Too bright. I felt bad knowing that I was bound to disappoint her. She smiled. "This is good. See how you ask the right questions? You *are* the novice."

The llama beside her blinked, big-eyed, at me and looked more thoughtful as she gnawed on the splintered remains of my pencil. Fragments of it dropped forgotten from her mouth. For the first time, her expression wasn't completely skeptical.

Llama girl smoothed her fingers over the animal's white fur. "Humankind without wisdom..." She shook her head. "Even the earth trembles at the thought."

Her llama moaned like a plaintive toddler.

"The Wise Woman is dying. Find her soon or all is lost." The bell atop Llama girl's hat jingled as she turned to leave.

"Wait! I don't understand. What *all* is lost? Find her? Where?"

"Follow your instincts."

Did she know how hard I'd been trying to ignore my troublesome instincts over the past few years? Did she really expect me to dust them off and use them like a rusty compass to locate one woman among billions? "My instincts are gone."

She glanced back and almost smiled. "You'll find her in the desert under a palm tree."

Chapter 2
Aftershocks

Ollie lifted a chunk of plaster off me. I lay on the floor, still stunned. The colors of night faded away, as if Llama girl's world had been nothing more than a watercolor, taking with it the storks and crooning frogs. The afternoon sun glinted through our shattered news-room window.

"Sophie!" Ollie brushed bits of plaster off my face. "Are you all right? Say something?"

"The llamas..." I muttered.

"Llamas?" He squinted at me. "Lay still, kid. You must have a head injury." Ollie hollered for our printing press operator. "Swede! Call 911! Sophie's delirious. We've gotta get her to the hospital."

Swede picked his way through the rubble and pointed vigorously toward where Main Street used to be. "How in tarnation do you expect an ambulance to get across the Grand Canyon out there?"

Swede tended to exaggerate. So, despite my pounding head, I tried to sit up.

"Don't move," Ollie ordered, and the two of them set to arguing about toppled cell towers and busted landlines.

"I'm okay," I mumbled and leaned up to look out of our missing front window. The chasm wasn't anywhere near as big as the Grand Canyon–more like a deep, deep, very deep ravine. Later, it would come to be known as the Main Street Gorge.

Ollie rubbed his neck. "Anyhoo, leastwise she isn't bleeding."

"Not visibly." Swede is not an optimist. "She could have a concussion. Internal bleeding, or—"

A third aftershock hit.

Plaster hailed on us. Ollie swore, and both he and Swede ducked under my worktable. This time I had the good sense to scoot under my desk. I huddled under it, getting kicked by some invisible force and hoping Llama girl had been merely a hallucination from getting conked on the head.

On the tile, right beside my knee, jiggling like water on a hot skillet, was the eraser end of my blue line pencil. I grabbed it and, despite my quaking universe, inspected the distinctive bite marks.

When the earth finally stopped doing a hula dance, we crawled out from under our hiding places. Without a word, like migrating geese fleeing winter, we headed out of the building. Ollie kept his arm around me as the three of us shuffled over hunks of plaster, broken glass, and scattered office equipment. We gingerly stepped over what used to be our front door and went out into the sunlight to check on our neighbors and stare into the chasm.

Across the great divide, Maggie sobbed as she struggled to climb over a pile of red stones. Those stones had been set in place a century before she was born. An old maid with no children, the Emporium was all she had. She cried her way over each stone as if they were dying children.

One by one we all gathered on our respective sides of our groaning world and stood in awed silence.

There would be time for our tears later. Even Maggie stopped crying as we stared down into the abyss, at torn sewer pipes burbling into the pit, upside down stoplights, fizzling wires, cars wedged on their sides at the bottom–alarms blaring uselessly, and huge chunks of sidewalk and pavement strewn two stories below our feet. We shouldn't have stood so near the edge. What if it happened again? But none of us could turn away from the massive lightning-strike gash that ran up the center of our hometown.

So, is this what happens when the Earth grieves?

"How far does this thing go?" Mr. Larsen hollered to Ollie, pointing down the length of the fissure.

Ollie shook his head and shrugged. "Won't know 'til we get a hold of a radio." He turned to Swede and asked about the newspaper's prize possession, our antique printing press. "Did the Heidelberg survive?"

Swede rubbed the back of his neck. "Yah, I'll have to dust the plaster out of her, but I expect that ole' press would survive a nuclear bomb."

"We need to put out a special edition. And I don't care if I have to send the story to the AP by carrier pigeon. We've got to get word out to the rest of the world." Ollie rubbed his hands together. And I knew why. He was literally standing on the biggest story of his career. "Sophie, you don't look so good. You up to working on the story?"

I couldn't write. Not now. I had a groaning world and two-toed llamas prancing through my brain. When I'd crawled out from under my desk, I'd noticed a green smear on my computer screen. Either that was llama spit or I'd gone stark raving crazy. I didn't try to explain. "How can we write without electricity or internet?"

"The old-fashioned way." He looked positively excited at the prospect. "There's an old Smith-Corona typewriter in the storeroom."

Swede snorted. "Yah, and I suppose you plan to run the press by hooking a couple plow horses up to a flywheel?"

Ollie gave him a drawled out an emphatic Norwegian no, "Nooowh, I've got a back-up generator in the storeroom. I'll siphon the gas out of my car if I have to. We're gonna get this story out to the world."

I heaved a worried sigh. "For all we know, the rest of the world has been hit, too."

"Yah, you might have something there." Ollie scratched at his graying stubble. "Find our radio, Swede. I saw it in the printing room yesterday."

Just then Mr. Larson came hurrying through the debris toward us. Looking like a balding middle-aged rapper, he held a small boom box to his ear, and shouted out bits of a news report. "8.7 magnitude. Shook the whole Mississippi region. Iowa. Missouri. Illinois. Tennessee. Arkansas. All the way to New Orleans. First quake of this magnitude to hit the continental U.S. since 1964 when a 9.2 hit central Alaska."

We gathered close to listen. To mourn. To share our shock.

"Lord, save us..." He lowered the radio and in a solemn tone announced, "They're saying the Mississippi has changed course." I shivered as he continued relaying the report. "The entire eastern half of the country is experiencing tremors." He set the radio on the ground as if he didn't want to hear anything more.

A cloyingly sweet scent of donuts wafted from Mr. Larson's apron, so ordinary, but amidst the crumbled buildings and devastation it seemed grossly out of place. Nausea nearly gagged me.

An earthquake that big might've hit our farm. Suddenly I had to find my brother. "Ollie, I've got to go check on Danny."

"Right, kid, I'll drive you."

"No, I'm okay. You stay and write your story."

"You sure?"

I wasn't sure of anything, but I said, "Yeah," and waved goodbye. I stepped over a fallen street sign, avoided a tilted fire hydrant gushing into the chasm, and crunched on an incredible amount of broken glass as I dashed back into the newsroom for my purse and keys. With a deep breath, I slipped out the back door of the office. Our parking lot had a few snake-sized fissures, but there sat my jeep in one glorious piece, untouched by the chaos around us. That jeep was five years older than me and sported more than one rust spot, but as I grabbed hold of the faded green metal and slid into the driver's seat it felt like being cradled in the arms of an old friend.

I trembled—the aftereffects of shock I suppose. It took a moment or two before I could stop shaking enough to get the key into the ignition. I cranked the engine, put her in gear, and headed home. Wind whipped my hair and blew tears sideways across my cheeks.

Our farm lay due west of the new Main Street Gorge. I put the jeep in four-wheel drive to navigate over the dips and wrinkles and debris in the streets. Outside of town, I went off-road to bypass a fallen power line. A mile later I gunned it across another small fissure. The whole time I couldn't get those words out of my head, *the entire eastern half of the country is experiencing tremors.*

I held my breath for the next five miles. Then, in the distance, like beacons of hope, stood all three of our neighbor's silos, and off on the left Jakob Anderson's big red barn still stood in one piece. The familiar tree line of Mill Creek Woods still crowned the hill and the bridge still spanned the creek.

I sighed with relief. My heart almost returned to a normal rhythm, until I glanced in the rearview mirror and saw a llama in my backseat. I stomped on the brakes and nearly spun into the creek.

Dust flew around us and the llama herder materialized in the passenger seat. "Now are you going to go find the Wise Woman?"

Once the dust settled, I shifted into first and yanked on the parking brake. "Out!" I pointed feverishly. "Both of you. And no spitting." I glared at the long-necked llama.

To my surprise, they both vanished. A second later they reappeared beside the jeep staring at me. I didn't like Llama girl's long-suffering expression, staring big-eyed at me as if I were a slow-witted child.

"Taste the wind, Sophie." Irritation colored her normally melodic voice. "The scent of death approaches. You *must* seek the Wise Woman."

"About that—"

She shook her head against my argument before I could even speak it. "Blossoms of disillusioned womankind taint the breeze, turning it sour. Life as you know it is slipping away. Growing darker by the minute."

The thing slipping away is my sanity.

I pressed my lips tight, wishing her away. Only she didn't

go. "No," I said firmly. "I'm going home to see if my brother is okay."

"Do you not remember the Dark Ages?"

This from a girl of fourteen?

"No." I gripped the steering wheel. "Not firsthand."

"I remember." She sighed and leaned heavily on her staff. "It was a time of unfathomable cruelty. Violence. Hopelessness. Disease. People bent their minds toward death, toward brutal domination and conquest. These were their fondest aspirations."

"That was hundreds and hundreds of years ago. It's over."

She shook her head. "Not so long ago in the history of humankind. In those days they did not design medical equipment." Pain whirled in her dark eyes. "Instead, they used their knowledge to build instruments of torture, iron masks, and barbed chastity belts for their women. Canons and catapults, racks and slow blades for their enemies."

The afternoon light dimmed as if a dark cloud passed over us. Mill creek evaporated. In its place appeared a village with cobbled streets, thatched huts, and stone shops. The putrid stench of sewage flowing through open gutters burned my nose. A narrow street echoed with the sounds of jeering. Villagers goaded a woman forward, shouting, throwing stones, and spitting. Her hands were bound with leather straps. A rusty iron mask in the shape of a shrew's head was clamped over her head. Her husband thrashed her legs and back with a stick, driving her through the crowded marketplace.

"Stop!" I shouted.

The village disappeared. In its place stone walls rose up, musty moldy walls without windows. A man lay naked, strapped to a wooden torture table, his captors savored his agony as they inserted a huge metal corkscrew and began to twist it.

Like the man on the table, I gasped and couldn't breathe.

More horrifying images flashed before me. Llama girl showed me beaches strewn with dead and dying bodies—a senseless slaughter of men, women, and children, as horned raiders from the north plundered a coastal village. She showed me faces turned black with disease, and motherless children wandering through filthy streets until starvation took them.

I clamped my eyes shut.

Even so, I could not escape. My chest constricted until I thought I would suffocate. "Stop! Stop," I choked. "No more. Please."

"This and worse awaits your world," llama girl said quietly, and the awful visions subsided. "Wisdom is bleeding out of the earth."

Sick to my stomach, unable to respond, I bent forward and pressed my hand against my hammering heart. *How?* "How can one woman from a small town in Minnesota do anything about such horrors?"

She thumped her staff on the ground. "Next time it will be far worse. Human beings' tools are more ingenious now. Knowledge without wisdom is deadly." She rested her hand on her llama's neck, lacing her fingers through the long hair as a mother would tousle her infant's curls. Sorrow veiled her words so that I barely heard her. "If you fail, I doubt anyone will survive."

Would we all be destroyed? Just our world? Or hers too? I still didn't have enough breath to fully form my question. "Anyone?"

She didn't answer.

The old llama blinked her long lashes and issued a low moan that meant I didn't want the answer, just that it was too awful to contemplate.

"Okay. I get it." I took a deep breath and straightened. "Find the Wise Woman."

Llama girl raised her chin, and hope glistened in her eyes. She closed the distance between us and laid her hand on my shoulder as if blessing me. "Go, daughter. Quickly. While there is still time."

"Show me where she is." I met her gaze evenly. She was sending me on this mission. I had a right to demand answers.

As if my request pleased her, she smiled. Quick as lightning, another vision opened. No more dark ages, I saw her—my first glimpse of the Wise Woman—a woman very much from our era. I had expected a hospital bed, IV tubes, and heart monitors, or at the very least someone sitting lotus style on a silk pillow in an austere Buddhist monastery.

Not this!

No hospital bed. No Tibetan monk's toga. She had on a bathing suit. And sunglasses. Just as llama girl had said, the Wise

Woman sat beneath a palm tree. But this woman didn't look sick at all. More like an aging movie star stretched out on a chaise lounge, sunning under a wide-brim hat. For a dying woman, she looked darn good. Maybe llama girl had clicked her vision remote controller to the wrong channel?

"That's her?" The corner of my mouth twisted up skeptically. "The Wise Woman?"

Llama girl let go of my shoulder and vanished.

Twenty-six minutes later, I skidded to a stop in front of our farmhouse. Danny saw me from the field and sprinted my way, tearing recklessly through rows of young corn as if it wasn't all his hard work that did all that planting. He shouted something at the top of his lungs, but I couldn't make it out. I chewed my lip. Not wanting to be the one to tell him what was going on, or that I'd be leaving.

I knew my brother. That frantic run didn't look anything like the smooth wide-receiver run from his high school days. That ground-thundering run was burning up with fear.

The screen door creaked open and bounced shut. Marla came out of the house with the baby on her hip. "Thank God, you're home. I've been worried sick. Been trying your cell phone. There's no signal. Power's out. Everything shook like crazy. The bathroom mirror broke. Is that a bruise on your forehead? Are you okay?"

I nodded and turned back to watch my brother.

Marla kept talking. "After we heard the radio say it was an

earthquake Danny took off to check the fields. Said you'd be home soon. How he figured that I don't know."

It was like that with Danny. He wasn't born with my strangeness, except when it came to me. They say some mothers have an intuitive bond with their children. In my case, my brother always seemed to know when I was in trouble or needed help.

He ran up breathless and doubled over, worry pinching up his forehead. He clapped a hand on my shoulder. "Tell me."

"It's bad in town." I explained about the Main Street Gorge.

Danny leaned in close and narrowed his gaze at me as if he knew I was holding back. "And?"

"And I need to go pack." I went inside the house and tore through my dresser, flinging underwear and socks into a duffle bag.

"Why?" he asked, as I stuffed clothes into the bag.

"There's something I gotta do." Instead of meeting his gaze, I folded a t-shirt and shoved it into the bag. "I can't explain. You'll think I'm crazy."

"When have I ever thought that?"

"Fair enough." My brother had always believed me, always trusted me, no matter what crazy thing I'd seen or done. This one was bound to push his trust too far. "I'm sorry, Danny. This time I can't explain. You're going to have to trust me. I have to do this." I paused, squeezing a pair of socks in my fist, picturing the dark ages falling on him and Josh, crushing their souls with ignorance and savagery. I tossed the socks in my duffle bag. "I have to go. It might make all the difference for Marla and baby Josh. You. Me. Everybody. Unless I fail. Then it won't amount to anything at all. Either way, I've got to try."

Danny raked his hand through his hair. "How long?"

That was just like him. No lectures. No accusations that I'd gone off the deep end. Just, *how long*? He was the best brother in the whole world.

I stopped and stared at the floor. "I don't know."

Marla, who looked every bit as skeptical as a certain llama of my acquaintance, said, "You can't just up an' take off. It isn't safe. Especially now with the earthquake and everything." She nudged Danny. "You can't let her." Joshie started to cry.

I squared up and faced him straight on. "Danny, you remember the day Jace almost drowned?"

He nodded.

"It's like that."

He whistled out a stream of pent-up air. He knew the whole story—the real one. The story I'd never told *anyone* else.

"Only this time it's bigger. Worse. Way worse."

He took Josh from Marla. The baby snuggled against his chest and calmed down. "Marla, honey, I'd like you to get some sandwiches together for Sophie to take."

And that was that.

My sister-in-law shook her head and went off to the kitchen mumbling something about us being reckless lunatics.

A simple nod and Danny knew the gratitude I felt. "I'll call as soon as I can. Do me a favor. If I'm not back in a few days, call

Ollie for me and tell him I'm sorry. Tell him Becky Larson knows a little about layouts and graphics. Maybe she could fill in while I'm gone."

Turning away, I opened my top dresser drawer, searching for one last thing, Mama's locket hidden in the back corner. It was hard to know what to bring when hunting a Wise Woman. I unfolded Grandma's lace-edged handkerchief, opened the locket and stared at Mom's tiny photo. She'd been gone for years, but I could still feel her hand on my shoulder, reassuring me, like she did the day Jace and I drowned. Just seeing her face gave me hope this Wise Woman hunt might not end in disaster. I snapped the gold heart shut, coiled the chain, wrapped it securely in the handkerchief, and tucked them into my pocket.

Marla came back and thrust two sandwiches tucked in plastic bags at me. "Don't go," she said sternly.

"I love you, but I have to do this. Danny will explain later." I hugged her, put the food in my duffle bag, zipped it, and slung it over my shoulder like a soldier headed for war.

I paused beside Danny and smoothed my hand over Josh's plump little cheek and twirled one of his soft curls one last time. Then I brushed past them into the hallway. I hated goodbyes. When Danny and I lost our parents, first mom and then two years later dad, well, that was enough *good-bye-ing* to last me a lifetime.

He grabbed my arm. "Soph, wait!"

Against my better judgment, I turned back and hugged him. "I love you, Danny. You're the best big brother a kid could ever have." I kissed baby Josh on the cheek and turned away, fighting the moisture filling the corners of my eyes. Tears would be disastrous. He'd never let me go if I cried.

So, I pushed away and gave my brother a brisk pat on his shoulder, the kind of sturdy thump Dad used to give us on the first day of school or the first time we went to climb up the high dive at the public pool. It meant, *Go on then. You'll be fine.*

Only I wished I hadn't done that. That one gesture threatened to resurrect ghosts I'd fought every day for the past three years to keep buried. *I couldn't risk thinking about Dad right now. I had enough on my plate without digging into that heartache.*

Before Danny could change his mind and decide I'd lost my marbles, I hurried out of the door. The screen door bounced just like it always did. Danny caught it before the second thump and stood there on the porch, hugging Josh, watching as I climbed into my jeep and drove off to hunt for a Wise Woman.

Chapter 3
Wandering Dreamer

Since most of the deserts in the U.S. were situated in the Southwest, I drove in that direction. Plus, I didn't dare risk traveling toward the catastrophic earthquake scarring the Mississippi region. According to the news, most of their major highways were closed and multiple fires and floods threatened that part of the country.

As darkness fell, a bright moon lit my way on the backroads, the radio faded in and out with intermittent static. I'd grown weary of earthquake news anyway, so I switched it off. To keep myself awake, I recited aloud a poem my mother had taught me about the moon. O'Shaughnessy's magical words danced from my tongue.

"We are the music-makers,
And we are the dreamers of dreams,
Wandering by lone sea-breakers,
And sitting by desolate streams; —
World-losers and world-forsakers,
On whom the pale moon gleams:
Yet we are the movers and shakers
Of the world for ever, it seems."

Mom must've thought that poem would reassure me. *Dreamers of dreams*, Yeah, she knew early on that I had strangely vivid dreams even though I'd rarely spoken about them. *Sitting by desolate streams*—yeah, I guess that fit me, too. I'd certainly learned to keep my peculiarities to myself. It made some people nervous, and they tended to steer clear of me. But a *mover or shaker*?

Not me.

I was a college dropout from a little town in the middle of Laura Ingalls-Wilder's Minnesota prairie. I was nobody! And for sure I wasn't someone who llama girl should have entrusted with a task this important. What would happen if I failed to find the Wise Woman? Or failed to accomplish whatever it was a novice was supposed to do?

Would civilization come tumbling down?

I flipped the fuzzy radio back on. Anything to distract me from those thoughts.

By the time the sky turned pre-dawn gray, I was heading south, yawning my way through Iowa.

Iowa. . .

Endless corn fields.

Clueless deer wandering across the highway.

More corn fields.

Me, I couldn't look at cornfields without feeling eight years old again. And that was all good, because when I was eight, she was there, my mother.

"Do you see it?" I could still hear her voice as we drove by fields of knee-high corn. "Look there, Sophie. It looks like a man running on stilts." She pointed at the furrows of corn transformed into the long legs of a circus performer running beside the car. She was like that, my mother, able to make a bunny out of a bland white cloud, or turn it into a frightening pirate ship, depending on her mood.

While Dad drove, she entertained my brother and me in the car by reading stories aloud, filling our heads with the antics of *Huckleberry Finn*, or Dorothy Gilman's *The Amazing Miss Pollifax*. My favorite was wacky *Mrs. Piggle Wiggle* and her bizarre solutions for reforming naughty children. I didn't know how my mother read without getting carsick, but she managed, and our family car trips turned into adventures in more ways than one.

Morning emerged on the flat horizon like a pink rose blooming at the edge of a dull woolen sky. Rose turned to bright magenta, and before long yellow light lit up the green stalks of corn. I yawned and tried to stretch my back.

Under the brilliant sun, an hour or two west of Des Moines, a gnawing feeling hit my stomach. Not just hunger, *doubt.* Common sense and a wicked lash of reason flogged me mercilessly.

You haven't a clue where you're going, do you?

Hunting for a Wise Woman?

I mean, how rational is it to drive off to who knows where in search of some mysterious woman with no known address? Your blood sugar could be off. Diabetes does run in your family, you know.

"Yeah, could be." My stomach rumbled in agreement. Maybe a large stack of pancakes smothered in syrup would cure me. I could always turn back after breakfast. A mile down the road I spotted a gigantic sign for a diner and truck stop and nearly skidded off the highway.

The sign featured a six-foot, shaggy, neon-outlined llama. Granny Jo's Mama-Llama Café. The cantankerous creature winked! Yep, it winked, and raised her hairy motorized front hoof toward an arrow that flashed the words "*next exit.*"

Who uses a llama for their logo? I'd never seen a sign like that before—ever. On the other hand, I'd never trekked across the backcountry on a harebrained assignment given to me by a hallucination before.

So, this is the way it's going to be, eh?

I turned off the highway and followed the road to the truck stop, muttering, "I'm hungry enough to eat a llama, sans the fur and spit. Granny Jo better be more than a figment of my imagination."

I parked in front of the restaurant, and it seemed solid enough. Judging by the décor, the place dated back forty or fifty years. Aside from the fact that Granny Jo's cleaning staff could have used a refresher course in mopping, the place looked okay and smelled even better. I slid into a worn maroon vinyl booth and patted my hands against the metal-rimmed Formica table. A *real table*. Whew! My chances of getting actual food just jumped up a couple of notches.

The waitress handed me a plastic-covered menu. Surprised that it didn't have a llama on it, I made a joke about their unusual billboard.

"What billboard?" She scrunched up her nose, sniffing at the extra exertion my question caused.

"The big sign on highway 71 coming down from the north."

She smirked.

Good gravy, this wasn't a pop quiz. I pointed out the window. "You know, the gigantic six-foot blinking neon llama?"

"Llama?" She squinted sideways at me as if I'd just gone cross-eyed. "Dunno. Sounds to me like you need some coffee, hon."

"Maybe so." I gave up and ordered an orange juice along with two strips of bacon to go with my pancakes and eggs.

She left, and an amazing fast five minutes later, returned carrying my breakfast on one arm like a mother who has learned to balance an infant on one hip while wrangling two other rambunctious toddlers with her free hand. She dealt the plates out on my table and stood back, surveying her handiwork. "There you go. This ought to get you going the right way." She topped off my coffee and plopped down a small dish of prepackaged cream. "Granny's motto is, a good breakfast'll carry you for miles. Get you to your destination quicker. And that's what we all want, isn't it?" She glanced at me pointedly.

Oh, so now she was Miss Talkative.

Before I could respond, the window beside me shook violently as a Peterbilt semi, pulling an enormous double trailer, rumbled by the diner. The truck clattered and hissed across the parking lot to fill up with diesel. When I turned back to my waitress, she was gone. I sat alone with two steaming plates of food. The aroma of bacon and hot syrup wafted up and teased my nostrils.

I have to say, if you're ever traveling west of Des Moines on I-71, odd giant llama sign aside, Granny Jo's cooking was well worth the slight detour. The hearty farm breakfast silenced my grumbling stomach and gnawing doubts. I paid my bill and pulled back onto the highway humming along to an old country western song that demanded, "whiskey for my men and beer for my horses."

There had been a palm tree in my vision of the Wise Woman. The way I figured it, she had to be in one of three places known for their palm trees, Florida, California, or Arizona. I mean, after all, llama girl hadn't said, "*Fly* off to find the Wise Woman." That meant the old gal wasn't in Europe, China, the Middle East, or the Caribbean. If she had said that, I'd be off the hook. She'd need to find a richer novice to do her bidding.

When I got to Kansas City, it was my last chance to decide. East to Florida? Or West to Arizona and California?

Something in the vision held a cue, only I couldn't quite put my finger on it. The closer I got to the junction, the more uncertain I felt about which way to go.

Why West?

After all, didn't the three wise men come from the East? Dalai Lama lived in India—East.

Then why was I instinctively thinking of turning west?

I took my foot off the accelerator.

Hmm...

Was I unconsciously running away from this assignment? Who could forget about Jonah? Sailing off in the opposite direction didn't work out too well for him. Luckily, here in Kansas, there were no giant sea creatures waiting to swallow me whole.

A semi barreled up behind my jeep and laid on his horn. The earsplitting blast sent a jolt of adrenalin burning through my veins. Granny's pancakes sloshed like lead ballast in my stomach.

In a flurry of rattling metal and puffs of brown diesel smoke, the eighteen-wheeler went around me, his huge tires spit minuscule pebbles around the edges of his mudflaps. He had one of those yellow signs on the back of his double trailer. "How's my driving?"

"Rude." It seemed like a feeble response, but I didn't have time to compose a sufficiently scathing answer.

Above the eye-level how's my driving sign was a large advertisement for coffee, the presumably product this rowdy trucker carried. Instead of Juan Valdez with his iconic hat and donkey, this brand featured a painting of a dark-haired young woman who bore an uncanny resemblance to llama girl, and her sacks of coffee beans were not strapped on the back of a mule. No, you guessed it, they hung over a conspicuously large and alarmingly familiar white llama. Scrawled across this tableau was the slogan: *Make the Wise Choice.*

Owing to an acoustical anomaly of some sort, it seemed as if that surly llama bleated at me just as the semi blew his horn again.

When the truck slowed and turned right at the next junction, my doubts vanished. I followed the sun (and that rude semi) west, to the land of cowboys, gold miner's dreams, and with any luck, the Wise Woman.

Before long, the truck disappeared into the watery mirage of heat-soaked highway stretching ahead of me. It didn't matter. I knew now where I was going, and certainty settled over me.

An hour later, when I wound through Topeka, missing an exit, doubling back, and finally catching I-35, I was equally certain someone was following me.

Chapter 4
No Such Thing as Coincidence

A white F-150 remained in my rearview mirror all the way from Topeka to Wichita. It didn't matter if I sped up, breaking the speed limit, or slowed to a crawl, the white truck maintained a distance of about two football fields. At Topeka I took the I-40 exit. I grimaced when he took the same exit.

Coincidence?

I think not.

I had that jittery feeling. You know, the one you get when

you come home late and discover the front door is unlocked. You automatically think, *someone might be in the house.*

The door creaks open, and every rattle and pin drop scares you senseless. Then, after you've checked behind every door, under all the beds, in the closets, and shone your flashlight into all the shadowy corners and found them all empty, don't you love that big breath that comes? That blessed intake of relief tastes incredibly sweet and refreshing.

Yeah, well, sometimes someone is lurking behind you.

And you can kiss blessed relief good-bye forever unless you do something daring to escape.

I have to lose whoever was stalking me.

So I stepped on the gas, whipping in and out of traffic, heading toward an exit and then speeding past it, until I took a screechingly reckless turn off the freeway going north onto Hillside Street. Anyone following me would never suspect I'd go north. After all, we'd just come from the north. From Hillside I took a hard right onto Central, heading back east toward I-35. I'd have to pay to take the tollway, but better that than ending up as yet another crime statistic in a body bag. Or worse, disappearing forever.

Cruising down Central, there wasn't a white pick-up anywhere in sight! Whew! I high-fived my dashboard and congratulated my trusty old jeep. "We did it. Excellent leg work!" Before getting on the tollway, I needed to take a quick detour for gas and to use a restroom. I wheeled into a gas mart.

As a reward, I gave the jeep gas with extra additive in it.

Ten minutes later I strolled out of the convenience mart carrying two extra bottles of water and munching on a hotdog that tasted a little like it might've been roasting on those rollers since last week.

Just then, a white Ford F-150 pulled up to the gas pump diagonal from mine. Hotdog forgotten, mustard and relish dribbling onto the pavement, I nearly stumbled off the curb.

It couldn't be.

Except it was. I knew it in my heart of hearts it must be. The dust pattern on the fenders matched mine too closely. The driver's door opened.

My stalker.

For some reason, I'd always imagined a stalker would be an ugly, hunch-backed, middle-aged man with grizzled hair and bitterness pinching up his face. That was not rational. The faces of serial killers in the news looked alarmingly normal. More often than not, evil came packaged quite pleasantly. Perhaps we ignore this fact in the desperate hope that evil will be easy to spot.

I certainly didn't expect the guy following me to climb out of his pick-up looking achingly innocent in his clean white cotton shirt. You can bet your last nickel I didn't expect him to hit me with a hesitant half-shy smile, just as if he hadn't been following me for the last two hundred miles, carefully hanging back no matter how I adjusted my speed. I frowned back at him with the fiercest, huffiest, *I'll-kick-both-your-shins-clear-back-to-Topeka-if-you-come-anywhere-near-me* frown.

Here's the scariest part. If somebody found my college journal and read those embarrassing pages where I listed exactly what my ideal man would look like, this stalker guy was it. Tall, muscled, broad-chest, dark wavy hair—not a checkmark missing, right down to his Tony Lama boots. Yeah, and he even had that rugged farm-boy look with hints of intelligence.

Way too much of a coincidence.

Visions and dreams are one thing. Coincidences . . . well, those are just plain spooky.

I yanked my receipt out of the pump, tossed the hotdog in the trash, my appetite had evaporated, tossed the water bottles behind the seat, and peeled out of that gas station as if the devil was on my heels.

Maybe he was.

Pushing the jeep to her max, I crossed the New Mexico state line sometime after midnight. My eyelids drooped and reluctantly fluttered open whenever I realized sleep was sneaking up on me. I rolled down the windows, hoping a desert breeze whipping my face would wake me up. Instead, the lukewarm air had a soothing effect, so I cranked up the radio. It didn't pick up much of anything except weak news reports and sporadically a station that ran heavy on Norteño accordion music.

Hanging onto the steering wheel, I stretched my back and leaned forward. In New Mexico the sky drifted up like an airy cathedral, expanding so much it scarcely held down the oxygen. Jagged mountains loomed far off on the horizon. Barren rocks and sand stretched unimpeded for hundreds of miles. Nothing separated heaven from earth on this long flat stretch of road. Tattered cacti stretched their arms worshipfully toward the magnificent splash of the Milky Way—billions of stars glittering on inky silk.

I felt my smallness in the universe. I was one tiny insignificant human riding on this ball of dirt and fire across the vastness of space. Who was I to be hunting a Wise Woman?

I settled back against the driver's seat and focused on more corporeal issues, like stewing about the fact that those distant headlights in my rearview mirror probably belonged to the guy who was following me.

I almost didn't see the coyote dash across the road in front of me and stop right in the center of the pavement. I slammed on my brakes. I swerved, spraying gravel as my tires skidded onto the shoulder. Wide awake now, my heart jogged a polka double-time along with the accordions and trumpets sputtering from the jeep's radio.

That mangy coyote stared at me, his yellow eyes reflected eerily in my headlights, and then he walked off into the stillness of the night, completely unconcerned that he'd nearly met his ultimate fate at the hands of a very tired, very rattled, Wise Woman hunter.

My radio hissed, and a flurry of Spanish faded in and out. Pinprick-sized headlights moved toward me. I eased back onto the road and floored it, putting as much distance between me and those headlights as possible, just in case they belonged to my stalker.

A dozen or so miles later, the speed limit dropped to thirty-five as the highway passed through a small town. A few scattered lights illuminated the windows of the houses. Most of those came from the cool blue-gray flicker of TV screens.

I'm not sure if what happened next was a sign or not.

Probably not.

Nevertheless, there it was—a goat standing on the side of the road. A goat, not a llama. But it had long scraggly white hair, floppy ears, and short pointy horns. This odd-looking goat wore a red collar and a bell around its neck. There was no swirling cloud or colored smoke to signal that this was delirium or another of my funky dreams. It occurred to me that I might've fallen asleep. So I braked and patted my cheeks to make certain.

Wide awake.

Not a dream.

Still, what was a goat doing out here in the middle of nowhere? On the other hand, I reasoned, folks here in New Mexico might be comfortable letting their animals wander around freely. That could explain the coyote lurking down the road. Maybe he smelled dinner.

The goat stood like a herald in front of a dimly lit row of small, white-washed, adobe bungalows—a motel called *Catch Some Zzz's*.

Miraculous sign or not, stopping for some rest seemed like a good idea. I did a U-turn and pulled into the motel parking lot. It felt good to get out of the jeep, to move my legs, and rejoin civilization. As I headed toward the office, the goat followed me, her cowbell clanged loud enough to wake the entire town. She bore very little resemblance to llama girl's shaggy sidekick, unless you wanted to count the annoying personality. She kept nudging me with her nose.

I didn't want the pesky thing to get the idea she could try out those stubby horns on my backside. "Git! Go home. Shoo." Whisking my hand at her had no effect.

Lacewings and June bugs swarmed the porch as the motel office lights blinked on. The screen door opened. "Cut it out, Pricilla!" The proprietress clapped her hands and explained, "She's our watchdog."

"Aren't you worried about coyotes getting her?" I hurried in the door.

The woman coughed and waved away an invading moth. "Nah, honey, don't you worry about her. Sure, we got some renegade coyotes 'round here, but Pricilla's not afraid to use those horns when she has to. And don't get me started on those hooves of hers. The old girl knows how to take care of herself." Stepping behind a counter, she opened a drawer, rifled through it, and pulled out a ballpoint pen. From the rooms behind the lobby, the fuzzy sound of applause echoed across the linoleum floor as a late-night talk show host chatted to his audience. She pointed the pen at the doorway where Pricilla stood behind the screen watching us. "Yep. Somewhere out there is a one-eyed coyote. Prissy kicked an eyeball clean outta his head."

I chuckled.

"I'm not kiddin' you. She's a survivor, that one." The motel owner tossed her salt and pepper braid behind her shoulder and pulled her bathrobe tighter. The fabric was decorated with grinning suns and sleepy moons. Appropriate for an innkeeper, I thought. One of the happy suns smiled up at me from her enormous left breast, while a sleepy moon hung in the loose folds where her right ought to be. Before I realized I'd been staring, she plopped the room rental forms on the counter. "Cancer."

Red-faced, I bent over the form. "I'm so sorry. I didn't mean to be rude."

She shrugged. "We all got scars, honey. Some just show more'n others."

I felt naked then. As if her weary eyes were peering into my dark places. Places I pretended didn't exist, like the fissure in my soul where my mother had once dwelled. An oozing wound, an empty gash, where that missing part of my heart ought to hang.

I don't have scars.

I don't!

The goat bleated at me as if she sensed the lies I told myself. Her bell tolled for my hidden grief. I wanted to snap at her, *what do you know about it*? Instead, I kept my mouth shut and tried to remember my license plate number to fill in the blank spaces.

The proprietress yawned and plunked a key on the dented wooden counter. "Number four. In the middle. Linen's fresh. Just changed it last week."

Last week would have to do.

I left, gingerly inching around Pricilla, who sniffed my jeans. Not wishing to be taste-tested, I retreated posthaste and grabbed my duffle bag out of the back of the jeep. While making my way across the parking lot, a white pick-up pulled in. I didn't look a second time. Didn't need to. My stalker's tires crunched over the gravel. The motel key stuck as I fumbled with the lock on number four, jiggling it frantically until at last it spun through the tumblers. Before he turned off his headlights, I had opened the creaking wooden door, dashed inside, slammed it shut, and slid the chain bolt in place.

The room needed air.

I needed air.

The searing New Mexico sun beating down on the bungalow had baked in sixty years of dust, body odor, and mold. The whiff of desert air that had floated in with me sank in the heaviness of the room. I couldn't open a window. Everyone knows that's the easiest way to for an intruder to get in.

I leaned against the door in the darkness, thinking, listening. The seesaw buzz of cicadas grew deafening as I strained to discern his movements. I heard his truck door shut, the soft crunch of his boots against the gravel, and...

Where was that annoying watch-goat now?

Shouldn't she be ringing her bell, bleating a warning, jabbing him with her pointy horns, kicking out his kneecaps? I peeped through the Venetian blinds.

Watch goat—my ass.

Stalker-guy squatted beside that traitorous fraud and patted her hairy neck as if they were long lost friends. In the office doorway the motel clerk looked on, smiling as broadly as one of the happy suns on her bathrobe.

"Come on, lady, send him packing," I whispered.

She didn't. Instead, she held the door open as he went in to rent a room. He waited like a perfect gentleman for Priscilla, the two-timing goat, to prance in first. Then he slipped up with his little *I'm-only-here- to-rent-a-room* act and glanced sharply in the direction of bungalow number four.

Definitely a stalker.

This did not bode well.

I let go of the blinds and scrambled along the wall to find the light switch. The dresser lamp blinked on, casting a weak yellow haze over my accommodations. The front window was fitted with an air-conditioning unit. I turned the knob, and it quivered into motion, squeaking, whining, and rewarding me with an erratic thump each time the fan rotated.

The bathroom window was high, too high and narrow for him to climb through—safe to open. Unfortunately, grime from years of rust and disuse had jammed the crank. Lowering the lid on the toilet, I used it as a stool, climbed up, and pounded the heel of my hand against the old handle. It budged, ever so slightly. Encouraged, I hit it harder.

The window burst open. As it did, the toilet seat slid sideways on its brittle plastic moorings.

Funny how, in moments like these, physics came to mind.

Theorems governing vectors and directional forces suddenly became important. *Too late.* Falling toward the bathtub, I clutched at the shower curtain. The moldy old vinyl ripped off the rings like a zipper and did little to impede my fall.

If stalker-guy didn't kill me, my clumsiness probably would.

In a way, I was glad I hadn't turned on the bathroom light before crashing into the tub. The dim light gave me a moment to recuperate before realizing the dark thing moving across the slippery white porcelain beside me was a cockroach the size of a small mouse.

I'm not an alarmist.

Really.

Nor was I the type of girl who screamed at scary movies, wasps, or big spiders. Cockroaches were another thing entirely.

I yelped. Leaped out of the tub. Yelped again. Did a jig, brushing wildly at my clothes and hair. The yelping may have tapered down to something like, "Gross! Gross, gross, ick. Gross!"

After my heart settled down, and that hideous thing from some germ-infested black lagoon crawled back down into the drain, I felt slightly embarrassed.

It was quite possible that I overreacted.

Possible, but to be fair, we didn't have cockroaches that size in Minnesota. It took a moment or two for me to compose myself and get rid of that *something is crawling on me* feeling. I reassured myself that at least now I had a cross-breeze cutting through the stagnant air.

The worn brass chain-lock seemed like pretty flimsy protection. I figured I'd fortify the place by pushing the dresser in front of the door. It was a good idea, except I didn't notice the little brass lamp sitting on top of it had a very short cord. As I pushed the dresser further from the plug, the lamp failed to come with it and took a nosedive. It clattered against the concrete floor.

More physics.

The bulb shattered with a muffled pop, plunging me into darkness.

I stood there massaging my throbbing forehead to the tune of the whine-thump-squeak coming from the limping air-conditioner, wishing I had paid more attention to details. While calculating how much I would owe the motel lady, I heard the unmistakable sound of boots on the concrete stoop in front of my bungalow. That detail I didn't miss.

He rapped on the door. "You all right in there?"

"Go away."

"I heard noises. I thought—"

"Stay back. I've got a gun. If you so much as jiggle that door handle, I'll blow a hole straight through the door and you." I didn't have a gun. I grabbed the brass lamp and held it in both hands ready to swing for a home run if he tried anything.

In those infinitesimal seconds, all other sounds disappeared.

No cicadas.

No air-conditioner.

No goat bells.

There was only him and me, separated by peeling paint and a dried-out piece of hollow-core door.

I could tell he'd planted his hands on the wall beside the doorframe and leaned in. *That's how it is when you're scared.* Even the brush of his palms against the adobe sounded loud.

He exhaled slow and easy. "Good."

What in blazes did that mean?

"Good?"

"Yeah." His boot scuffed softly as he let go and stepped back. "Keep it handy."

Then he walked away.

Chapter 5
Wars and Rumors of Wars

Unbelievable! I slept in. I expected to wake up every few minutes fretting over stray sounds, the soft turning of a doorknob, footsteps large and small. Except I didn't. I flopped down on that squeaky mattress, worn out and confused, clutching that stupid lamp base, which really wouldn't have done much to protect me from stalker-guy, but at least it was something. Next thing I knew, sunlight was squeezing in around the blind slats. My roommate, Godzilla the cockroach, might have done a tap dance on my spine during the night and I wouldn't have noticed.

The clock's soft green readout blinked forward one digit.

Ten-thirty!

I moaned and sat up, raking my hair back from my face.

The lamp base slid down the depression in the mattress and bumped against my thigh. Scattered shards of glass winked up at me from the floor, a cheery little good-morning chaos.

After a quick prayer of thanksgiving to the King of the Universe for giving me rest and keeping me safe during the night, I glanced at the dreaded bathroom. I had no desire to survey the rest of last night's damage, but nature called. I carried the lamp with me just in case I met up with one of the motel's six-legged guests. First, though, I peeked out at the parking lot. The white Ford was gone! Hooray! I peed much easier knowing that.

Motel Lady looked different in the daylight. The white hairs in her braid showed more in the glare of midday, making her look grayer and older. She seemed less alert and more withdrawn, as if the nighttime was her natural habitat. I wondered if she was even the same woman. Maybe they were twins, one sister for the day and one for the night. I missed the lady with the sleepy moon/happy sun bathrobe.

This one hardly glanced up as she punched numbers into a calculator and answered my question about a place to eat. She muttered while tallying up my damages. "Twenty-two fifty for the shower curtain, and three dollars for the broken bulb."

I handed over my credit card and tried to draw her out. "So, where's your trusty watch goat?"

She glanced up. Her brow pinched together like she thought maybe I was completely bonkers. I held my palm at horn level, pretending to pat the animal in question. "You know, the little white goat with spiky horns and a bell? Fearless Priscilla?"

She just shrugged and handed me my receipt.

By eleven A.M. this part of New Mexico was already hot, not unbearable, just *wishing-for-a-breeze* hot. I slung my duffle bag into the back of the jeep, and that was when I noticed the army of red ants gathering under the shade of a raggedy old Live Oak tree—legions of big red ants! A dark-red moving carpet marching in unison. In my whole life, I'd never seen that many insects in one place. The soft humming of wings drew my attention to another army, or rather an air force of flying black ants swarming in the branches of the old oak.

A teeny tiny bugle must have blown that very instant. The air force took flight. Masses of flying ants dive-bombed the red army.

This wasn't a particularly safe place for spectators, I mean, that many ants could sting the life out of a rhinoceros, except it was impossible to look away. I had to know what would happen. In that instant, I felt as if I was God watching World War II.

Tiny warriors wrestled with one another in miniature hand-to-hand combat, tumbling and stinging, stabbing, death locks until their foes lay curled up and motionless in the dirt.

Just then, an airborne stormtrooper buzzed off course and landed on my shoulder, injecting me with poison the moment he touched down. I slapped off the kamikaze bomber and stepped back, out of the line of fire. I didn't like playing God anymore—it itched too much.

The bite prickled and started to swell. Histamines jetted

through my bloodstream, declaring war. Just like the ant armies, my white blood cells charged into battle against the invading foreign proteins. I smoothed my hand over my shoulder trying to cool the assault and scowled at the mess of warring insects rolling on the ground in a vicious kill-fest. What a sickening waste of perfectly good ants.

Yet, war was an undeniable part of life. Part of me, too. I couldn't even stop my own body from warring against itself.

How could I stop humankind from brutalizing themselves?

Preserve wisdom?

How?

It seemed like a hopeless delusion to suppose one woman might hold back the inevitable tide of destruction. I couldn't stop these ants, much less humans. I abandoned the ants to grapple with their fate alone, unobserved, with no historian to mark their tragedy. Unless...

Do ants pass on the stories of their battles?

Perhaps young ants will one day hear about the Great War held under the old live oak tree—if any of them survived to tell the tale.

A wounded bystander, I drove off to hunt for breakfast. The diner wasn't hard to find. It was the only one on the main highway through town, and a dozen vehicles were parked out front. Almost all of them were trucks, mostly two-tone jobs hailing from previous decades. There among them sat a very familiar white Ford F-150 with Kansas plates.

Him.

A stalker's truck ought to be black, not white. My fingers tightened around the steering wheel. "Black, like a big ole cock-roach."

Chapter 6
Esperanza's Cocina

My stomach grumbled, reminding me that there might not be another place to eat for a hundred miles. It was broad daylight, a public café, *what could happen?*

I have a very opinionated stomach, almost as opinionated as my ovaries during certain times of the month. Not only that, but the ant bite started to throb. Apparently, my histamines were bombing the snot out of the ant's assaulting protein. A big red hive the size of Mount Vesuvius emerged on my shoulder.

Hungry, uncomfortable, and ready to do battle as fiercely as any insect on the planet, I yanked open the door of Esperanza's Cocina.

Stalker-guy was inside alright, sitting at a booth in the back, a newspaper spread open to hide his face. As if I wouldn't notice his gleaming white t-shirt, the too-new jeans covering those long outstretched legs, and his Tony Lama boots casually crossed as if he were lounging in his own kitchen.

I straightened my back, trying to stand as tall and intimidating as possible, marched over to the counter, and sat down.

"¡*Hola!*" A waitress smiled and handed me a menu.

I did my best to smile pleasantly in return. "May I have some ice in a bag, please?"

She tilted her head quizzically as if I'd asked her to hand over the formula to turn straw into gold. It was a good thing I hadn't asked if they had any Benadryl.

I pointed to the welt rising on my shoulder. "Ant bite."

The newspaper rustled. I glanced in his direction, but he whipped it back in front of his face.

"Ice? *Por favor*." I asked and pointed to a glass of ice water in front of a customer two stools away from me at the counter.

She nodded and dashed away, returning with an older man who could easily be mistaken for llama girl's father. He had the same all-seeing eyes and a similarly embroidered shirt, except this guy had tied back his black hair and wore a cook's apron. "You want breakfast, yes?" he asked, waving his spatula like a wand.

Maybe it was a trick question.

Wary of wands and llama girl lookalikes, I narrowed my

eyes, trying to focus through him in case he was an apparition. He seemed solid enough. "Yes, please. But first may I have some ice? There was an ant war, you see, and I was a casualty." I pointed to the fiery lump bulging unattractively at the upper edge of my tank top.

"Loco ants." He shook his head and made a "tch"-ing sound as he slid open the ice machine, scooped chunks into a dishrag, and wound the corners to form a bag. Thrusting the makeshift ice pack at me, he added, "Ants—they go crazy. Every year gets worse. Not ants only. Coyotes. No *asustado. Vicioso.*"

"Vicious?"

"Yes. It is so. *Y los buitres, también.* The coyotes, *y* vultures —*comportarse loco.* They are forgetting the difference between what is dead and what is alive." He shook his head and contemplated the floor, sadly, as if mourning the remains of the squashed insects under the ice machine. "*Todo es fuera de equilibrio.*"

A few of the other patrons in the café murmured their agreement.

"What?" I demanded. "*En inglés, por favor.* What did you say?"

"The balance, she is slipping." He shrugged. "Is true, we cannot stop evil. You, me, we are... *solo somos humanos.* Only human, yes? This is for God to do, *verdad?*" He bowed his head momentarily, and it seemed like all the other patrons did, too. "We can only help to bring it into..." He parodied a set of scales using the spatula as a weight. "*Equilibrio.* This is why you must hurry, yes?" He studied me expectantly.

My jaw did not drop—I've never understood that expression. My jaw remained firmly connected to the rest of me. It may have flopped open a bit, sort of like a stunned fish. I mean, how did this guy know about my hallucinations or visions or...whatever they were?

Nevertheless, I argued with this stranger. "I'm not so sure I'm going to be hurrying anywhere. Now that I've gotten some sleep and had time to think it over—"

"No." He grimaced and swung his arms wide encompassing the occupants of Esperanza's Cocina and beyond. "Es *una necesidad*. You must!"

A familiar, plaintive "maa-ah" startled me. I spun around on the stool. Priscilla, the motel watch-goat, stood at the door bellowing her stern opinion on the matter.

Apparently fluent in goat, the cook nodded and backed toward the kitchen, pointing with his spatula. "You will go. *Un momento*, I am preparing much food for your journey."

I glanced around. No one except me seemed concerned about the rather vocal barnyard animal trotting into their café. It was then that I observed the features of the other patrons. The man next to me, the children seated with their parents at the booth in front of stalker-guy, they could all be cousins to the cook, including the young waitress. All of them had the same distinctive aquiline nose, the same melted-bronze skin, and the same shimmering brown eyes capable of peering through walls and into souls.

Apparently, I'd stumbled into a llama girl family reunion—and they were all staring at me as if they knew exactly who I was, and what I was *supposed* to be doing. I pasted on a smile, held the ice pack with one hand, and waved at them with the other, real friendly-like, *a Miss-Minnesota-riding-in-a-parade* wave, not a *what-the-heck-am-I-doing-here-and-please-stop-staring-at-me* wave.

My illustrious stalker peeked out from the side of his newspaper. I waved at him, too. Why not? For all I knew, this was just another loco dream. It might have been. Everything seemed unreal, except the hive sizzling on my shoulder and the gnawing in my stomach. Those were painfully tangible. I sincerely hoped the food would be too.

Whenever something really upset me, I tried to make a joke out of it. Trouble was, nobody in Esperanza's Cocina was laughing or buying my bravado. Not a one of them waved back or even cracked a smile. You'd think we were at the Pope's funeral. An elderly woman shook her head and glumly studied the runny egg yolk pooling at the edge of her plate.

Priscilla, the friendly neighborhood goat, sauntered up, bleated nastily, and unloaded a pile of smelly green buckshot at my feet. So, I had a pretty solid idea of the general attitude. Obviously, the occupants of Esperanza's Cocina's expected a Wise Woman hunter wearing a flashy cape and a big 'S' on her shirt to zoom in and set their universe back into balance.

Instead, they had me—an unimpressive cape-less wonder.

They're expecting me to hunt down this illusive Wise

Woman, plug up the planet's wisdom leak, and save these folks from warmonger ants and crazy coyotes. Clearly, they thought the person destiny chose for the job didn't look too promising.

I felt bad for them.

A little girl leaned up to her mother's ear and whispered something. Her mom shook her head, and they both looked at me as if I'd just run over their family dog. The little girl's eyes grew so large and sad that I wanted to hide under the counter. Two stools down from me sat a guy with a sweaty bandana tied around his head, an eagle tattooed on his arm, and enough muscles to lift a concrete truck. He had a tear trailing down his cheek.

"Okay," I mumbled. "I'll do my best."

I tried to swallow the dumb lump of shame swelling in my throat, except it stuck.

They all studied me with such forlorn expressions I couldn't bear to look anymore. Instead, I stared at the menu like it was the most fascinating piece of literature on the planet. They kept watching me. I knew they did because my neck actually began to itch. Several more awkward moments passed before the cook returned and thrust a grocery-size brown bag at me and refused payment. "*Vaya con Dios*, little sister."

I thanked him and hurried out to the jeep. In a spray of dust, I whipped out of the parking lot and headed down the highway. And yeah, I headed west to the land of palm trees. I may not have a cape, but I was no quitter.

What was the worst that could happen? I might wander the

desert for forty years, never find the Wise Woman, run out of money and gas, and die trying, right? Except by then, the world might have blown itself to bits, right? Success sounded like an infinitely preferable option.

"I can do this. I can," I repeated over and over like the proverbial *little-engine-that-could* until finally, I decided food might help fortify me.

Unwrapping a tortilla, I chomped into a whole new experience—eggs, cheese, and a mixture of tomatoes and peppers. *Oooh!* Who would have thought scrambled eggs could dance such a sinful tango on my taste buds? If the bag hadn't been stuffed with several more of those things, I would have turned around and gone back to Esperanza's.

Instead, I headed straight into a storm.

Chapter 7
Devil of a Storm

"What?!" I flung my second breakfast burrito onto the passenger seat and slammed on the brakes.

A gigantic vortex of sand performed a frightening ballet across the highway right in front of me. Three stories tall, it whirled across the pavement sucking up debris, cactus, and an old tire from the side of the road. Then, as if it had all been nothing but a freakishly short nightmare, it spun out into the open desert and collapsed into a puff of dust. Hitchhiking tumbleweeds bounced out and went their way along with fluttering trash. The tire landed with a thump in a new resting place beside the demolished prickly pear.

My heart went berserk, stomping a mean flamenco against my sternum. Mama Nature wasn't done yet.

In the distance, materializing like evil genies, a half-dozen plumes of dirt and sand rose up and gyrated across the desert floor. Rising as tall as the mountains against which they were framed, these enormous frenzied dancers whirled and undulated crazily and then vanished as swiftly as they sprang up. Oddly enough, not a cloud marred the brilliant turquoise sky.

With a white-knuckle grip on my steering wheel, I pressed the gas pedal. "This is not good. Not good at all," I muttered in accompaniment to the manic thrumming of my heart. Scanning barren patches along the road, I watched for telltale wisps of dust fanning up behind the sagebrush and dry scrub, wisps that might suddenly coil up into a towering column and take me and the jeep for an uninvited spin.

Dust devils.

Now I see how they got their name. These twisters, whirlwinds, or whatever they were could do some serious damage if they hit your car. These things bore no resemblance to the little whirligigs that occasionally twirled across our Minnesota cornfields before planting season. These looked like giant ghostly sand tornados, and I planned to steer clear of them.

There had to be a logical explanation for these eerie apparitions. Wind currents trapped on this side of the mountains, perhaps?

Sure.

That seemed reasonable. Wind currents might also explain

the many dark-winged predators floating high above the horizon, drifting like string-less kites on the odd indiscernible eddies. Vultures? Ravens?

I swallowed hard and glanced with disinterest at the remains of my breakfast on the passenger seat. My stomach turned into a scaredy-cat and huddled behind my liver—*not conducive to digestion*. So, chili peppers and cheese were out of the question. Cowardly tummy aside, something felt wrong. The air smelled of changing ions, and I had the distinct impression the easy part of my journey was over.

I didn't need psychic ability to draw this conclusion. The clues were stunningly obvious. The electrical sensation in the air got weirder, and it felt as if a reverse wind were sucking the oxygen away.

On the upside, those monstrous dust devils disappeared entirely.

During the next fifteen minutes, the cheerful turquoise sky faded. A somber wash of brownish-gray muted the once lovely blue. Whitecaps of a herculean thunderhead cloud boiled up in the westerly sky, rising over the tops of the mountains. A sensible jackrabbit raced like mad to dive into its hole. Even the bugs must have found hiding places, because there weren't any striking my windshield.

I glanced in the rearview mirror and sighed. An all-too-familiar white truck appeared on the horizon behind me. "Perfect!" I smacked my hand against the steering wheel. "Dust devils, stalker devils, and—" I was going to be cute and say, "a devil of a storm," but something in the road ahead grabbed my attention.

Coyotes.

Blockading the road.

My brakes screeched. The jeep skidded a little sideways.

What?!

For a second, one tiny fleeting second, I hoped they might be friendly. You know, like fluffy llamas and plump geese. I glanced to the side of the road hoping there might be a shepherd of some kind nearby.

Nope.

Renegades.

And those bared teeth meant they were definitely not a friendly crew.

I didn't realize coyotes ran in packs, and I thought they only hunted desert rats and maybe a jackrabbit or two. They were supposed to be scrawny and malnourished, weren't they? Not as big as bulked-up wolves and certainly not interested in tangling with a full-grown jeep and its occupant.

Yet, there they were, slow-walking down the middle of the road. Coming toward me like a badass road gang from Mad Max. Obviously, this burly bristle-necked pack had found more than a few bunnies to nibble on. And it looked like they were on the prowl for bigger game. Now I understood what they meant at Esperanza's about the *loco coyotes.*

I'm the praying sort.

Only this time there was no time to put all the words into a nice orderly request. It flew out in a desperate yelp. "Uh-oh...God, help!"

The biggest coyote lowered his head and trotted toward the jeep with a faster pace. A few more strides and he'd be able to jump up on the hood. And I swore I could see him grinning, all smug and growly, as if he thought I'd be easy pickings.

Cocky coyote.

His attitude got my dander up. *Dander*—I didn't even know what that was. I *did* know this—I wasn't going to let that mean-eyed, snarling, rat-catcher intimidate me.

Not gonna happen, Mr. Tough-guy Coyote.

If these devils wanted to play chicken, they'd tangled with the wrong girl. I pressed reassuringly on my shivering stomach. "Take it easy. Mama's got this." I gripped the wheel, revved the engine, put it in gear, and stomped on the gas pedal. If one of those mangy curs decorated my front grill, so be it!

Okay, at the last minute I dodged. The thump-*splat* idea made me squeamish. Unfortunately, at high speeds, my old jeep didn't weave very efficiently. It swerved and tipped onto two wheels for a second, thudded back down on all four, and that was when I may have run over a coyote's toe, or tail, or something. I thought I heard a loud, wounded-sounding yipe. With my tires screeching and all that high-pitched barking, I couldn't tell for sure.

I blew past them like a big clumsy version of Roadrunner. A few of them chased after me for a moment, but then it was over. I didn't look back again or check the rearview mirror. I couldn't. My poor, petrified stomach needed attention or she was going to regurgitate breakfast.

I tried to burp up some of the air I'd gulped and rubbed my

trembling belly. Trying to affect a calm I didn't feel. "We got through it. Everything will be fine," I muttered.

Inside, a more instinctual part of me shouted back.

Fine!?!

Have you gone off your Fruit Loops?

Everything is not fine. Not fine, at all. What was that? An ambush?"

"The worst is over," I breathed slow and steady. "Everything is going to be all right." And for several seconds, I almost believed it.

Then I heard the first rumble.

Distant at first, but it rapidly filled the entire desert with trembling. This was not the sound of a rumbling train or thunder. Nor was it the terrifying din of an approaching tornado—I've heard that. No, this was bigger and deeper. My bones vibrated, and I forgot to breathe when I heard it.

I prayed again, this time wordlessly. My stomach squeezed into a knot and dove for cover behind my ribs. Three seconds later, I understood why. The massive tidal wave of dust rolling across the desert made me want to run and hide too.

Instead, I froze.

Mouth open.

No breath coming in or going out.

Help.

I'd never seen anything so terrifying in all my life. It was a wall of dirt hundreds of feet high. And it was headed straight for me. My foot slid off the gas pedal. I had no idea what to do.

Then, it was as if llama girl, or an angel, or somebody

whispered in my ear, "No *time for fear. Do something.*"

Everything slowed to a crawl. A calm determination settled over me—the determination to survive. With raw clarity, I calculated the possibilities and assessed my options.

There was a sandstone outcropping less than a half-mile off the road. That might provide at least a little protection from the gigantic brown tsunami rushing toward me. I'd also be out of the way in case other vehicles were still moving blindly on the highway. Shifting into four-wheel drive, I tore across the desert sending up a spray of dust behind me, bouncing over bushes and rocks, racing to outrun that towering wall of dirt.

The roar grew louder and louder as I gunned it toward the rock formation. Particles of sand pelted my windshield with increasing speed and force, but I knew this would be nothing compared to when that giant swell hit. Skidding to a stop beside the stone ridge, I edged forward, positioning the jeep under a slight overhang and yanked on the parking brake. Then I hurried to batten down as much as possible, securing the window flaps in the rear. Before I could find anything to stuff in the gaps and torn places, the tidal wave hit.

Headwinds thundered over the outcropping like a runaway freight train. The jeep rocked violently. Dust gushed through the cracks and crevices in the cloth top, stinging my eyes, making it hard to breathe. I hunkered over, pulling the neck of my t-shirt up over my nose and mouth. Peeking out, I couldn't see any farther than the end of the hood. The world became a dense reddish-brown flurry. The roar from the maelstrom drowned out all other sounds, save one.

A thud.

Something hit the roof, jarring the whole vehicle. At first, I thought the strong winds must've chipped off part of the small overhang and it had fallen on the ragtop. I shielded my eyes and glanced up. Thank goodness for the roll bar, but the wind was either scooting the stone chunk around or something alive had landed up there.

When claws pierced the fabric and the padded paw of a very big cat dangled from my ceiling, I had my answer. Ignoring the extra dust flying around, I reached back in the rear compartment beside the toolbox and grabbed the jack. An instant later, the mountain lion widened the slit.

One look at the size of that paw and I nearly choked as my heart tried to exit through my mouth.

I gulped back the sharp tang of terror, and with the flat end of that jack, I shoved her pointy toes back up through the torn roof. She shoved back.

Whoa! Lions are super strong!

I could appreciate her need to get out of the storm, but somehow I didn't think a lion her size would sit quietly in the back. No, I figured it'd be a sweet deal for her.

Shelter and a meal.

She growled at me, confirming her reservations, and plunged her sharp unmanicured appendage back through my roof, batting at me as if I were a scared mouse. Maybe I was, but I also possessed a rousing desire to live. I swung that big ole jack as hard as I could and connected for a home run.

She shrieked. Really loud. Really angry sounding. Cougar

screams have the effect of temporarily stopping all blood flow in their opponent.

I nearly fainted. But right about then I saw lights coming straight at me.

UFO? God to the rescue? Angels?

Actually, I figured I was done for, and what I was seeing might be the bright lights at the end of that death tunnel everyone always talked about. It wasn't until I glimpsed a flash of white paint through the whirling sand that I realized this was just another devil, and his headlights were barreling straight for me.

The mountain lion must have been curious too. She stopped trying to shred my roof and padded down the windshield onto the hood. The jeep sagged forward under her weight, and her tawny tail glided across the glass like a slow mop, then curled upward with the dark tip twitching. Her muscles flexed fluidly as she moved. She was huge and all muscle, finely honed muscle, perfect for the purpose of taking down her next meal.

Beautiful.

Terrifying.

Strange to tremble in fear of a creature and at the same time sit awestruck by her perfectly designed killing power.

Her ears stood at attention as she peered out at the approaching vehicle despite the whipping dirt. The truck came to an abrupt halt only a few feet away. His horn blared, but my feline visitor remained unimpressed. She stood her ground or, in this case, my engine cover.

Stalker-guy emerged through the dust waving wide-spread arms.

"Are you crazy?" I said, shocked that he'd try such a suicidal maneuver. He moved in closer, and I saw he had a bandana covering his face, but no gun. Not even a baseball bat. What was he thinking? I clenched the jack. Crazy stalker or not, if the cat attacked him, I couldn't just sit there and watch him get eaten. I'd have to go out there and clobber...

The cougar arched. Her haunches tensed, and light reflected off of some very big teeth as she let loose a blood-curdling scream. I lurched back against my seat. Hair on my arms prickled.

She's gonna tear him to bits!

I couldn't bear it.

I flung open my door and stood up.

Amidst the chaos—the shrieking lion, sand pelting my skin, stinging my eyes, this guy's rumbling truck engine—an amazing sound bellowed out of my wimpy lungs. One solitary command thundered forth and trumped all that noise. "NO!"

And I meant it.

The cat flinched. She pivoted and immediately riveted her attention on me. I stood, pinned between the jeep and the flappy little cloth door, face-to-face with a full-grown cougar. I stopped breathing and hoped an angel or two might come and stand with me.

I didn't see an angel—*something better came.*

Despite the dirt whipping around us an incredible calm flowed through me. "Go on then," I said. "Get down. Go home."

This time I didn't even raise my voice, yet the sound pierced the roar of the raging storm.

The cat drew back, her eyes wide and ears at full attention. Her mouth opened as if to scream at me, but no sound came out. Her posture shifted sideways and hunched. Wary. She hated me. I could see it in her deadly pale eyes as she stared. And yet there was something else.

A begrudging fear.

Or was it respect?

With an aggravated growl, she jumped down from the hood. No deadly leap with claws bared. She got down like a dog shooed off the couch.

Astonished, my calm evaporated. My knees wobbled as I ducked back into the jeep, quickly shutting the door. Who could predict what she'd do now? Trembling, sucking air as if I'd just run a marathon, I leaned over the steering wheel, straining to see.

The cougar blended in perfectly with the whirling sand.

Stalker-guy edged away from her, down the side of my jeep. A moment later, my headlights illuminated the silhouette of the big cat, padding in a tight circle. No doubt she regretted not scratching my eyes out when she had the chance. Finally, she put her head down and skulked away.

My passenger door flew open, and stalker-guy flung himself into the seat and yanked the door shut. He gasped for air. "What the hell was that?"

I kept hold of my trusty jack. "I don't know," I said, pleased he grasped the situation so clearly. "I assumed she was a friend of yours. You know, a creature from the seventh circle."

"Not funny." He coughed. "She could've killed you."

He had his nerve scolding me. "Um, hello. Didn't I just save your sorry skin?" A flush of annoyance helped me stop shaking. The cab was dustier than ever, so I held my shirt over my mouth while I argued. "She was sizing you up for a mid-afternoon snack. What did you expect me to do? Ask if she wanted ketchup?"

"I saved you," he said. With that handkerchief tied over his mouth and nose, he resembled a bank robber from the old west. His gaze shifted pointedly to my torn ceiling. "She was on *your* roof."

Duh.

I shrugged. "So I noticed." I didn't have to answer to hold-up men or stalkers. "I had it under control."

"Where's your gun?" he demanded.

Shielding my eyes from the dust, I studied him, trying to do the math. *Does he want the gun so he can kill me? Or does he want to shoot the cat? Anyway, it doesn't matter, because I don't have a gun.*

"What do you want it for?" I ventured.

"What do you think I want it for?" He barked. "To scare off that cat!" *You idiot*, his tone inferred. "She might come back any minute. Where is it?"

"The gun? Or the cat? I think she went that way—"

I stopped talking when his eyebrows slanted into a not-so-happy angle. But I figured any stalker worth his salt should have his own gun. With a shrug, I said, "Don't you have one?"

He used that slow measured cadence teachers employ on denser pupils. "If I did, do you think I'd be sitting here asking for yours?"

I swallowed, which wasn't a good idea considering all the dust collecting in my throat. "I lied." It came out in a low garble.

"What?"

"I lied about having a gun." I barked.

"Terrific." He adjusted his bandana. "I don't suppose you have any duct tape, either?"

What? For gagging me. Was he totally crackerjacks?

I shook my head.

"I'll be right back. If she attacks again, put it in gear and drive away. She can't stay on your roof if you keep moving."

Keep moving? Where? In this dust?

I could drive off a cliff and wouldn't know until it was time to shout *Geronimo.*

He leaned up, checking the ground beside his window for our friendly neighborhood kitty before opening the door. I noticed the remains of my burrito stuck to his backside but decided against saying anything. I had enough grit in my teeth from talking. Besides, the wind would probably blow it away before he went very far.

He pushed my wobbly door shut against a burst of whirling sand and, like a ghostly shadow, he passed in front of my headlights before disappearing near his truck. He came back carrying a roll of gray duct tape in one hand and an oversize pocketknife in the other. I edged against my door still gripping the jack tightly.

He tossed the knife onto the dashboard. "This wouldn't do you much good, but keep it with you just in case..."

I relaxed significantly when he ripped off a piece of duct tape and plastered shut one of the slashes in my ragtop. This guy was nothing if not thorough. He continued taping up everything and re-taping any places that came loose. It cut down the dust in the cab considerably.

He even mended some of the old tears on the side flaps in the rear. "I don't know if this will hold when the rain hits, but it'll help."

"Thanks!" I smiled and set the jack on the floor beside my seat. "You're pretty nice for a stalker."

"Stalker?" Somehow he managed to look genuinely offended. "What do you mean?" He pulled down his neckerchief giving me the full force of his displeasure.

I tried smiling at him, but his glower didn't let up. So I decided a little sarcasm might be in order. "Oh, my mistake, wasn't that you? Behind me? Ever since Kansas?"

"Okaaay." He drew it out and took a deep breath. "I can see why you might've drawn that conclusion. I *was* following you, but that's not the same as stalking."

"You say potäto," I muttered.

"No. I generally say potāto." He came down hard on the "tay" sound. "Calling me a stalker infers criminal intent. I don't have criminal intent. Therefore, I am not stalking you," he insisted.

I shrugged. There didn't seem to be much point in debating the legalities. Anyway, I generally lost in a war of words. "Seems like you were."

"Well, I wasn't."

"Okay. Fine. You're just an ordinary guy who followed a woman you don't even know hundreds of miles across the country."

He shook his head. "You don't believe me."

"What difference does it make? Right now, we're stuck in the middle of some freakish storm with a hungry lion padding around out there waiting for the cafeteria to open up." I pushed my thumb against the plastic window and felt the patter of dirt striking it. "*You* tried to help me with the cat. I saved your life. *You* taped up my roof. *I'm* grateful. Looks like we're even now. You can go home."

"I'm not a stalker." He must have a habit of beating dead horses. "Nothing could be further from the truth." He leaned against the door staring out at the storm and those boots of his were tapping irritably against my floorboards. He looked all broody and insulted. "I would never stalk anybody."

"Good. Glad to hear it. You thirsty?" I reached behind my seat and grabbed a bottled water, unscrewed the top, and offered it to him.

He declined. "You first."

"My mouth feels positively muddy." Water had never tasted so good. I swallowed more and handed it over.

He drank without putting his lips on it and then scowled at the bottle, obviously still miffed about me maligning his character. Something about the way he cared what I thought of him made my insides go a little swoony.

Make up your mind, sister.

I reached for the water. My impish subconscious must have planned this move just so I could touch his hand as he relinquished it.

"Okay," he says as if he was about to surrender something far more important than my half-empty Dasani. "I can explain this much—I'm supposed to protect you."

I nearly dropped the bottle. It slipped, but he caught it and wrapped it snugly back in my fingers. I looked up at him confused. "Protect me?"

He stunned me further with those magical green eyes of his. Without consulting me, my heart started singing mushy songs. My devious stomach tiptoed out of hiding and twirled around like a dopey schoolgirl. All this inner cheerfulness distracted me for a split second or two.

Lucky for me, my skeptical nature pranced to the forefront of my cerebrum. "What do you mean protect me? Did my brother send you?" No, *wait, that's impossible. How would Danny know this guy? Or what direction I'd taken?*

"I don't know your brother. And I can't say anything more about this."

Now it was my turn to frown. Darn my mousy brown eyebrows, they never intimidated anyone. He didn't even squirm. *Okay, Buddy, I've figured it out on my own. There's only one possible explanation.* "Llama girl sent you."

His brow furrowed far more impressively than mine did. He looked at me as if he thought I was loopier than Grandma's rug. "Llama girl?"

"Okay, if not her, then who?" I demanded, losing patience. "Who sent you?"

He turned away to study flecks of sand as they pelted the window.

I waited, tapping my fingernails against the stick shift.

"Listen up, Buddy, or whoever you are. You better tell me what's going on, otherwise I'm going to clobber you with the same jack I intended to use on that mountain lion that nearly ate you for lunch."

"I could've handled that cat. And my name is not Buddy."

"Fine. I'll just keep calling you stalker-guy."

He winced. "It's Ryder."

"Ryder?" I peered at him suspiciously. "Oh, I get it. You're making that up, right? Like the song, *Riders in the Storm.*" He rolled his eyes. "Okay, so that's not it. Wait! I know. Isn't that the guy's name from *Lord of the Rings*?"

"I think you mean Strider." He exhaled loudly, clearly annoyed. "And no, my mother was Irish—it's a family name. Now can we please move past this."

"Okay." I raised my hands in surrender. "Ryder it is. Unless you prefer Buddy?" Funny how those nice eyes of his can appear warm and fuzzy one minute and hard and grumpy the next. And stubborn. He didn't even crack a smile.

So serious, this one.

I ignored his silence. "The point is I have a right to know who put you on my trail."

He remained stubbornly mum.

"There's a lot more at stake here than you realize." I tapped on my steering wheel. "So, spill it, Ryder. Or you may be excused from my jeep."

"I'm fully aware of what's at stake," he said gravely.

"You couldn't possibly know anything about it. I'm dealing with things that are..." I let go of the wheel and crossed my arms defensively. "Well, let's just say things that are a tad out of the norm. So—"

"Yeah. If you ask me, it's all downright bizarre." He turned, studying me, all intense-like. I will admit that I liked him looking at me as if he thought I was someone to be admired. Except I might've been reading into it. He was probably thinking that all the freakish happenings were on account of me. After all, didn't he just kind of call me bizarre?

He shook his head. "A cougar. Those coyotes. Unbelievable! And this storm—"

"Hey! I had nothing to do with this crazy storm. And your pal out there, the cougar—" I placed a hand over my chest and stuck three fingers in the air, taking the Girl Scout oath. "She was not invited to this party by me. So, stop frowning."

"I'm not frowning." He continued to glower, just not quite as hard.

Then I remembered the coyotes. "So, you saw that pack of overgrown coyotes, too? Listen, I don't know what possessed them to congregate in the road. And if you're with one of those secret animal protection societies and I accidentally hurt one of them—"

"That's not the issue." He flopped back against the seat, his jaw locked tight, staring out the window again. "It's this whole situation. Me following you, because..."

I waited for him to stop staring outside and add something to that *because*. Flying dust can't possibly be as fascinating as all that.

"I'm not going to bother explaining." He was still watching sand batter the windows. "You wouldn't believe me, anyway. I don't even know if I believe it myself."

I felt sorry for him. Poor guy, he actually thought he had hold of something more bizarre than the stuff I dealt with on a regular basis. "Try me," I said softly, and with a weary sigh added, "I'm the maven of strange."

He turned to me then, focusing hard, as if, for the very first time, he could really see me. "Yeah." He nodded and looked away, as if looking at me was too sad. "Yeah. Poor kid. You probably are, aren't you?"

I'm not used to empathy. It fluttered frantically inside me like a trapped moth. I tried to shake it off with a smile, and make some sort of joke, only I couldn't.

How did he know my secrets?

Chapter 8
Road Signs

"We better get moving. It'll be pouring soon." As if Ryder's words cued the rain, a giant mud drop splooshed onto my windshield and another struck the hood.

I tried to shake loose from the confusion engulfing me.

How much did he know about me?

And how?

How could he know *anything*?

What he said next captured my full attention. "Since you're driving this rattletrap, it might be a good idea if I—"

"Rattletrap?" I gestured at the army green interior. "This is vintage! An old friend." I patted the dashboard. "And I resent—"

"Yes, fine. Vintage. I get it. Thing is if we don't get back on the highway—" He pointed flippantly at my worn metal dash. "Your old friend here is going to sink up to her rusty axle in mud. And, while we're on the subject, how about you taking a turn following me for a change? It'd be a little safer in the downpour."

"Downpour? You can't tell by a couple of drops—" To illustrate the futility of my protest, rain began peppering the jeep. Big mud covered drops pinged against various body parts as if my vintage friend was an out-of-tune marimba.

Ryder turned those dangerous green eyes of his on me and leaned close, forcing me to concentrate. "Even if we hadn't just been through a major dust storm, which is generally followed by a thunderstorm, it's *you* we're talking about." He ticked off on his fingers a short history of my travels. "You've got dust devils and mountain lions after you. At this rate, I figure we're in for one heck of a deluge, don't you?"

My lips pursed up and twitched from side to side in what, I realized, was an unflattering imitation of my brother when he stewed over something. "All right, you have a point."

"And you'll follow me?"

The thought of bouncing back across the desert, alone, in dim light, facing a thunderstorm head-on, added considerable appeal to his offer. "Sure, I guess. For a while."

"Great, Sophie. Then, maybe you should tell me where we're going?"

"Hey! Wait a minute. You know my name." I squinted at him, suspicious again.

"Of course, I do." His fist wrapped around the door handle like he was ready to go. "So, getting back to those directions—"

"Listen up, Ryder Buddy, if that is your real name. I'm not going to follow you anywhere unless I get some answers."

"There's no time." The rascally rain sided with him and increased tempo.

I stuck to my non-existent guns. "For all I know, you could be driving me straight into a trap."

Those eyes of his widened with indignation. "I wouldn't do that." I wish his eyes were not so pretty. A boy really shouldn't have lashes that long.

I looked away. "Yeah, well, how do I know that?"

His voice softened. "I told you Sophie, I'm your protector, not your stalker."

"Potäto." I stared stubbornly straight ahead.

He rumbled like a grumpy bear. "We *need* to go." When I didn't concede immediately, his shoulders stiffened. "Now!"

"Not unless you tell me what's going on. Who sent you? And how you know my name? You know, just a few little life-threatening details like that."

"I can't. I'm not even supposed to be talking to you."

"Too bad. Go on then. Have a nice trip." I waggled my fingers in a flippant toodle-oo.

Ryder did a twitchy thing with his lips, just like Danny and I did when we were thinking. Except in the end Ryder's mouth clamped into a tight straight line, mashing my irritating objections between them. He exhaled, a big noisy puff of air, and

I knew then I'd won. "Okay," he said. "Since you were headed west, I'll assume that hasn't changed. We'll continue west and stop in Gallop for dinner. I'll explain what I can then."

That would have to do. I nodded.

He opened the door. "But I'm picking the place."

"Aye-aye, Herr Commandant." I saluted.

My stalker-turned-lion-tamer rolled his eyes and banged the door shut, which didn't amount to much since it was mostly cloth. Although I was impressed when he made sure the handle latched tight before dashing through the rain to his truck.

Did I say rain?

This was a mud bath. Big drops plummeted through the dust cloud, mixed with dirt, then collected in globby brown spitballs and splatted against my windshield. The wipers smeared this muddy mess back and forth, unable to clear more than a small hazy swatch for me to see through.

We crawled like blind caterpillars across the trackless rocky dunes and sagebrush, unable to see more than a few feet at a time. Finally, the storm turned into real rain, and a cleansing torrent washed away the grime.

The desert changed faces. Now, instead of bumping over rocks and barren earth, we splashed through rivulets and gullies streaming with water. My trusty "rattletrap" crossed these obstacles with ease, but Ryder's truck got stuck twice. Nothing that a little spinning out, backing up, rolling forward, and spitting muck all over my windshield, didn't cure.

If you ask me, I should have been in the lead. Things would

have been a lot cleaner. My advantages didn't last for long though. Faster and faster, the rain fell, until my wipers, fanning at full speed, could scarcely keep up.

Finally, we rolled onto the highway with our oil pans inexplicably intact. As Ryder had predicted, the thunderstorm developed into one of those 100-year type floods dumping buckets of water over the jeep. I leaned forward, ignoring the steady drip leaking through the duct-taped ceiling and soaking my right shoulder, and strained to see through the gray downpour.

Every dip in the road became a potential flash-flood situation. My brother's safety rules bleeped across my brain. *Special Danny news bulletin.* "We interrupt your next regularly scheduled thought to bring you this warning: do not attempt to drive through water that is more than six inches deep or midway up your tires. Warning! Do not do it, Sophie! You could be swept away."

"Okay, okay," I muttered, cutting off Danny's stern warning. "What am I supposed to do?" I didn't have a yardstick handy, and even if I did I wasn't about to get out there and measure. As we headed down the next slope it sure as heck looked deeper than six inches.

I tapped the brakes. If Ryder's truck started floating downstream, I'd know not to cross. Mercenary of me, I know. I like to think, if that actually happened, I would've found a way to rescue him. I shuddered, picturing him being swept away in the dark rushing water.

Drowning.

It all came back, far too vividly, the desperate strangling sensations. I wanted to stop that from ever happening again. Not to me. Not to anybody.

For years after Jace's death, I made it my mission in life to prevent drowning. As soon as I turned fifteen, I qualified for my lifesaving certificate. Summers were spent atop a lifeguard platform, red bathing suit, zinc smeared on my nose, making sure the kids in our town never suffered that horrifying experience.

Then my mom got lung cancer. As she slowly suffocated, I realized my fight was a losing battle. I couldn't save the world.

I couldn't save anybody.

Not even my own mom. All I could do was sit by her bed and hold her hand while she drowned in her own lung fluid.

And now, here I was, bobbing like a cork in the ocean on my way to who knows where, with wind, rain, and some unknown force fighting to hold me back.

What did I think—that I might win this battle to save wisdom?

How?

God help me, I wasn't even sure I could get myself across the next low place in the road. Worse than that, I didn't have the slightest idea which road to take next.

I swiped angrily at my eyes. Rain dripping from the ceiling must have made them mist up. Too bad I couldn't wipe away the worry that Llama-girl had picked the worst possible novice for this job. The sharp salty scent of fear rose in my nostrils. Pins and needles tiptoed over my scalp and spine. My airways squeezed so tight that big 'ole mountain lion may as well have been sitting on my chest, all hundred and fifty snarling pounds.

"Breathe!" I ordered myself. "The world isn't drowning just yet." I fixed my eyes on Ryder's blurry red tail lights. For now, I would just follow. And like Scarlet O'Hara always said, "I'll think about the rest of this crap tomorrow."

By the time we got up the mountains to Gallop, the trapezius muscles in my shoulder felt like chunks of granite. Rain had thoroughly drenched the clothing on my right side. My hair and skin bore a nice gritty coating of dust and sand. Not a pretty picture. I desperately wanted a steaming hot bath, a soothing cup of tea, and room service. After that, I planned to indulge in a long luxurious rest between clean sheets, the five-star variety, spotless and silky. No more sandpaper sheets washed sometime last week that smelled like overheated gym shoes.

Ryder had other ideas. He pulled up beside a fast-food restaurant, a squat cinder block building with a flat roof and a hand-painted sign on the wall that promised: Hamburgers, Tacos, Chorizo, Hot Dogs, and Deep-Fried Shrimp.

Reluctantly, I disembarked and trudged across the dilapidated macadam parking lot, avoiding potholes the size of washtubs that had discarded food containers and straw casings floating in them. I met Ryder under the red eaves. Water drained over the fascia board and splattered onto the narrow walkway.

Moisture mixed with the unmistakable smell of mustard and grease. "*This* is your idea of dinner?"

He gave me a cautious smile. "I felt like a burger." It sounded more like a question than an answer.

"Well," I huffed. "After that drive, I feel like hell. That doesn't mean I have a right to stab you in the eye with a pitchfork. Look at this place."

"Oh, come on." He gestured at the parking lot. "Check out all the cars. The food must be fairly good."

"Hmm." Despite feeling dehydrated, I needed to relieve myself. With trepidation I glanced around, imagining the condition of the restroom. Ah, there it was, tucked away at the back of the building like a gas station built in the fifties. A red door labeled *el baño* in faded black marker was decorated with a plethora of flamboyant graffiti.

Why oh why hadn't I brought a gun? It would have come in handy warding off vermin crawling on the floor while I squatted over the john.

Ryder shoved his hands into his jeans, and his shoulders went up in a shrug. "Given the condition of our clothes, a formal restaurant seemed out of the question."

His shirt had muddy splotches all over it, and I glanced down at my soggy attire. Mr. Logical had a valid point. We fit right in at this joint.

"Burgers it is." I put on my best game face, except it crumpled a bit when I turned back toward the bathroom. "Listen, I need to... ah...use the restroom. I'd ask you to come in with me because you said you're supposed to protect me, and I'm assuming that includes keeping me safe from crawly things, too, except we don't know each other that well. So how about you go in there first? Build a campfire or something to hold the critters at bay. You know, rats, mice, cockroaches large enough to be ridden in a rodeo."

He grinned and then clamped his lips together when he saw how serious I was.

"You picked this place, Ryder. You're going to have to go in there first. I promise to call out the National Guard if you don't come back out in ten minutes."

He held up his hands in a fair imitation of surrender. "No problem. I'll run recon. Can't be that bad."

I smirked skeptically and followed him to the door. "Oh, and don't leave the seat up. I don't want to touch that thing."

"Seat down. Got it."

Four minutes later, Ryder emerged rubbing his still-damp hands on the sides of his jeans. "No paper towels."

"Shocker." I peeked in as he held open the door. "Bugs?"

"A few crickets. Nothing to worry about."

I didn't see how he could be sure, since the floor was littered with crumpled paper towels that had overflowed from the trash can. All kinds of creatures might be lurking under that heap.

"Oh," he nudged my arm and lowered his voice. "I wouldn't sit directly on the throne if I were you." He looked genuinely concerned.

"Right." Despite the faint light from a lone bulb, which was made even dimmer by fluttering lacewings, I'd already glimpsed the peeling wooden seat in all its staph-infected glory.

The door banged shut behind me and I squatted nervously. Ryder had obviously stood and done his business facing the opposite wall. While I, on the other hand, squatted facing forward and was treated to a clear view of the debris pile. *Newsflash.* More than a "couple crickets" occupied that small room. Hoards of the little pests hopped gaily in and out of the trash pile.

Then I saw her.

In the far corner, a magnificent gray spider tiptoeing gracefully across the silken strands of her elaborate net.

Spiders didn't bother me much. As a kid, I loved every word of *Charlotte's Web.* How could I be afraid of spiders after admiring the noble creature who saved Wilbur? I had always hoped to see some spider spell out words in her web. Silly, I know, but I wondered what this one would write if she could?

Keep going, Sophie!

Or, *Go home.*

I would never know. A more immediate quandary drew my attention.

No toilet paper.

Forced to drip-dry, I watched in fascination as the spider carefully wove her sophisticated trap. She incorporated lumps of mummified flies and hapless moths into the design. I waited, childishly hoping to see the shape of a letter, or maybe even an arrow telling me which way to go, south for Arizona, or further west for California.

That was foolishness, of course.

I zipped up my jeans and ran water over my hands. No soap. Big surprise. The mirror was the hazy kind made from polished aluminum rather than glass. I sighed at my distorted image. My hair was a mess, and I desperately needed a shower. In this bathroom, there wasn't much I could do to remedy my appearance. So, I turned for one last look at the spider.

Light caught on the glistening strands of her web. I forgot about the water dripping from my fingers. My mouth hung open. I kicked paper towels and crickets aside for a closer look.

"Ryder!" I hollered. "Come here. You gotta see this!"

The door wasn't locked because, naturally, the lock was broken. "What's wrong?" He cracked open the door. "You alright?"

"Come in. You've got to see this."

Ryder stood beside me, studying the silvery web. "Is that...?"

"Yeah," I whispered, without shifting my gaze, unwilling to risk losing the image. "A star."

"But...how?" he murmured. "What?"

"Yeah. Exactly."

"Th-that can't be." He stuttered. "Not possible."

I pointed. "Those look like rays coming out of it, don't they?"

"Maybe," he said skeptically, and moved closer to me, studying it from another angle. "Most webs have radiating lines, right? Granted, these are..." He stiffened. "She filled in some of the rays, didn't she?"

"And underneath the star, isn't that a—"

"Rectangle." He drew in a deep breath. "You know what it looks like, don't you?"

"Charlotte's Web," I whispered reverently. *And an answer to my fears.*

"No, it's a..." Ryder stepped back shaking his head. "A flag," he whispered.

"Yes, it is." I grinned, and I would have hugged Char-lotte if she wasn't a squishy little spider who probably would've reciprocated by giving me a nasty bite. "You hungry, Ryder?"

"But that's..." He stared at the web. "Shouldn't we call a news team or something?"

"You can if you want. I'm going to go eat."

He hesitated and followed me out of the restroom, pointing back at the red graffitied door, shaking his finger. "That's the Arizona state flag."

"Yep." I smiled, and it was exactly what I needed. I felt so relieved that I thought joy might come bursting out of my fingertips at any minute.

"But it's in a..." He turned and stared at the door. "In a spiderweb."

"Could be a trick of the light. I'm ravenous, aren't you?" I looped my arm through his and towed him down the walkway to the front of the building. "Bet you six dollars I can eat a whole deep-fried cactus."

He didn't respond. The rain had stopped. The moon skated out from behind a dark cloud. A hundred crickets tuned up their fiddles and began the dissonant chorus of evening.

Before we went inside, Ryder muttered, "That's more weird stuff, isn't it?"

"What's weird? Deep-fried cactus?" I pretended to study the bill of fare painted on the wall outside. "I don't see it on the menu, but I'm sure if we ask—"

Ryder rolled his beautiful green eyes heavenward, and yet he didn't seem to notice the billions of stars blinking on in the aftermath of the storm. I looked up at the heavens and smiled.

God, I love your universe.

I really really do.

Chapter 9
Around the Bend

I couldn't figure this guy out.

Ryder was not good looking like some smooth-faced actor. He was way more sunburned and farm-boy than that. He looked more like the boy next door, the kind of guy you would definitely trust if he wasn't your stalker.

Except he's way too serious.

Yeah, but he was also kind of funny in his own way.

Like for instance, he ordered two jumbo cheeseburgers. Two! Then, he just sat there and stared at them. Not because he was too busy talking, mind you. He wasn't talking at all. I, on the other hand, chattered enough for both of us, happy because now I had proof that I wasn't a delusional nutcase headed in the wrong direction.

Okay, on second thought, Ryder is good-looking, in a rugged, he worked-in-the-oil-fields sort of way. And that quirky half-smile of his grows on a girl.

He said he was a geological engineer. I weaseled that much out of him. Haven't the foggiest idea what that means, except he spends most of his time looking at sedimentary rocks instead of women. Which I figured gave me an edge, not that it mattered. I had *things* to do.

Dating wasn't one of them.

Sigh.

"These onion rings look pretty good. Want one?" I interrupted his mental vacation and tempted him with a crispy golden circle. "They smell kind of shrimpy flavored, but otherwise edible."

He shook his head and took an absentminded bite of burger number one.

At this rate, we would be here until Christmas. "You want a take-home sack? I can get you one." I slid out of the booth, but he caught my arm.

"This isn't a joke, you know." He looked more than a little upset.

I sat back down and waited for him to unload whatever was bothering him. Frankly, I'd expected it fifteen minutes ago.

"I don't know if I'm going crazy or what." He raked his fingers through his hair. That wasn't good because grit from the dust storm sprinkled his shoulders and food tray. "Spiders just don't do that. They can't. It's impossible."

"Didn't you ever read Charlotte's Web?" I smiled like little Miss Sunshine.

His eyebrows pinched up in an unmistakable warning for me to stop making jokes. "This is serious."

"Look..." I wanted to comfort him, to say something philosophical and brilliant, except I had nothin'. So I shrugged. "The web was there to help me—that's all there is to it. A road sign. End of story. Let it go. To be honest, I'm surprised you could even see it. If we went back in there now, I guarantee you it would be gone. That's the way it works."

"Maybe that's how it works for you. Not me. There are things in this universe you can depend on." He thumped his finger on the scarred blue tabletop. "Math. Physics. The laws of nature."

"I see." I twirled the onion ring on my finger. "That certainly explains why you like rocks."

"Don't patronize me." He pressed his lips together in a thin impatient line.

"I'm not." I took a sip of my Coke and pointed the crispy circle at him. "Why does that spider bother you more than a mountain lion plopping down on my roof, or those coyotes on steroids?"

"Those things are explainable." He pointed in the direction of the infamous bathroom. "There's a spider in there . . . weaving flags." He propped his elbows on the table and rested his forehead in his hands. "That defies explanation."

"Hmm. Yeah, well, you know what else is unexplainable? Why a guy like you is following a girl like me—a girl who *loves* spiders that can weave messages. That's the big mystery, and you promised me an explanation. So let's have it, Ryder. Why are you here?"

He swallowed, and not because he'd taken a bite. Nope, his Adam's apple bobbed up and down as if he was trying to gulp down a golf-ball-sized case of nerves. "I'm not supposed to tell you. But now..."

He looked up at me like a stranded boy scout who'd just lost his handbook, his pocketknife, *and* his compass.

"Are you gonna tell me or not?"

"I can't. He told me not to—"

"He?!" I blurted. "*He*, who?"

"A guy in a suit."

"*Some guy in a suit*? That's it? Did you catch a name or a company?"

"No, but he had a slick laptop with some sort of governmental emblem on it." Ryder indicated the size of the laptop with his hands. "It was high-tech. *Very* high-tech. Not like anything I'd ever seen. Ever. Anywhere." He shook his head again. All that dust was going to totally ruin his food.

"A laptop?" I squinted hard at him. "So what?"

"Not just *any* laptop! There's not a computer store in the country you could walk into and find anything remotely similar. The tech was like something out of..." He clammed up for a second or two. "That doesn't matter. It's what I saw on it that convinced me to accept this assignment."

"Okaaay." I studied Ryder, wondering what could've been on that spiffy laptop that had him so worked up. He looked shaken, and this from a guy who looked tough enough to run offense in college football. Whatever he saw, it shook him up and now one little spider web was ripping a major hole in his confidence.

What in the world did suit-guy show him?

Unless...

"Wait a minute. Were llamas involved?" I asked.

"Llamas?" He frowned at me as if I'd completely lost what remained of my marbles.

"You know, big and hairy animals with long necks." I stretched my hand indicating their great height. "They tend to spit when annoyed."

"No! No llamas. And I can't tell you anything else, Sophie. I can't." He shook his head and stared at his uneaten burgers again. "I've probably said too much already. Broken all kinds of covert regulations. And if I don't clam up, they could send me to some sort of black-ops prison for the rest of my life." When he finally looked up at me, he wore an expression that looked so desperately lost I felt like crying for him.

Except then he went and stuck a pin in my sympathy balloon.

"It's just that after all that weird spider stuff, it feels like I'm losing my mind. I—I just don't know what's real and what's not."

Welcome to my world.

In the jeep he'd seemed to accept all the oddities of my world. I'd thought there was a chance this guy might understand. Instead, the very thing that reassured me shook him up.

Why couldn't he appreciate the wonder of it all?

I'd accidently squished the onion ring in my fingers, so I tossed what was left of it onto my paper plate. "Okay, sure, I get it. My weird stuff is too much for you. In that case..." I dusted the crumbs off my hands. "Maybe you should go back to Kansas, or wherever you're from, and hang out with your reliable physics books and your dependable laws of nature."

"Maybe I should," he mumbled.

I stood and looked down at him for a moment. "*Via con Dios*, Ryder. It's been fun, but I have work to do." I started to walk away, then turned back. "And for your information, it's not easy for me either. Nothing has ever been dependable in my world. *Nothing!*"

"Wait." He bolted out of the booth and caught hold of my arm, pulling me back, holding me close for a second.

But then, as if my skin had scorched his fingers, he let go. It left him standing smack dab within kissing distance. I swear, the poor guy looked like he didn't know what to do, kiss me or bolt out of there like a bull in a rodeo chute.

I possessed an itsy-bitsy stubborn streak. That was the only reason I can think of to explain why I didn't step back and give the bull room to run. Instead, I smiled defiantly up at poor confused Ryder and waited for his next move.

He didn't budge, just kept searching my face. If the man expected to get an answer from me, he'd be standing there till next January. I wasn't even sure what the question was.

Hoisted by my own petard.

I actually had no idea what a petard was, but all that gazing into one another's eyes made me a little bit nervous. Consequently, I turned on the chatter. "You're looking kind of pale, Ryder, buddy. You gonna faint?"

Nope.

Ryder didn't faint. He leaned down and her kissed me—surprised the socks off me!

What happened to Mr. Logical?

Kissing certainly did not seem like the next step in our equation. It was, however, rather nice. Kinda sweet. Tender even. Which was why I decided to kiss him back. With considerable enthusiasm.

Who knew geological engineers could kiss like that? He was kissing me like—

Oh-no!

I did the math and figured it out.

Darn him!

He was kissing me goodbye. Not just *any* goodbye, he'd kissed me like I was a doomed woman—giving me the kind of lip massage a guy would lather on his girlfriend if he thought she was scheduled to die in a plane crash that night.

He stopped to catch his breath. "Sorry."

Oohh—ewh! Now, he's apologizing.

That frosted it.

I backed out of kissing range.

"You're sorry?" I peppered my tone with enough sarcasm to make even the chef at Esperanza's Cocina catch his breath. "That was a *sorry* kiss, was it? My mistake. Here I figured it for a *nice-knowin'-ya, I'll see you at your funeral* kiss." Just to dig the pin in a little deeper, I mustered up the silkiest sultriest voice in my repertoire. "Tell you what, if I survive all this, why don't you look me up and test out one of your *not-sorry* kisses."

He winced.

Good!

He should wince after kissing me like that, when all the while he planned to abandon me to my fate.

I turned sharp and walked away, leaving good ole *kiss-'em-and-leave-'em-to-fend-for-themselves* Ryder standing there blinking. I strode out of the restaurant and glanced back through the window, expecting to see Ryder dialing 911, calling a search party to locate his missing tongue.

Instead, he stared blankly at the one and a half uneaten cheeseburgers on his tray, probably counting something solid and predictable, like how many sesame seeds were on his bun.

What did it matter?

There wasn't room in my life for half-hearted stalkers or would-be bodyguards. The crisp New Mexico night air slapped my cheeks. Time to get back on the road.

Three hours later, I was driving across stark lunar terrain

that literally glowed in the dark. Well, it wasn't entirely dark. There was starlight. And I wasn't dreaming. Unable to believe my eyes, I blinked several times. A few miles back I'd passed a sign welcoming me to the Petrified Forest, or maybe it was the Painted Desert. I had no idea what that desert was painted with, but no kidding, it glowed in places. Really, it glowed—blue unearthly gnome-shaped mounds, ghostly red and white striped rock formations, and barren gray moonscapes—the most unearthly scenery on Earth. Plus, the sky was purple out here.

Purple!

Forget Area 51. This place had to be the work of aliens. Either that or God has a whimsical sense of humor.

I pulled over. Without a doubt, I'd taken a wrong turn. How else had I ended up on a two-lane road in the middle of extra-terrestrial territory? I wasn't even certain I was in Arizona. Maybe the Bermuda triangle had blown over and swallowed me up. It didn't look much like Wise Woman territory. There wasn't a palm tree in sight.

A map would've come in handy. Unfortunately, I hadn't thought of that before leaving civilization. After all, I had my phone. Only, the signal had dropped an hour ago from one bar to no bars out here in intergalactic country. So, unless the local squirrels opened a convenience mart nearby and carried old fashioned paper maps, I was on my own. No signal. No compass. No soothing feminine voice talking to me from an onboard computer. It was just me and the stars under this eerie purple sky.

I pulled back onto the dark road and kept driving.

All roads lead somewhere, right?

Not necessarily.

Just about the time I was ready to surrender to tears, I spotted a green highway sign. The white letters gleamed under the illumination of my headlights and promised a major metropolis called Holbrook was only nineteen miles away.

It didn't actually say "major metropolis." Chalk that up to the sarcasm racing through my veins—the kind that flooded my bloodstream whenever I felt anxious or annoyed. At that particular moment, I was both.

After what seemed like way more than twenty miles, about the time I was thinking about doubling back, lights twinkled on the horizon. *Civilization!* A few more miles and I could identify the outline of buildings in the distance—Holbrook.

Cute little town. But closed. Not even a café or a gas station with a sign still blinking. Ghostly dark. Everyone had gone to bed. Not a bad idea, considering the day I'd had.

On the far edge of town, a lone motel sign flickered against the blackness, a neon beacon guiding me to port, tempting me with the promise of a warm shower and clean sheets. Morning would be soon enough to find my way out of this mountainous maze. I'd be fine after a little rest. I didn't need a llama to tell me where to go or a stalker to watch over me. I pulled in.

After taking the longest shower in history, thankfully without the intrusion of any cockroaches, I towel dried my hair and snuggled into bed, clean and content. Right before I drifted off to sleep, I speculated on where my erstwhile protector might be. I'll admit, I wouldn't have minded seeing Ryder's white truck in the parking lot below my second-story window.

Except he wouldn't be there. Couldn't. It would've been impossible. After all, I was lost. Not only that, there hadn't been any lights in my rearview mirror for miles and miles. Not a one. I figured Ryder must be heading the opposite way across the New Mexico desert, making his way back to Kansas.

My stomach flopped dejectedly against my spleen. Neurons bleeped a telegram to my cortex. *Desperately need a plate of chocolate chip cookies.*

I sent a reply. "Chocolate does not cure everything." My cortex was not convinced. I shut my eyes, hoping sleep would overtake me and carry me away into the languid clutches of Ryder-free dreams.

Darn his green eyes!

I sat up and gave the mattress a sturdy punch. Then I lectured myself, even as my legs carried me off the bed and over to the heavy drapes. "This is pointless and stupid."

Nevertheless, I lifted the edge of the curtains to check the parking lot and immediately wished I hadn't. Knowing for certain he wasn't out there felt worse. Much worse. I let the drapes fall back into place, blocking out the yellow light from the nearly empty parking lot, and scuffed slowly back to bed.

Oh well, it doesn't matter.

Really, it doesn't.

I wouldn't have time for men after I found the Wise Woman anyway. Who knew what life with her would entail? Seminars, lectures, expeditions to the Himalayans, treks across the Andes, appearances at the U.N.—I'd be way too busy for Ryder.

I tried counting sheep, except they morphed into obstinate llamas—llamas making fun of me and refusing to jump over the fence. Then, those cantankerous long-necked fuzzballs morphed into big stinky camels. Next, they melded together and formed one gigantic camel blocking my path in the middle of the desert.

When I first went to sleep, I'd been cold. That happens when one sleeps too close to an air-conditioning unit. Yet in my dreams, I ended up crawling across the hot sand toward that enormous pile of rocks shaped like a camel's hump and head. The desert heat nearly suffocated me. I woke up tangled in the blankets, sweating and thirsty. I tossed off the covers and sat on the edge of the bed, trying to cool down. My damp hair had dried into a wild mess. Checkout time was noon. I glanced at the clock and moaned. That gave me exactly twenty-three minutes to drink some water, unsnarl my hair, and throw on some clothes.

While eating breakfast—a breakfast, I might add, that was not scrambled up by any of llama girl's relatives—I browsed an Arizona map and guidebook. I'd picked up in case I lost my cell phone signal again. There would be no more wandering around mountains and eerie moonscapes. The booklet was full of ads for restaurants, and right there on page seventeen was a full-color photo of last night's bad dream—Camelback Mountain! A gigantic stone camel. There it was, adorned with palm trees and swimming pools, sitting smack dab in the center of the Valley of the Sun. Phoenix.

Home of the Wise Woman.

It didn't say that last part in the booklet, but I knew, just knew that had to be it.

After breakfast, armed with my trusty guidebook and map, I drove 180 miles more through winding mountains and finally descended into the sprawling Valley of the Sun. The Phoenix metroplex. According to the guidebook, which was slightly out of date, more than 4.6 million people inhabited that desert oasis.

My mission: locate one Wise Woman amid that burgeoning sea of humanity.

Two or three times I thought I saw Ryder's white truck behind me, except I couldn't be sure. Traffic got hectic as soon as I hit the city, and getting to Camelback Mountain wasn't as easy as I thought it would be. It isn't a mountain at all, more of a big rock hill surrounded by thousands of houses and businesses.

Once I got there, I cruised up and down the winding roads trying to find the Wise Woman's house. I had the absurd idea I'd know it when I saw it. Ha! What I needed was a radar that would beep when I got close or a bloodhound sniffing the way. Instead, I went on instinct. Which meant I wound around Saddle Rock and Cliffside Drives, hunting, hoping, driving past the same houses two and three times, and getting more and more frustrated. Hadn't I just been on Echo Circle a half-hour earlier?

The afternoon slid past four o'clock and turned smoldering hot. I was close—so close I could cry. Yet, I may as well have been two thousand miles away. Frustrated, I considered stopping, standing in the middle of the street, and yelling, "Hey! Anybody seen a Wise Woman?" I didn't though. Primarily because I valued my freedom. I was pretty sure Arizona had its share of mental health facilities, and I'd prefer not to spend the next two weeks in one. So, I kept driving. There was a dying Wise Woman somewhere on that giant rock pile, and I needed to find her.

I thumped the steering wheel.

I will!

I was so busy renewing my determination that I almost missed it—I slammed on the brakes. Before they even finished screeching, I rammed the jeep into reverse and backed up in front of a house with a Spanish tile roof.

Oh yeah, this had to be the place.

How did I know?

Some people put a statue of a lion in front of their homes as a symbolic guardian or a tough-looking bulldog with a ring through his nose. This homeowner went a different way. Beside the gracefully arcing driveway of *this* house stood a half-size iron replica of the orneriest llama in my acquaintance, same furry long neck, same lofty mocking expression as if she was in on some secret joke. It pleased me to note that one of the haughty tyrant's long ears had rusted and bent sideways, making her a rather comical substitute for a royal lion.

Not so lofty now, eh?

I pulled into the driveway and parked. The house looked like something Frank Lloyd Wright might have designed. The warm sand-colored adobe matched the stone it rested on, and its smooth flowing lines blended elegantly with the mountain's contours. I stared, took a deep breath, and reconsidered. A place like this had to cost a fortune. How could a Wise Woman live here?

Wise Women were humble people, right? They lived in monasteries and communes. They wouldn't flaunt their riches with a sprawling house on the side of a mountain in an exclusive neighborhood. I hadn't really expected to find a commune on Camelback Mountain, but this...

Hmm.

I tapped my steering wheel and stared.

The more I thought about it, the more I knew it had to be her house. No one with enough money to buy a place like this would put a tacky llama statue in their yard unless they were the Wise Woman. There was no mistaking that stringy hair or that smug expression. Only one llama could have posed for that goofy statue.

So, what if she's rich?

I had a job to do. I parked, climbed out of the jeep, walked slowly up the circular drive, and stood in front of a daunting pair of oversized wooden doors. Suddenly, I felt grubby and out of place. I didn't knock right away. My stomach cowered near my backbone. I rubbed a muscle knotting and twitching in my neck. This was it. Time to sink or swim.

Go on.

You can do it.

That was Daddy talking in my head. As often as I tried to avoid thoughts about him, sometimes he was just there. I could almost hear him say, "*This is no different than climbing up on that high dive and jumping off.*"

Sure.

What's the worst that could happen?

Oh, I don't know, she could call the cops because a crazy woman was standing on her porch talking to herself. Or worse, she could tell me to go away—that she didn't know anything about any Wise Woman.

Jump already!

So I did. I grabbed the big black iron knocker and gave it a firm rap. It thumped against the thick wood and echoed like a sledgehammer. I started to sweat, badly, and not just because it was hot.

A few minutes later the door opened. I had expected a servant, or at the very least, an adult. Instead, a little girl in a pink bathing suit greeted me, her wet hair dripping onto terracotta tiles in the entryway.

"Hi!" She grinned, unembarrassed by her missing front teeth. "Come in. Gramma's been waiting for you." She clasped my wrist and whisked me into the foyer, shutting the door. "This way." Her bare feet left damp tracks on the floor as she scampered ahead into the cool darkness of a large room. I stopped, stunned. A broad expanse of windows, shielded from the sun by a long, low overhang, opened onto a breathtaking view of the city.

"Come on!" she called, waving me forward as if I were a cumbersome jet she needed to maneuver into position on a runway. Obviously, she'd confused me with someone else, and now I was traipsing through a stranger's house.

In for a penny...

I followed the little girl out through the back door, where she abandoned me, took a running leap off the decking, and did a cannonball into the pool to join two other children.

Then I saw her.

On the far side of the patio, my quarry, the last hope of humankind.

The Wise Woman.

Her wide-brimmed hat drooped over her face, mimicking the shade of the palm trees behind her. The same graceful palm trees I'd seen in the vision.

Identical.

The exact same saguaros and sandstone rocks in the background— everything was exactly as llama girl had shown me—even the haze and smog wafting over the city in the valley below.

Children splashed, giggled, and shouted as they played in the water, completely ignoring me as I walked quietly up to the chaise lounge and studied the Wise Woman of our world, the guardian of wisdom.

She stirred and folded back the soft straw brim of her hat.

Dark sunglasses hid her eyes during those brief seconds of silence hanging between us. Finally, she lowered the glasses. Her mouth quirked to the side and her eyes crinkled at the corners. "So, you've finally come."

I kind of had a speech planned, something like, "*Hello, my name is Sophie. A girl and her llamas sent me to find you. Apparently, I'm supposed to be your novice.*" Except now that I really thought about it, that sounded dumb. And seeing her, *knowing she really existed*, paralyzed my tongue. I suppose, underneath it all, I'd wondered if she might turn out to be an illusion, a figment of my imagination. My brain lurched stupidly. Here was the Wise Woman, and I had nothing to say. I'd traveled two thousand miles to stand here speechless.

Now what?

She waited for my response, snowy hair framed by the straw hat, her clear blue eyes assessing me, the corners creasing in jovial lines as she watched my mouth stuttering short sounds, failing to form a coherent word.

She leaned forward. "How *is* llama girl?"

Chapter 10
Shadow of the Albatross

I ducked into the shade to escape the scorching sun. "It's true then? You're the last Wise Woman? And..." I tried to swallow, but my mouth felt drier than a dust devil. "And so, um, that means I really am the novice?"

At first, she didn't answer.

I realized then that all along I must've secretly hoped this journey might turn out to be nothing, a figment of my imagination. My shoulders sagged under the stifling heat and the weight of certainty. I drew in a deep scorching breath. "Isn't there *anyone* else besides me?"

She glanced away, watching the children in the pool, as if

my question made her uncomfortable. Turning back, she smiled wistfully. "There *were* others. Once." She shrugged. "You are the only one who came." She stood and held out her arm to me. "Come inside. You must be hot and exhausted."

I hesitated, not knowing how to respond to a stranger putting her arm around me. So, I blurted something totally off subject. "I was followed."

"Well, of course you were." She answered calmly, guiding me toward the house.

"Of course?" I questioned. "Surely, you can't think it's perfectly normal for a man to stalk me halfway across the country?

She laughed to herself as if she knew something I didn't.

My steps faltered and I stiffened. "Does that mean you know who sent him? And why?"

"There are always counter forces, my dear. Opponents. Some might even say enemies." Yet, she still smiled as if we were discussing the weather. "Distraction is one of our opposition's favorite weapons." She flicked her hand through the air like a magician banishing my concerns as if that answered all my questions.

It didn't.

Distraction?

My jaw tensed, as I followed her into the house. Nothing—*none of this* was as I expected it.

The woman who was supposed to help me keep our world from falling into the next disastrous Dark Age led me into her perfect perky yellow and white kitchen and poured me a glass of iced tea. She was as wrong for this job of saving the world as I was. What could a woman like this, wealthy, pampered, perfect, understand of the hardships the rest of us faced? I sat down at the counter and stared at the amber liquid sparkling in the tumbler.

"You're thirsty."

I nodded.

"Then drink."

I lifted the glass, but it seemed dreadfully wrong to relax over refreshments when llama girl's plans were falling apart right before my eyes.

The world is doomed.

She studied me for a moment. "I understand. You'd feel better if you'd found me sitting cross-legged on a cushion humming a mantra, wouldn't you?"

I glanced at her over the rim of my glass. "I didn't expect..." I waved my hand at the sunshine-y kitchen, the granite countertops, and gleaming stainless-steel appliances. "All this."

"Oh, I see. You're disappointed I didn't take a vow of poverty." She sighed. "You expected to find me cloistered away in an adobe hovel, didn't you? Living off the desert, surviving on prickly pear, wild honey, and locusts." She chuckled, evidently pleased with some private joke.

I shifted uncomfortably and gulped a mouthful of tea. The sweet lemony liquid bathed my throat and stripped away the dust and grime of my long hours on the highway. "Not locusts,"

I said, in almost a whisper.

"That's a relief. They're not nearly as tasty as one might imagine." She stifled a smirk and poured a glass for herself.

I supposed I should've been grateful we weren't squatting on the dirt floor of an adobe hut. I ran my finger over the polished cat's eye granite. And yet...what could a woman like this teach me about wisdom? Look at this place. And that designer hat she tossed so casually on a nearby chair. Those sunglasses—it would take me a half-month's salary just to pay for those.

I didn't come all this way for fashion tips or decorating secrets.

"Okay," I drawled. "What now? How does this Wise Woman thing work?"

Her fingernails tapped absently on the counter as she scrutinized me. "I prefer the term Wisdom Keeper."

I fidgeted. I wasn't fond of close inspections, particularly when it felt as if my flaws were standing up to take a bow. "Look, I've come a long way." I tried to sound frank and business-like. "I'm sure I look dusty, rumpled, and in desperate need of a shower. It wasn't an easy trip. Things happened. Strange things. But I hurried because llama girl and her furry friends seemed to think—"

I stopped, impatient, but not callous enough to say *those* words.

"What?" Her eyebrows shot up. "Did she tell you I'm dying?"

Unfortunately, my silence answered more brutally than I

could have.

She blew air between her lips. "Pffft! I'm in perfect health. See for yourself." She stepped back, allowing me to assess.

She looked fine, but I didn't have x-ray eyes. What did I know? There was no point in responding. *Death is a tricky booger.* It didn't always show up on the outside. She knew that as well as I did.

"I'm in superb health." She insisted with a little more vehemence than necessary. "Although, I suppose, something unforeseen..." She stared out the window to where the children played. "*Could* happen."

It can't be easy to look squarely into the mirror of your own mortality, to see the fatal crack splintering and wonder exactly how much time is left.

"Did llama girl say anything else?"

I shook my head. "Just to hurry."

"That could mean anything, months, even years."

"Sure." I conceded. Although, if that was true, why did I feel this intense sense of urgency?

She sniffed pointedly at me. "Shoot straight with me or we won't be able to accomplish anything."

I didn't know how to respond to her scold, so I scrawled a question mark in the moisture condensing on the outside of my glass. She stood silent as well, watching her grandchildren, glancing around her kitchen as if storing up all the memories it evoked.

We weren't getting anywhere. I tiptoed back into the

conversation. "Your granddaughter said you *knew* I was coming?"

"Bridget." She whispered, and her lips rested in a soft smile as she glanced out at the little girl splashing in the pool.

"You're right," I said with as much cheeriness as I could muster. "It could be years. There must be mountains of things I need to learn." I gauged her reaction, waited for a response but got none. I sighed heavily. "Look, ma'am, I don't have any idea what I'm supposed to do now. Llama-girl just said, 'Go and find the Wise Woman.' So, you tell me, what's on the agenda?" I paused expectantly.

Still, she ignored me.

Irritated, I tried to draw her out. "I do have things to get back to, you know... *a life*."

Why she thought *that* was funny, I cannot say. "A life." Her sardonic laughter didn't bode well. "Very well, *novice*." She leaned against the counter and studied me. "How do *you* think it works?"

"Oh, I see, answer a question with a question." If my quasi-mentor wanted straight shooting, she was about to get it. "No, thank you. I played that game with my professors in college. It's slow and tedious."

"It can be, can't it?" She grinned full out then, all the crinkles and lines springing into action. She slapped her hand on the counter. "I like you!" She declared this as if it was a long-awaited verdict, lifted her glass to toast the happy discovery, and then drank heartily. "This might not be so bad after all."

“Wonderful,” I muttered and sipped my tea.

“Let’s start again, shall we? I’m Naomi.” She presented her hand.

I did the same. “Sophie.”

“Ah. Of course.” There was that enigmatic half-smile again. Naomi set her tea on the counter and opened the fridge. “Well, Sophie, what would you like for supper? How about a nice chicken salad?” She plunked a head of lettuce on the counter. I must’ve been biting my lip pensively or something, because she paused and squinted at me. “There’s no ceremony, if that’s what you’re thinking. No crystal ball handed down through the ages. I don’t have a magic scepter to thump you over the head with. Taa daa! Here you go. Here’s all the wisdom of the world.”

My stomach curled up like a disconsolate child and drooped near my spine to mope. Surely, I hadn’t come all this way for nothing. “Nothing?”

“I didn’t say *that*.” She shook her head and mumbled something as she delved back into the refrigerator, and I thought she said something like, “Wisdom without experience leads to madness.”

“There must be something,” I urged. “A manual? A list of guidelines? A website? Something? What about a book?”

“A book?” She laughed, pulled out a package of celery hearts, a large carrot, and shut the refrigerator. “A *book*.”

Naomi turned and concentrated that squinty assessing look of hers on me again, making me afraid all the weird parts of my brain were marching forward, and in their best Minnesota-country-girl voice, introducing themselves. "Howdy-do, ma'am, I'm Miss Sophie's good pal, Insecurity, and this here's our cousin, Awkwardness."

She leaned in, studying my face. "Llama girl told me you ask the right questions."

Was that respect?

I gulped. I distinctly heard respect in the Wise Woman's tone. It took me a minute to boot my countrified self-consciousness offstage and wrap my head around her words. "Wait. Are you saying, there *is* a book?"

"Oh, yes. There most certainly is."

"A manual?"

She chuckled again. "Not exactly."

The back door flew open. "Gramma! Gramma!" The little girl dripped water on the floor and shouted. "Matt won't stop cheating. We're playing Marco Polo, an' he keeps peeking."

"Hmm." The Wise Woman rested her hand against her cheek and tilted her head. "And what would you like me to do about that?"

"Tell him to stop peeking."

"Did you tell him?"

"Yes, but he keeps doing it." Bridget huffed her shoulders and pursed her lips for a moment. "Oh, I know what—you could make him sit on the deck and listen to one of your stories."

The Wise Woman sighed softly. "Tell you what, you go back outside, and I'll be there in a minute or two to tell all of you a story."

"*All* of us?" The little girl stepped back.

"Yes. Unless, of course, you think you can manage the situation without me?"

"Um, okay. I think I can manage." The little girl backed out of the door and splashed into the pool. Her threats to her brother echoed through the window. "If you don't stop cheating, Gramma's gonna come out here and make you sit on the deck while she tells you a really *really* long story."

The younger boy must have capitulated, because shouts from the backyard sounded far less hostile.

"I thought kids liked stories?"

"They do. Although, I think they enjoy swimming and video games a bit more." She placed a package of frozen chicken in the microwave to thaw. "What about you?"

"Swimming is great. Minnesota is pretty cold most of the year, but I—"

"No." She leaned across the counter again and stilled my hands in hers. "*Stories*, my dear, do you like stories?"

How should I answer?

Should I mention how often as a child I'd hidden out in my room with a book? Or that I used to climb our oak tree and imagine the world below was the lost island of Robinson Crusoe? Or that I loved it when my mother read aloud, her voice carrying me away to England where I galloped on the back of Black Beauty or off to Switzerland to climb the Alps with Heidi.

Did I like stories?

No.

I craved them.

I craved them so much it felt as if I must have them or die of mental malnutrition. Nonchalantly, I swirled the ice cubes in my glass and shrugged. "Sure. Yeah, I like stories."

She squinted again and nodded, seeing straight through my guarded reply.

As I squirmed under her knowing scrutiny, a quick rap resounded from the front door and someone hollered from the foyer, "Hey, Mom! It's me."

"In the kitchen, Ashley." Naomi turned on the tap and began to wash the lettuce.

Spiked heels clicked against the clay tiles as Naomi's daughter walked briskly into the room. Tall, blonde, and meticulously groomed, I wondered if maybe she worked as a runway model for Saks business clothes. In that ice blue suit she could've held court with the president and his cabinet. Ashley kissed the air by her mother's cheek and turned to greet me.

I squirmed uncomfortably on the bar stool, smoothed my wrinkled t-shirt over the waistband of my cutoffs, and finally surrendered to the lost cause. "Hi! I'm Sophie." I shoved my hand out in greeting and plastered on a smile.

Ashley performed a two-millisecond appraisal of my rank, title, and social standing, squeezed out a glazed smile of dismissal, and turned back to her mother. "Thanks for watching the kids. The nanny will be back tomorrow."

"No problem." Naomi plunked the lettuce in a colander and dried her hands.

Her majesty, Ashley, strode out back to collect her children.

Naomi's smile was self-conscious, almost apologetic. "My daughter."

"I gathered."

Ashley returned with her three little munchkins marching in line behind her, wrapped in towels, sloshing in their flip-flops, and leaving a trail of pool water. Bridget grinned up at me and waved. The oldest boy complained about having to leave, but the youngest detoured into the kitchen and darted up to Naomi, offering his grandmother an irresistible wet pucker. "Bye, Gram-gram!"

Then his sister dashed back and added her kiss to Naomi's wet cheek, throwing in a soggy hug. "I love you, Gramma."

Naomi tugged the little girl into a tighter hug. "I love you always."

"Hurry up, Bridget!" Ashley called from the foyer. "We're running late. Tell Gramma thank you, and let's go."

Bridget waved at me and scampered away shooting a question to her parent. "Mamma, did you meet the novice?"

There was no answer.

Ashley walked slowly back to the family room where she had a clear view of the kitchen counter. Blanched, she stared at me and then at her mother. Her lips moved, and I scarcely heard her whisper. "Is it true? She's the—"

Naomi busied herself with a towel, wiping up the floor. "Yes, dear, Sophie is my novice. Don't worry about it. Run along, darling, you're late."

"But if she's here—"

"Ashley, I'm fine. Nothing is going to happen overnight. Call me tomorrow. We'll talk about it then."

Naomi's daughter took a stutter step toward us, but the children started bickering. She glanced in their direction, and then back at us. I felt sorry for her as she battled one of those moments that divides and tests us so grievously. The children's escalating commotion won out. Ashley's posture sagged and those six-inch Italian heels suddenly looked grossly uncomfortable as she clomped toward her restless children.

I wanted to weep for her, but it wasn't my place.

Naomi, though, watched her daughter's departure with more than pool-water moistening her cheeks.

My presence here meant the unthinkable. I was the harbinger of death, a giant albatross darkening their lives. There had to be something I could say, something to fill the clumsy moment. My mind considered the unsuspecting faces of her grandchildren. Except the little girl, she was different.

She knew.

"Your granddaughter, Bridget, she's perceptive. Couldn't she have been the novice?"

"I'd thought it was possible."

"But not her mother?"

"No." Naomi propped her hands on her hips and glanced around her kitchen as if she couldn't quite get her bearings. She swiped at her cheek with the back of her hand. "I'd hoped, of course." She shook her head slightly. "It simply wasn't to be. By the time Ashley was seven or eight I knew she wouldn't be the one."

"Why isn't Bridget your novice?"

"Too young, I suppose." Naomi shrugged and laid chicken breasts into a baking dish. "Who can say? You were chosen. That's all there is to it. The remarkable thing is..." She paused and sprinkled herbs over the meat. "You came."

Chapter 11
A Secret Room

Naomi put the chicken in the oven and gestured to me. "Come. I'll show you to your room."

I followed her down a hallway. The walls in this part of the house were painted a muted pomegranate—a strange shade of red that drew me in and swallowed me up as we walked deeper into the bowels of the house. I felt like a thief tiptoeing through a dragon's lair in search of treasure. We passed several rooms, dusky chambers with plantation blinds strategically angled to minimize the late afternoon sunlight.

I paused in a doorway, straining to identify a splash of white I'd glimpsed through the louvered slats. My steps faltered.

It couldn't be . . . him!

Could it?

No.

Ryder hadn't been behind me on the road to Phoenix. I'd checked. Besides, there were millions of other white trucks in the universe.

And yet...

I hurried to catch up to the Wise Woman. "That guy, the one I told you about, the guy who followed me—I think he's parked on the street out front!"

"Doesn't surprise me, my dear. You mustn't let it trouble you." Indifferent to my alarm, she turned down a long dark passage. "Did you really expect he would give up so easily?"

Yes!

No.

Maybe.

I shook my head. I supposed there was a chance it wasn't him. Even as I denied it, I knew, somehow, he had managed to find me.

"Never underestimate your adversaries." Naomi cautioned as if reading my mind, and then dismissed him with a shrug.

"Adversary?" I asked. "You mean, like an enemy."

She laughed. "Not exactly an enemy. But at the moment, though, we must turn our minds to more important things."

A set of keys dangled in her hand, and we approached a

narrow door made of solid oak. "*This* is your room," Naomi whispered reverently and traced her fingers over an enormous black antique lock.

Thoughts of Ryder evaporated.

My room, she'd said. This doorway looked suspiciously like a Spanish dungeon. I'd read *The Count of Monte Cristo* and didn't fancy being locked away or trying to dig my way out with a spoon.

I edged back.

Naomi held up a large ornate iron key. The handle itself was cast in loops forming the symbol of a gothic cross. She hesitated before jamming it into the keyhole. "I salvaged this lock from one of the crumbling old trunks that had housed The Wise Woman Chronicles since before the Middle Ages. It dates back to the 14th century. As long as one keeps it oiled, the locking mechanism will work as well now as it did then."

The latch clicked noisily and finally released with a soft clunk. She pushed open the door. "My will stipulates that this lock, the key, and everything inside this room, belongs to the novice." She motioned for me to enter. "It's yours now."

I stood there blinking as if standing in the muted light of a medieval forest. A mound of dragon's jewels would not have stunned me more. I couldn't move.

Naomi walked past me and gestured with her arms wide. "It isn't a hammock on a porch, but I think it's rather nice, don't you?"

"This is incredible." I stumbled toward a massive four-poster bed with vines and leaves carved into the dark woodwork, and a canopy hung with mossy green gossamer veils. "Way better than my hammock. Wait!" I turned sharply back to my hostess. "How did you know that I like to sleep on the porch in a hammock?"

Naomi grinned, apparently anticipating the moment I would step into that particular snare. "Yes, well, I believe when you were given a vision of me, I had a simultaneous vision of you on your porch in a hammock staring at the moon."

"But—"

She waved away my question. "Perhaps llama girl opened a visual portal of some sort."

I shook my head. "Couldn't have been a portal. It wasn't nighttime in Minnesota when I saw you. And what I saw was you laying on a chaise lounge exactly as you were when I saw you this afternoon. She showed me the future."

Naomi nonchalantly dismissed my concern. "Time is a funny mechanism. Not quite so linear as everyone thinks."

Across from the bed stood the most amazing cabinet I'd ever seen. Plump, heart-shaped apples were carved into deep wine-red hardwood and polished until they glistened. Sculpted leaves and vines twined thick and lush around leaded glass compartments of various sizes. Naomi pressed a switch on the side, and light, soft as fairy dust in the forest, illuminated hundreds of leather spines.

I edged closer. "Are these The Chronicles?"

"Yes." She opened one of the compartments. "The entire

case is temperature and humidity controlled. The glass restricts UV light. I had a specialist in manuscript preservation design it. Before they were passed down to me, these priceless journals and books had been kept in cedar trunks and stored in a warehouse. Think of it. Centuries of irreplaceable writings at the mercy of the weather." She ran her fingers over the leaves sculpted on the corner of the bookcase. "I had a cabinetmaker reuse any of the carvings salvageable from the old trunks."

"Apple tree," I echoed her reverent tone.

She touched a delicate, five-petal flower tucked in among the leaves. "And blossoms."

I noticed a snake cleverly woven through the twining branches. "This symbolizes the tree in Eden, then?"

"Very good." She tilted her chin in my direction approvingly. "Yes, the Tree of Knowledge of Good and Evil. Eve made that fatal decision to introduce knowledge into the world. Then she enticed Adam to join her in her disobedience. Their sin resulted in the two of them being cast out of the garden. Ejected from paradise, thrust into a world of decay, pain, and death, they took with them knowledge—unbridled, unrestrained knowledge. One might think knowledge would be a help to them, right?"

I nodded, picturing them struggling to learn how to build fire and make shoes. "They would need it to learn how to do things."

"Except, in the garden, they'd already learned many things. How to prepare food. How to groom the garden and tend the animals. God even made clothes for them out of animal skins before they even left the garden. By the way, he would've had to slaughter an animal to make those clothes. Imagine seeing one of their pets flayed open just so they could be clothed."

I cringed, remembering how I always hated it when we sent our pigs and cows off to the slaughterhouse.

Naomi directed my attention back to her. "Consider the name of the tree Eve ate from."

I responded hesitantly. "Knowledge of Good and Evil?"

"Yes. Technically though, hadn't they already been introduced to good? After all, they lived in a peaceful good garden, they had plenty to eat, perfect weather, no weeds, and the animals weren't vicious. And they walked with God, who is most assuredly good."

"Yes..." I gripped the book tighter, staring at the words, struggling to find my way through the maze she was weaving. "All good."

"So, what did they primarily gain knowledge of?"

"Ohhh..." I sank back against the chair. "*Evil.*"

Her mouth quirked up to the side in an expression I had begun to recognize as semi-approval. "With her sin, Eve brought us knowledge. Yet without wisdom, that knowledge was used primarily for evil. Point in case, one of the first things humans learned to do outside of the garden was kill. And then to lie. And to blame. All because Eve chose knowledge. God held Adam ultimately responsible, but is it any wonder that it falls to Eve and her daughters to try to balance knowledge with wisdom?"

"Does it?" *They hadn't taught* us *this in Sunday school.* Skepticism was a trait I had trouble hiding. "Balance it, how?"

"Perhaps counterbalance would be a better word. This world relies upon a precarious balance in all things. Male does not exist without female, and vice versa. There is no day without night, nor light without dark. In this world, it is through the lens of evil that good is made evident. That lens helps us *begin* to comprehend the radiant goodness of God."

"I get it," I said. "Opposites."

"Yes, but not always opposites." Naomi pressed her hands together, prayer-fashion, two forces warring against one another. "Many aspects of our world war against each other. For instance, rain versus sunshine. Too much rain creates a swampy treeless bog. Too little and the sun-scorched earth cracks and becomes barren sand dunes. Both have their place in nature, but neither are inviting habitats for humans. Knowledge, in and of itself is neither useful nor detrimental. The trouble is, without wisdom to guide its usage knowledge becomes dangerous. Ultimately fatal. The Wisdom of God stabilizes knowledge and teaches us to use it beneficially rather than for destruction. Do you understand?"

I hadn't forgotten llama girl's demonstration of the ingenious torture devices used in the dark ages when everything was out of balance and horribly askew. "I suppose that's why I'm here."

"Yes." Naomi relaxed her shoulders and nodded. As if reciting a mantra, she repeated, "And it is why Eve and her daughters must do all they can to preserve and increase wisdom until God finally transforms the universe and restores perfect peace."

I took a deep breath and pointed at the cabinet. "It looks like you've done it. Preserved wisdom, I mean. Other than that, I don't see how we can do anything to bring the world into balance—you and I? Seriously, do you watch the news? It's gone crazy, and we are just—" I shrugged my shoulders. "Two women. We're nobodies in the scheme of things."

"So it would seem." Naomi's hands dropped to her side. She glanced briefly out of the window and sighed heavily before facing me. She stood like a penitent child, with her head bowed in shame. "I'm afraid I haven't done a very good job of it. I had personal distractions, and what little I did do was spent safeguarding the manuscripts. I neglected more important matters."

"Wait—wasn't that the point? To preserve wisdom?" I waved my hand at all the books. "It looks like you did that very well."

"Yes, I built a cabinet. Except there was more to the job than that—much more." She clasped my arm, tugging me toward the cabinet and some invisible purpose. "Don't you see? I ought to have preserved it in the hearts of our sisters. I failed in that. And now women's place in humanity, our role in the universe, in the spiritual world—all these things have been lost. Distorted. Traded. It's almost too late." Her voice broke and her eyes welled with the threat of tears.

Why was she so distraught? I wasn't the kind to give up without a fight, only I wasn't exactly sure what battle she was talking about. "Too late for what? It seems to me women are doing better than ever," I protested.

She let go of my arm. "Are we?" Her features surrendered to gravity and drooped in sad mournful lines.

"Well, yeah. I mean we can vote, and—"

"Oh yes," She cut me off. "A century ago, here in the states, we won the right to vote." She heaved in a deep breath. "And we do get paid on a more equal basis now. And here, a woman can pursue any career she chooses. We aren't required to wear dresses in the workplace. The double standard isn't quite so glaring anymore, which means a woman's morals are no longer inequitably questioned by society."

I forced a smile in the face of her gloomy sarcasm. "Um, well, that's all good, isn't it?"

"Is it? There are dozens of countries where we have no such freedoms. Where millions of women are still treated like expendable chattel. Even if we callously ignore their suffering, those wins are mere trifles. Trifles!"

Trifles?

Was she going all Gloria Steinem on me?

I stepped back. But she moved closer, bearing down on me intently. Twisted with sadness, her features suddenly bunched, and the muscles tightened into the hardened lines of a warrioress. "Those were paltry aspirations. *Feeble* in the face of what we could've accomplished! *Mere nothings* compared to what we could've been—compared to what we really are inside." She stepped back and straightened to her full height. "Women have altogether forgotten our place in the divine. We've surrendered to the world and forgotten our true powers."

Our true... what?!

I swallowed nervously and backed up, bumping against the curling tail of the cedarwood serpent. "Um, we have *powers*?"

Please, please God, don't let the Wise Woman be a crazy person.

"See? Even you don't understand." Her shoulders sagged, and sadness conquered her features once again. She dropped into a chair beside the cabinet. "I *have* failed."

"No, don't say that." I wasn't sure if she'd failed or not, but I didn't like to see people crushed under guilt. I knew what that was like. I knelt by her chair. "Look, I'm here now. You can teach me all about these mysterious superpowers women have. You can explain our place in the...the universe, or whatever it was you called it."

"Our place in the divine," she murmured and shook her head, staring at her hands clamped together in her lap. "It's too late, Sophie. I've let all of you down. Not just you. All women, everywhere. What's even worse is that I was allotted a time in history when I might've made a tremendous difference. The world was ripe for growth. Instead, I let doubt win. I got distracted. Tangled up in the weeds of life. Procrastinated. And now—" She bowed and pressed her face into her hands. "Now, it's too late."

Her sorrow nearly broke me, and her regret twisted my stomach into such a tight squeezy knot that my heart cried out for me to *do something. Do something now!*

I had no tricks of my own. So I did an impression of my Mom. I mimicked my mother's soothing voice and her calm sureness. "Listen, Naomi," I said and patted her knee just the way Mom used to do. "Llama girl could've sent me here two years ago, maybe even five years ago. Except she didn't, did she?"

Naomi glanced up at me and waited, squint-eyed, for me to say more.

"She sent me to you *now*—to *this* exact moment in time. I don't understand llama girl, and I can't even begin to know *what* she is. Or *why* she exists. All I know is that four days ago she appeared in a vision along with her strange flock of llamas, sheep, goats, and geese, and they sent me here to find you."

Naomi's nose twitched. "She has geese now?"

"Yeah, and maybe some ducks. The important thing is that God must have something to do with all of this, because the whole way here there were signs. Big signs." I remembered Esperanza's Cocina, the spiders web, the cougar. "And...well... there were miracles. Lots of them."

The Wise Woman was listening, really listening. It looked like some of that grief, regret, or whatever was, began to lift. I smiled my cheeriest smile, the one reserved only for important occasions. "That's why, instead of giving up, I think you should begin teaching me."

She straightened and studied me for what seemed like the

longest two minutes in history. Finally, she nodded. "Very well."

"Whew! Good. Because I've come a really long way." I took a breath. "So where do we start?"

The corner of her mouth twitched. "At the beginning."

Chapter 12
In the Beginning—הקודש רוח

Looking back on it, I think that first lesson was the most difficult. It shook my world more violently than the earthquake that ripped Coldwater in half.

"The beginning?" I asked, meandering blindly in where angels dare not tread.

"You *have* read Genesis, haven't you?"

I nodded, getting a little nervous. Sure, I'd read Genesis. But I crossed my arms warily, hoping she didn't intend to ask me about any other books in the Old Testament, like for instance, Leviticus. I had yet to trudge all the way through that one.

Did she expect me to know the entire Bible?

"Are you listening?" Her hands were on her hips and her eyebrows imperiously arched.

I am now.

I nodded.

"Do you remember the part in Genesis where it says, 'Let us make man in our own image?'" She emphasized the word *us*.

"Uh," I hesitated. "Yes. I think so."

"Hmm." She frowned. "Perhaps you'd better read it again." She pulled a thick leather-bound Bible from the shelf, flipped it open, and handed it to me.

Her nose wrinkled at my hesitation. "Just read those two verses, 26 and 27." She tapped the page. "Aloud."

Impersonating an obedient student, I cleared my throat and dove in. "And God said, 'Let us make mankind in our image, in our likeness—'"

"Stop," she interrupted. "You may skip all that fish, fowl, and cattle stuff. Move on to verse 27."

I bent over the book, attentive to her finger pointing to verse 27. "So, God created mankind in his *own* image, in the image of God he created them; male and female he created them."

"There! Do you see it?"

"See what?"

She exhaled impatiently and drummed her finger on the sentence. "It's right there."

Apparently I was a slow understudy. I squinted at the verse.

"Male and Female." She swung her hands wide as if encompassing the whole world. "Together *they* created fathers, mothers, and eventually children, right?"

I nodded dutifully.

She tapped her foot. "Created in God's image. So, who is this triune God—this Holy Trinity, this *us* who created family, fathers and mothers? Let's see, we have God the Father, God the Son, and...?" She ticked them off on her fingers and waited, watching me with the expression of a shrewd old owl observing a young mouse crawling on the ground.

God the Father.

God the Son.

And...

"The Holy Spirit." My eyes must have opened wide enough to allow a blast of wind straight through to my brain. "You don't mean the Holy Spirit is..."

God the Mother?

It couldn't be.

I'd grown up a good little church-going girl, our congregation reciting the Apostle's Creed every week. Naomi kept talking, but I couldn't concentrate.

Is it possible we have a Heavenly Mother?

Has She been there all along in the person of the Holy Spirit?

Stunned and shaking, part of me cried in joy.

I felt like a lost orphan who'd just found her missing parent. Another part of me got shaky and nervous—I'd never heard this doctrine before. *Was it heresy*? I was pretty sure the Coldwater Church Council would think so. Then again maybe no one had ever pointed this out to them either.

Deep inside, though, another part of me smiled serenely and sighed with relief. It was as if I'd subconsciously understood this truth all of my life but had never fully looked at it before now.

Each of those parts of me pulled in different directions. *It was a lot.* Spots swirled at the corners of my vision, and my temples drummed uncomfortably. I sat mute, nearly drowning in joy and awe, bewilderment and shock.

No longer an orphan.

I had a whole and perfect family. God was a whole and perfect family. And I belonged to them.

I didn't know whether to jump up and dance or to faint.

"Think, Sophie." The Wise Woman stood over me, gesturing as vigorously as if she was speaking, not just to me, but to an auditorium full of novices. "Does it make sense that not one of the three members of the Godhead would be feminine? Is woman such an inconsequential creation that she fails to be related to any aspect of this same God who said 'let *us* go down and make humans in *our* image, male and female'?"

I shook my head and laid my hand over the words in Genesis. "It says so right here. Why have I never seen this before?"

She smiled as if I'd pleased her. "It's not only in Genesis, Sophie. It's everywhere in the scriptures if your eyes are open."

"Everywhere?" I blinked.

"In the Old Testament, the Holy Spirit is referred to as

Ruach HaKo'desh. Her name is not merely grammatically feminine. It is figuratively and allegorically feminine, and it occurs more than ninety times throughout the Bible."

"Why was I never told this before?"

Naomi sighed and dropped into the chair next to mine. She wore a grave condolences expression. The face that people wear when they have to dish out the bad news that someone you loved has died. "I believe..." She reached for my hands and clasped them in hers. "God allowed it to remain hidden for many years. And for a very good reason."

I pulled out of her grasp. "What possible reason could there be for hiding something as important as this?"

Naomi glanced away as if she were gazing into the past. "Think of how you felt about your earthly mother. Not as you did when you were a teenager trying to escape being bossed around. Think instead about how you felt as a young child when she was your whole world. And how you feel *now*—now that you are mature enough to appreciate the countless good things your mother did for you. The nights she sat up with you when you were sick or the times she went to bat for you against a mean teacher at school. Or how she taught you the names of all the flowers blooming on the mountain behind your house."

Had Naomi noticed the lump in my throat? I bowed my head, wondering if she knew my mother was dead.

Naomi leaned close as if confiding a secret. "God the Father and His son, Jesus, are very protective of the Holy Spirit, just as you are of your mother, and the way most men are of their mothers and wives. Why do you think Jesus warns in both Matthew and Luke that blasphemy against Him and the Father can be forgiven, but blasphemy against the Holy Spirit will not be tolerated? Bad mouthing Her is the one unforgivable sin."

I looked up, blinking. I had always wondered why that was unforgivable.

She nodded solemnly, stood up and paced. "That may be why God has allowed Her identity to be obscured all these centuries—for the sakes of those who might foolishly blasphemy Her and damn themselves. He is, after all, extraordinarily loving and merciful."

"However..." She stopped and leaned against one of the large carved posters of the canopy bed. "There is another reason why it has been hidden for all these centuries." She spoke so softly I almost couldn't hear her.

I knew the reason, felt it in my bones.

Opposition in all things.

"Evil."

"Yes." She slowly traced her finger over the corner bedpost, a carving of a serpent winding its way up the tree trunk. "Counterforces. There are always counterforces. The evil one would like nothing more than for women to remain blind to our potential. To keep us stumbling in the dark, uncertain of our value in the spiritual world, and even worse, for us to stay completely ignorant of our powerful role model in the person of the Holy Spirit."

I massaged my throbbing forehead, trying to understand.

"Isn't that all the more reason for them to teach this in church?"

She sighed. "How did you expect them to do that, when as early as the first Nicaean council clerics began purging the Spirit's feminine nature from canonical writings? During the conflicts between Gnostics and Traditionalists, they nearly annihilated it. Men decided it was acceptable for women to personify virtue, modesty, and beauty—which is odd because men can be every bit as beautiful as women. And women certainly haven't cornered the market on virtue. But they simply could not accept that any part of God was feminine. They balked at the idea that the female aspect of God represented wisdom. Although anyone who reads Proverbs 8 cannot doubt it. Perhaps if the Holy Spirit only represented comfort and assurance, they would not have had such difficulty, but the magnificent Holy Spirit is also the fiery powerful testifier of truth."

Naomi's hand slid off the bedpost. "Consider the historical context. Early church leaders accepted women and honored them as equals in Christ. Mary Magdalene holds the honor of being the first person greeted by the resurrected Christ. The Apostle Paul considered Pricilla a coworker in his ministry. She and many other women served as leaders in the early churches—Chloe, Lydia, Apphia, Phoebe of Cenchreae, Nympha, the mother of John Mark. It was not until the 3rd and 4th Centuries that women began to lose esteem in the churches.

Naomi leaned forward, resting her forehead against the wooden post. "Religious scholars, who had detached themselves from God and relied upon academics rather than the truth-testifying power of the Holy Spirit, translated the feminine aspects out whenever possible. Some of them may have been concerned about losing power to the women in the church. The ancient histories available to us are riddled with arguments and contradictions. It is equally likely that women during the Dark Ages faltered in their understanding and lost their way."

"Then it wasn't hidden just because of men?" I had a thousand questions, but that one burst out.

Her hands lifted, offering me an empty shrug. "Does it matter? Blame is seldom useful. No doubt both sexes made errors. Whatever the cause, many generations lost their connection with our Heavenly Mother—with the Holy Spirit. And they suffered because of it. People suffered terribly during the dark ages."

I remembered all too vividly the awful visions llama girl had shown me. "What happened to make things change?"

She brightened. "The printing press came along and spurred a revival. With it, Lady Wisdom returned to the Keepers and humankind slowly emerged from that horrid darkness." Naomi's brightness faded. "But by then the true nature of our gifts and abilities had disappeared into obscurity, and woman's connection to the divine seemed to be erased from our collective memory. So, despite the enlightenment, in many ways, humans are still trapped in ignorance and darkness."

Gifts?

Abilities?

Trapped in darkness?

Am I asleep and this is all some distressing dream?

Questions and more questions mounted up like a soaring tidal wave rushing toward me.

I closed the Bible and set it aside. My stomach felt as if I'd been punched. I clamped my lips between my teeth, fighting a shakiness that threatened to consume me. I struggled to sort through her words, to somehow set my world back on steady feet.

Only I couldn't.

Because Naomi kept talking. "Instead of embracing our nature, women fought to compete with men. Women failed to recognize their strengths, except to use them for gain. Our foremothers lost out because they envied what men had. They disregarded their innate gifts in favor of trying to be like men. We fell into competition with them and ignored the incredibly powerful gifts and potential that we might've developed and offered to humanity."

Powerful? How?

If that's true, what is woman?

What am I?

I squeezed my eyes shut trying to grasp her meaning.

"Consider the possibilities, Sophie. What might our world be like if women had welcomed our true nature? Centuries have been lost because we didn't comprehend our connection to God. Oh, if only men had understood the truth about womankind—and our relationship to the Holy Spirit. They needn't have feared us. They could've encouraged the training of our gifts. By cloaking the truth and relegating women to the back seat, men lost out on the good we might have accomplished together. Not only that, it crippled Christian doctrine. The Trinity is impossible to comprehend if one ignores who the Holy Spirit is. I suspect in some small way attempts were made to rectify the loss of a female connection to God by deifying Mary. Sadly, that only muddied the waters. Is it any wonder—"

Dizzy. I wanted to grip the sides of my head. Instead, I stood abruptly and stumbled, clutching at the bookcase to steady myself. It was then that I realized my cheeks were damp with tears.

"Oh dear, I've said too much." Naomi stepped back. "I should've explained it more gradually."

I hid my face from her, staring into the open section of the bookcase, pretending to study the titles.

Her voice flowed over my shoulder, soft and soothing. "I'll go check on dinner."

Chapter 13
Wanted: One Fairy Tale Decoder Ring

Have you ever been so overwhelmed after learning something new that the entire planet seemed to wobble on its axis?

That new concept might be perfectly wonderful, a first-rate mind-blowing epiphany. Except even epiphanies can shake one's foundation. For me, silence provided the greatest steadying effect.

Note to self: it is not a good idea to close your eyes when your foundation is reeling.

So, keeping my eyes open to steady the room around me, after a half-hour or so I made my way back to the kitchen, and we ate dinner in relative silence.

I use the term, *relative*, because Naomi chose to play a confusing piano piece that kept hitting jarring notes. I winced.

"It's Prokofiev's piano Opus 22," she explained, even though I hadn't asked. I supposed she had it on so that we would not slice our chicken breasts in awkward quiet.

I would have preferred the awkwardness.

Complex rippling notes, verging on the melodic yet cleverly avoiding it, did not allow my mind to sink into silent meditation. Instead, those rackety clashing notes kept me on edge, my world still slightly askew. Had she chosen this on purpose?

I might have resented her for this auditory torture had not the chicken melted like little chunks of heaven in my mouth and the wild rice with carrots been the perfect companion for chicken smothered in basil, butter, and garlic.

Still, perfect chicken aside, why hadn't she chosen one of Schumann's pleasant symphonies? Or even seventies rock, or whatever was popular when she was a teenager. Hoping my voice might drown out Prokofiev's random dissonance, I broke the quiet between us. "This is delicious."

She inclined her head slightly, acknowledging the compliment but saying nothing.

"The books…" I started but faltered.

She glanced up, hawk-like, zeroing in on my floundering.

"They, uh, some of them looked very old." *Dumb. Dumb. Dumb. Of course they were old.*

I tried again. "Er, what I meant to say was that I noticed a large leather volume titled *Collection of Her Royal Majesty Elizabeth I*."

Naomi set her fork down and laced her fingers together. "We are the keepers of many ancient manuscripts. Some of the stories even harken back to before the flood, oral traditions passed down and eventually committed to paper. Copied and recopied as it became necessary."

"I see." *I did not see.* I just tried to sound like I did.

She could tell. That sideways grimace gave it away.

So, I cleared my throat and began again. "That particular book though, was it actually written by Queen Elizabeth? *The* Queen Elizabeth, you know, Henry the VIII's daughter?"

"The very same." Naomi beamed. "Our dear Bess made certain the English legends and fairytales were all properly collected. They might have been lost forever if not for her."

"Queen Elizabeth was a Wise Woman?"

"It's unclear. We know Henry's last wife, Katherine Parr, was the Wisdom Keeper at the time. What an amazing woman she was—married the old King, not for avarice but out of devotion to her countrymen. More importantly, she eagerly took over Elizabeth's education and training." Naomi leaned close to me as if divulging a hush-hush morsel of gossip. "Some say it was Katherine's tutelage that made Elizabeth such a brilliant strategist and prompted her caution about the advisors she gathered around her. She became queen at a young age and yet avoided becoming anyone's pawn. Remarkable girl, she turned a floundering, bankrupt little island into a flourishing empire."

Queen Elizabeth...

I shook my head, dazed. It seemed impossible that I should share a destiny with a woman like her. "Surely, she was too busy being queen to take time out for this Wise Woman stuff." I didn't mean for my comment to sound as if I thought *this* "stuff" was trivial.

Naomi leaned back in her chair. "We don't have direct confirmation. After King Henry died, Katherine remarried—this time for love. Sadly, that second marriage created a breach in her relationship with Elizabeth. Not long afterward, Katherine died. Whether Elizabeth formally accepted the role of Wisdom Keeper or not, is unknown. Evidently, she believed 'this stuff' was important enough that she attended to it in Katherine's stead." Naomi tossed her cloth napkin onto the table and regarded me warily. "More to the point, several queens have served as Wisewomen. For example, the Queen of Sheba, Makeda, was a Wisdom Keeper. Perhaps now you can understand why she was so determined to visit Solomon and test him."

"Uh-huh." I didn't know much about the Queen of Sheba except what I'd seen in the movies. Which wasn't much. I shrugged. "I always figured she was a rich society-queen, no pun intended, who decided to meet up with the excessively rich guy who everyone was talking about, King Solomon. That's the way things like that usually work."

"'Things like that.'" She scowled at me and galloped her fingernails on the table. "You're wrong about her. And while we're on the subject, what is this prejudice you have against wealth?"

One last carrot lay hidden in my rice. I chased it out into the open and stabbed it with my fork. "I don't know. Maybe, I think it would be too difficult to be wise, to truly understand things if someone hasn't suffered, at least a little."

"You suppose rich people don't suffer?"

"I wouldn't know." Piano notes vibrated the air behind us, a loud and dangerously dissident run on the keyboard that emphasized the momentary discord between us.

"Well then, it will please you to learn that several poor women have performed our office." Naomi set her silverware onto her plate nosily, lining up her fork, knife, and spoon uniformly. "Do you honestly think it's easier for a woman in poverty to do this job?"

I shoveled the last carrot into my mouth and chewed as thoroughly as I could while composing my reply. She stared at me with the same censorial grimace that wretched llama had given me when she had thought llama girl had picked the wrong novice.

Finally, I swallowed and confessed. "To be honest, I'm not even sure what it is we're supposed to do, much less what the qualifications should be."

Naomi tilted her head, resting heavily on her hand, and

spoke softly. I wasn't sure if she was talking to me or to herself. "You would have been thrilled with my predecessor. She had nothing. No bank account. No possessions of any value other than the collection. She spent her days wandering the desert, living in tents and huts, and yes, eating prickly pear when we had nothing else. Sarah was intent on gathering stories from the tribes of the southwest. She was convinced their old women were dying without having passed on their legends and knowledge to the next generation."

"Oh, I think I saw her book, *Legends of the Southwest.*"

She nodded.

"I don't understand. Myths? Legends? And you said Queen Elizabeth collected fairytales. What does all that have to do with preserving Wisdom?"

She sat up all of a sudden as if my question sent a jolt of electricity through the room. I'd seen that look before. It means *Hooray! You're not as thick as pea soup after all.*

"Excellent question. You see, the problem is that wisdom is obtained through experience. Ages ago, we learned to provide vicarious experiences for our children by telling them stories."

"Okay, relating experiences, I get that. But fairytales? What's the point?"

"Ah!" Naomi's face lit up, glowing in the sunset gleaming in from the open windows. "Fairytales are lovely little things with secret codes tucked inside. Take, for instance, the Princess and the Pea—"

"Didn't Hans Christian Andersen write that?"

Naomi nodded patiently. "Yes. A splendid fellow. We have him to thank for immortalizing a tale that had been told to children for years and might otherwise have been lost. But you're missing the point."

"What point?"

"The Princess and the Pea."

Piano keys plunked a wild staccato, intentionally missing the harmony by a mere half step here and there, driving me nearly mad. "What about it?"

"We were discussing the code hidden in—"

"Oh, you mean like the moral of the story."

"Not quite."

"Are you saying there's really a secret code? Do we drop out some of the words? Rearrange letters? Or—"

Naomi cleared her throat sharply. "You're making this somewhat frustrating."

"Sorry."

"Well, since you prefer to guess my meaning before I say it—you tell me, what is the message in The Princess and the Pea? You do remember the story, don't you?"

"Sure. There's this princess who gets caught in a storm and ends up sleeping in a castle on top of twenty mattresses, except the queen put a pea underneath the pile to see if she's really a princess or not. It keeps her awake all night and gives her a giant bruise."

"Close enough. And the message?"

I prevaricated slightly, putting on my best know-it-all

voice. "Aside from the obvious?"

She waved her hand, inviting me to spill those obvious cards on the table.

Uh-oh, I'd been bluffing. I didn't have any cards to show. I scoured my deductive reasoning cupboards and came up bare. Not even a bone. To be honest, that tale had always seemed a bit silly to me. I recalled an illustration from my tattered old copy of *Big Book of Children's Fairytales* featuring a girl in a frilly pink gown climbing a ladder to the top of a wobbly stack of mattresses.

Secret message...?

It seemed a bit preposterous. I gnawed on my thumbnail for a moment and ventured, "Real princesses are easily injured?" I quickly recanted. "No, if that was it, then why would she risk climbing the ladder and sleeping on top of twenty mattresses? I mean, if a pea under the mattresses can bruise her so badly, just think what would happen if she fell off that tall stack of mattresses. One false move and—"

"Good grief." Naomi rolled her eyes and grimaced. I didn't think her reaction was concern over the princess plummeting to the floor.

"You've missed the point entirely." She folded the monogrammed napkin she'd previously discarded and laid the perfect rectangle primly beside her plate. "Who is the princess?"

My mental cupboard doors flung open. A sugarplum! I knew! Without a doubt, I knew who the princess was. "Me!"

"Precisely." Relief flooded her face. "The princess is always us. You. Me. Every woman or girl who reads the story." Naomi leaned forward, elbows on the table, scrutinizing me intently. "So, tell me, Sophie, if I put a pea under your mattress tonight will you awaken with a huge black and blue mark?"

"Not likely." I chuckled. "I'm used to sleeping in a hammock, remember?"

"Then, what is this story really telling us?"

"You can't spot a princess by her looks? Don't judge a book by its cover, that sort of thing?"

Naomi sighed. "Think harder."

Thoughts whirled through my brain. Nebulous helium-filled puzzle pieces floated through my mind. The solution seemed almost visible, yet just out of reach. I sighed and shook my head.

Naomi relaxed against the arm of her chair and waited for me to come up with an answer. Time trotted by like a tap-dancing elephant until, at last, she gave me a hint. "The princess's carriage broke down in the middle of a raging storm. She trudged for miles, through wind, rain, and mud. Finally, she drags into the castle shivering with cold and soaked to the bone. Poor thing, she's worn to a frazzle. Even so, the prince develops a passionate interest in her, right?"

"Uh-huh," I muttered. "Ye olde wet t-shirt must've given Junior the hots."

One of Naomi's eyebrows arched in a warning to cut the smart-mouth comments. She patiently said, "That's when the sleeping arrangements were made."

"Ri-ight." I nodded, pretending I understood.

"Who doubted the princess's authenticity?"

"Junior's Mum?" I answered, a glimmer of where she might be going flickered in my mind.

"Who made her climb twenty mattresses? Who shoved a pea underneath?"

Ahhh, then I saw it.

"Her future mother-in-law!"

"Exactly." Naomi folded her hands together and rested them neatly in her lap. "There's your hidden message. This story warns every little girl that her future mother-in-law will test her. And some of those tests will be a trifle unreasonable."

Just then the Prokofiev CD came to an end. *Thank goodness*. The air between us fell comfortably still. In the ensuing silence, I began to feel slightly more intelligent. Flaws in Naomi's theory popped out at me. It was too bad I didn't have the good sense to keep my mouth shut. "You realize this means the hidden code failed."

She tilted her head quizzically.

I offered proof. "I can't be the only one who didn't get the message until you explained it."

Naomi rolled her eyes and dismissed me with a wave of her hand. "You've never had a mother-in-law. Besides, it's all in how it's told."

"I read it."

"Han's Christian Andersen's version, no doubt."

"So you're saying he blew the retelling?"

"Not exactly. The Andersen family was dirt poor. Even so, Han's mother insisted she was a displaced noblewoman until her death. It wasn't true, but I believe he grasped the point. The message is there. And, if you really analyze the story carefully, no other solid conclusion can be drawn." She shrugged. "Perhaps he might've directed the reader more firmly toward the point. That's where you come in."

I shook my head. "It's no good. Without you to interpret I won't be able to see any hidden messages, secret codes, underlying themes, or anything like that."

"In time it will become obvious to you."

"I don't see how. I still think the only obvious point in the story is that our real identities are not easily discerned."

She sniffed loudly. "That argument doesn't hold up. It infers that some of us are not princesses."

Well, she would have a problem with that, wouldn't she?

I glanced at her pointedly. "Some of us aren't."

"No. No!" She leaned forward flattening her hands on the edge of the table. "I explained all that. Some have simply forgotten."

I shrugged.

Naomi's light gray brows pinched together in an unequivocal, full-out, irritated scowl. "We're back to the rich versus poor thing, aren't we?" She huffed loudly. "Don't be difficult." Her nose went up, very princess-like. "And short-sighted."

I glanced away, surveying her superlative surroundings in

all their understated glory. It had been a very long four days. Not to mention the fact that my entire universe had just tilted permanently.

"I'm a bit tired. Perhaps my thinking is off-key." I thanked her for dinner, promised to be more receptive in the morning, and trudged with the weariness of her precious mud-soaked Pea Princess into the bowels of Naomi's castle, back to the forest that was my room.

"Tomorrow," she called to my escaping backside. "Tomorrow you will learn exactly how a story must be told. And how to truly listen." Her voice echoed down the hallway, winding eerily through the corridors, reverberating into my Spanish dungeon. Apparently, daughters-in-law were not the only women destined for testing.

Chapter 14
Sneaking Out

Sleep eluded me. So I flipped on a light, climbed out of that huge bed, and stared at the Wise Woman Collection. All these books—why not read one? I liked reading. No, let me amend that, I *loved* reading. So, why didn't I open the glass door and pull out one of those intriguing volumes?

I'll tell you why not.

If I had started reading it would be a commitment. It didn't take wisdom or rocket science to figure out why Naomi had laughed when I told her I had a life to get back to. If I did the Wise Woman thing, *this* would be my new life. My old life would fade away. Coldwater, my job, Danny and Marla, my friends—

Poof!

Gone.

And for what? To take care of some musty old books? And do what with them, save the world somehow? And what were these powers women were supposed to have? I felt so frustrated and confused that if there'd been a certain llama handy, I might've punched it. In return, I was pretty sure that particular llama would've stomped me to death and spit on my bloody remains.

Ryder's truck was still out there. Or at least it had been. I'd pretended not to see him when I collected my duffle bag out of the jeep. Later, when I happened to peek through the window while padding down the hall to brush my teeth, I noticed he was still parked on the street.

The more I thought about it, the more I felt it would be unkind of me, downright rude, not to go out there and make sure he was all right. He may think he was my protector, but really he was just a boy from Kansas. A very cute boy from Kansas. Well, not exactly cute, more like ruggedly good-looking. And not a boy. He looked about twenty-three or maybe twenty-four, I couldn't tell. Maybe he started college young. He did seem irritatingly smart and overly capable.

But what did I really know about him?

Was he even from Kansas?

I didn't know that either.

I stood there staring at him cataloging what I knew. He was a good-looking guy of *undetermined* age from somewhere in the

Midwest, probably, and he seemed fairly rational, except for the fact that he'd followed me here and refused to tell me the whole reason why.

Other than that, he was the closest thing I had to a friend on this camel-shaped rock pile. I decided to take him the cookies Naomi brought me before she turned in.

Yep, she'd brought me cookies just as if I was a twelve-year-old who needed a snack before bed—Ha! Now that I thought about it, maybe she was offering them as a bribe so I would stay and do my lessons tomorrow. I didn't know. She'd plopped them outside my door, and said, "Here are some cookies in case you get hungry."

Out of courtesy, I'd eaten one. I relented that much. I mean, after all, they were homemade chocolate chip cookies, and I was a sucker for the extra vanilla wafting off of them. Still, out of principle, I left the other two on the plate, untouched.

I cannot be bribed.

Sneaking out of Naomi's house proved a little tricky. Did she have an alarm system? If I opened the front door, would alarms start blaring and automatically send cops roaring up Camelback Mountain? Maybe I could find an alternate route out of the house? I crept through the living room into the foyer. Moonlight streamed in through the picture windows across the back, bright enough that it illuminated a large note taped to the front door. I set the plate of cookies on the foyer table and strained to read it.

Dear Sophie,

I left the security alarm off this evening in case you decide to leave. I wouldn't blame you, but I sincerely hope you'll reconsider.

All my best, Naomi

So, the cookies had been a bribe.

Humph. How did she know I'd been seriously rethinking this whole novice situation? I grabbed the cookies and opened the door. I needed to talk to someone sensible. Ryder would have to do.

I marched down the drive. He bolted upright in the cab as if he was shocked to see me. Before I got halfway down the driveway, he sprang out and rushed toward me. "What happened? Are you alright?"

Oh yeah, I just remembered he expects me to get killed or something.

"I'm fine."

Ryder stood close to me, checking all around us, shielding me like a bodyguard.

"Relax, Mr. Bond." I shoved the small plate up between us. "I come bearing cookies."

"Oh." He looked a little disappointed.

"Thought you might be hungry."

He shrugged, but I saw the greedy way he eyeballed those chocolate chip cookies. I lifted them higher so the vanilla could do its vamp-work on his nose.

He swallowed, which meant he was already salivating. "Not here." He glanced around again as if he thought someone might spring out from behind a cactus, then he put his arm around my shoulder and ushered me across the street to his truck.

It wasn't until we were ensconced in the cab and he'd shut the door that Ryder took a breath. "Okay, so what's up?"

"Oh, nothing." *Only a couple of million things.* "How did you find me?"

"I'm your stalker, remember?"

"Ha-ha," I said dryly. "Last time I saw you I figured you'd be headed back to the oil fields."

"I thought about it." He reached for a cookie. "Figured you were too important to leave you on your own."

"Uh-huh." I leaned over the console watching him chew. "Did it ever occur to you that if this mysterious guy in a suit with his fancy-schmancy laptop was really with the government, or the CIA, or whatever, he could've sent a troop of soldiers, or a pack of spies, or maybe even some Navy SEALs to protect me? Hmm?"

"Don't look at me like that, Sophie?"

"Like what?"

"Like you want me to kiss you."

"I'm not."

Except I was.

I was hungry for something to distract me, to make me forget about secret codes in fairytales and about superpowers women were supposed to possess but didn't anymore, and that my entire understanding of God had just been through a major overhaul. So, naturally, I leaned a little closer.

"All right, what's going on?" He studied me sympathetically as if I were his lab partner and I'd just failed a pop quiz. Not the response I was looking for. His ever-so-enticing lips spread into a kindly-smile. "I take it you found her, didn't you? The Wise Woman."

I pushed away with a sigh. "Yes."

"And?"

"And nothing. Let's run away together."

He laughed—sputtered cookie—and grabbed a napkin that, apparently, he kept handy for just such occasions. Very organized, this guy.

I gave him my sternest glare. "What's so funny about that?"

"*Nothing.*" He set the remainder of the cookie down.

"Something. You sprayed cookie all over your steering wheel."

"You caught me off guard."

"Good." I leaned over the console again and tried to do that come-hither thing that I'd heard girls were supposed to be able to do. I gave it my best effort.

Epic fail.

He busied himself wiping down the steering wheel.

Apparently, my come-hither-ing skills required a little more practice. I sighed. "I take it that's a no-go on my offer to run away."

He laughed again, this time more gently, and finally threw up his hands. "I give up, Sophie. You're adorable. You know that, right?"

"*Adorable*?" I squeaked. "Don't say that." I crossed my arm and frowned at the yucca plant blooming next to his truck. "Adorable is what you say about your best buddy's snot-nosed little sister."

"Yeah, well, you are neither snot-nosed nor my best buddy's sister. You're . . ." He thumped on the steering wheel. "A *problem*. Despite all the warnings that guy with the laptop gave me about keeping my distance, about doing this job without interacting with you. I can't! It's impossible. How am I supposed to do that? Look at you. You're so smart and brave, and cute, and you make me laugh, and . . ." Ryder leaned over the console this time, and touched my cheek with one finger, turning my face toward his. "There's just something about you that drives me half insane. It's about all I can do to keep from pulling you over here and kissing you until we're both senseless."

I struggled to hold back the smile threatening to burst out all over my face like the Fourth of July. My come-hither-ing skills must not be as useless as I'd thought. I was not crazy about being called a problem or cute—I'd rather be thought of as beautiful, but hey, I figured I could work with being his cute adorable problem.

So, I tested out the huskiest sexiest voice that I possessed, and said, "I could do with a little senselessness right now."

He didn't say anything right away. Ryder contemplated me for a long, rather delicious, forty-five seconds. It was forty-five seconds of *almost* kissing. He was so close I could practically taste those chocolate chips. "Sophie . . ." he whispered.

My cheeks flamed with heat in answer. "Yes?"

"You should get out of the truck right now and run back to the house."

"And if I don't?" I tried to make that sound sultry, although I was pretty sure it came across as stubborn.

He sighed and squeezed his eyes shut. For a second or two, I wondered if he was praying for help. Except then he turned away and leaned his head against the steering wheel. "Help me out here, Sophie. You have important work to do. You know that, right?"

I waited in the dark of that cab and didn't say anything.

"That guy showed me what happens to the world if you don't do whatever it is you have to do. I'm supposed to be here making sure that happens. Those Navy SEALs and the spy squads you mentioned—they can't help you. If throwing you in a holding cell and making you do whatever it is you have to do would've worked, I'm telling you those guys would have done it."

I pressed back against the seat staring straight ahead into the night.

He glanced sideways, and I could feel him watching me, waiting for a response. I didn't look at him. All the heaviness I'd felt earlier returned. All that uncertainty about what it was I am supposed to do washed over me like cold suffocating water.

"I know they would," he said quietly. "Because I asked."

That got me. It meant he'd asked laptop-man if there was any other way. He'd hoped they could send somebody else to do his job. "So, you didn't want this either?"

He waited to answer until I looked at him. "That was before I met you. As soon as I met you, it was all over. There was no way I could let you face this all alone."

I wished it was darker. I didn't want him to see my face welling up like some stupid crybaby. "Yeah, except I don't think I can do this...this... whatever it is." I waved my hand at the universe and the dumb yucca plant.

Darn! That came out sounding much squeakier and wobblier than I wanted.

I'd turned away and struggled to toughen up. "I'm not a Wisdom Keeper!" I blurted. "And certainly not a Wise Woman. I'm nobody. *Nobody!* I can't do this. I'm just an ordinary girl from Coldwater, Minnesota."

He laughed again, not the sputtery kind, the warm gentle kind of laugh that made me feel all melty inside. "Oh, Sophie, you're anything but ordinary."

I could tell he meant it. More importantly, some part of me realized it was the truth.

"Okay, maybe I'm not ordinary." I studied his dashboard as if it was that temperature-controlled cabinet full of books back in my room. "But I'm definitely not superwoman, and that's what they need for this job. Not me. You've gotta help me, Ryder. I'm over my head. There are no parameters for this job. No guidebook. No plan of action. And the Wise Woman, well . . . she is . . . she's a little kooky, to be honest."

"Kooky?"

"Certifiable. She insists there's a secret code in fairytales. She keeps harping on about the importance of stories and how we learn wisdom through stories. How is that supposed to help anyone? That isn't going to fix our upside-down world? It can't. It won't. It's hopeless." I clapped my hands over my knees and straightened.

It hit me like a bulldozer. Saying those things out loud, I realized I'd already made a decision.

I turned to him and calmly announced, "I'm going home, or I'll run away—*something*. I'm not staying here."

He drew in a deep breath. "That's it then?"

"Yep. That's it."

Parked on the street in front of her house, we had a clear view of the top of the rock pile, the camel's hump. Moonlight painted a reddish-pink ribbon on the edge of the giant sandstone. City lights obscured most of the stars, and only a handful of them still shone through. I wouldn't miss Phoenix. I wanted to go home to Minnesota and look up at the beautiful smogless night sky, glittering with stars, and the moon shining so bright you could count her craters.

"All right," Ryder finally said. "If you're sure, then we'll need to make a run for it. Going home isn't an option. They'll hunt you down there and try to force you to do whatever it is. We'll need to head to the Rocky Mountains. Someplace remote, maybe

Wyoming or Northern Utah. I've had some survival training. If we go right away, it'll give us a good head start on winter. We should be able to find some sort of cave or build a shelter, and we'll need to pack in supplies. If we get up high enough in the mountains, we might be able to survive what's coming."

Might survive?

That cold water that had been enveloping me burst. Exploded. I wasn't drowning anymore. No, instead my heart thundered like a doomsday drum. That toothy mountain lion may as well have been sitting on my chest.

I clutched his arm. "What do you mean we *might* survive? Survive what?"

He squinted as if he didn't understand the question. "You know, the stuff that's coming if you don't do—"

"What *stuff*!?" I demanded breathlessly.

"You know," he said. "The chaos and fighting. Volcanoes. Bombs. Riots. Food shortages. Looting. Starving people." My mouth gradually fell open, and Ryder rattled his list off a little slower. "Mobs. Fires. Anarchy."

I buried my face in my hands.

"Hey—" He laid his hand on my shoulder. "I'm sorry. I thought you knew."

All I could do was shake my head. Llama girl had told me if I didn't find the Wise Woman it would result in another dark age. Only Ryder wasn't describing a dark age; it was an apocalypse.

My mouth turned dryer than the rocks surrounding us. I tried to swallow but choked instead.

"You need water." He leaned over the seat, grabbed a bottle of water, and unscrewed the cap. "Here, drink this."

My throat was so tight I couldn't get more than a teaspoon down at a time. A couple of swallows later I could talk without coughing. "H-he showed you all that?"

"Yeah." Ryder's jaw muscles buckled and his lips pressed tight before he said anything else. "And worse."

How could anything be worse?

"Worse?" I squeaked.

"Yeah." He ran a hand across his forehead and eyes as if he'd like to erase whatever it was he'd seen. "I don't know how, but he had video of my family—cousins, my sister and her kids. Only they didn't look like they do now. It was of them in the future, a year or two, when the world is burning down."

"Actors maybe?" I suggested with quiet hope.

"I don't see how. It was them, *my* family. I recognized them instantly, only they looked thinner and sickly—ragged dirty clothes. My sister was huddling with her kids inside a house—my parent's house. I grew up in that place! Only in the video, half of it was rubble and the windows were all broken out." He shook his head. "Fires everywhere on our street. Gas lines busted and burning." He looked up at me his eyes watery. "It was literally hell on Earth."

I pictured Danny and Marla, Ollie and Swede, and everyone else in Coldwater struggling to survive in a world like that.

A hellish world that I had abandoned.

The trembling hit my shoulders first. I hunkered over,

shivering up and down. My face went next, crumpling up like an origami-gone-wrong. There was no stopping it. The floodgates opened. I came apart and officially fell to pieces—broke into a full-blown, chest-heaving, *please-don't-tell-anyone* ugly sob.

"It's okay." Ryder eased me over the console and cradled me in his arms.

"No, it's not," I blubbered. When I finished leaving a puddle of tears on his no-longer-crisp white t-shirt, I pulled back sniffling. He smoothed strands of my hair out of my eyes and wisely didn't say anything.

I swiped at my renegade tears with the back of my arm. "I suppose this means we can't really run away."

"No." He smiled sadly. "I don't suppose we can."

"I've got to stay and figure this thing out."

He nodded. "And I'll be right here if you need me."

"Good." I kissed his cheek and laid my head against his shoulder for a few seconds more. Then I got out of his truck and trudged off to learn how to be a Wisdom Keeper, or a Wise Woman, or whatever it was I needed to learn to keep hell from breaking loose on everyone I loved.

Chapter 15
Small Things

I WENT STRAIGHT back to my room, opened the cabinet, and started reading.

Sometime between midnight and morning, I must have fallen asleep. Pink light poured through the bedroom window. I awoke with books and papers strewn across my bed, drawings, journals, and stories.

Clutched in my hand was a poem, and on the sheets beside my leg lay sketches of a cold-eyed creature, part-bird, part-bear, drawn in violent colors—the Painbeast. I shuddered. The thing pierced some hidden part of my psyche with a too-familiar claw.

It comes each day,
Like morning,
The possibility of pain.

And when each misery appears
Nipping at my heels,
I turn and look.

Lest, with time, they multiply,
And, as days
Collect into years,

So do small wounds congregate,
Lurking in squalid puddles.
Breeding. Transforming.

Gathering in the murk behind my back,
To become a monstrous,
Snarling Painbeast.

Sliding out of the sheets, I sat on the edge of the bed, my feet pressed hard against the comforting coolness of the tiles.

That poem made me feel naked. Exposed. But more importantly, I felt understood. I wanted to know more about the woman who had drawn the creature that stared back at me from my dark places.

6 a.m., I wondered if Naomi would be up yet. She would know about the author. Movement outside the window caught my attention. My mentor knelt beside her flowerbed on a foam

garden pad, her head covered by her ridiculously wide-brimmed straw hat.

I looked back at the drawings on the bed and wondered why I hadn't been lucky enough to have the tutelage of the woman who wrote the poem. Gathering up my reading from the night before, stacking it in careful piles, I headed out to consult with she-who-was-supposed-to-confer-wisdom-on-me. With any luck, she might be able to tell me something about these other women.

Unlike Minnesota, there was no dew in the summer grass of Arizona. I missed that as I walked quietly across the small patch of grass beside the swimming pool. Naomi continued digging in a flowerbed beside the wrought iron fence, turning the soil over, lifting clumps into her polka dot gardening gloves, inspecting them for weeds and slugs. Without even turning around, without me saying a word, she began to answer my unspoken questions.

"As with prophets, not all Wisewomen are created equal. A few rise to greatness, some perform their duties in diligent silence, while others accept the calling with less enthusiasm."

"And you?" I strained to glimpse her expression under the shadows of the hat.

"Me?" She shrugged, but it failed to convince me of her indifference. "Oh, I suppose I brooded. Wondered, what was the point? Thinking back on it now, perhaps, I didn't take my calling seriously enough. But in fairness..." Her cheeks crinkled in a wry grin. "Well, you've met llama girl. Didn't you wonder if it was all a joke? Silliness? A hallucination?" She stabbed the spade into the soil and turned to smile at me. "The visions came to me in the sixties. What was I to think?"

"A bad mushroom."

"Crossed my mind." She chuckled and turned back to grooming the soil. "All it needed was a white rabbit."

I nodded, staring at my toes in the grass. I'd wondered much the same thing. Sitting down beside her, uncertain of what to say, I plucked a delicate stalk of grass loaded with Bermuda seeds and twirled it between my fingers.

Naomi took a deep breath and focused on the brilliant red-orange blossom of a Bird of Paradise. "I'm not being entirely honest with you. I suppose, in my heart, I knew. And I tried. I truly did. At fifteen, I went to live with my grandmother in a commune in the desert, and—"

"Your Grandmother? She was a Wise Woman?"

"*The* Wise Woman, yes." Naomi's eyes glistened with images from decades past. "She lived the part—in every way. Long hand-dyed skirts, gauzy blouses embroidered with tribal symbols..." Naomi's fingers rippled down her chest, touching invisible embellishments. "Suns, stars, wolves, birds, and what-have-you. The old gal looked like Merlin incarnate. She was just the sort of Wise Woman you were hoping to find."

I protested weakly. "Well, no, not really. I'm glad it's you."

She chuckled skeptically and dismissed my feeble offering with a wave. "You would've liked her. *Shinálí* grew her own food. Ate cactus and wild onions. Did you know there's an indigenous variety of asparagus that grows along the creek banks in southern Utah?" She twisted sideways, checking to make sure she had my attention. "Skinny stuff, but not half bad."

I nodded, encouraging her to tell me more.

"She even made her own cheese." Naomi's nose wrinkled up. "Stinky stuff. To this day I cannot stand the smell of Feta cheese. Especially not homemade."

I could not imagine my modern device-loving tutor eating smelly homemade goat cheese and scouring the desert for her next meal. "So, you weren't kidding about the locust."

"No." Naomi absently brushed dirt flecks off her knee. "But, oh, my dear, *Shinálí* could tell stories with amazingly vivid detail. She could make the story unfold before your very eyes. She might even be on par with Deborah."

"Deborah?" I tilted my head quizzically.

"Yes." She scrutinized me as if, surely, I ought to know who she was talking about. "Deborah from the Bible. You must have learned about her when you were a kid in Sunday School."

"Oh, *that* Deborah. The one who sat under a palm tree?"

"The very same. Do you know what I love about Deborah? She didn't really want the job either." She pointed her shovel at me. "There go your eyebrows again. Skeptical sort, aren't you? I'm telling you the truth. My grandmother told me all about Deborah. And I read the chronicles of her life. They're in the cabinet."

"What else did your grandmother say about her?" I waited, hoping Naomi might relate some of the tidbits left out of the historical account, savory little morsels.

Naomi glanced at me and smiled when she saw my eagerness to hear her account. "Very well, I'll tell you what I remember.

"Deborah married wisely. She loved her husband. He was handsome, smart, and fairly rich." Naomi tapped her shovel against the scalloped stone border loosening the clumps of dirt. "In those days, wealth made a woman's life much easier, she had the help of servants. Yet, even before she married, people came to ask Deborah's opinion. Can you imagine a young woman advising her elders? Unheard of in that culture—it wasn't done. But our Deborah had phenomenal tact. She could make people forget all about differences such as age. She was more than just wise. Deborah was also a prophetess."

"And she had something else..." Naomi paused, summoning up the essence of the story, organizing the elements of truth along with the right words to conjure the images to life.

I scooted toward her, leaning in so I wouldn't miss anything.

"She was pleasant to look at. Not so beautiful that she inspired envy or desire, but she had a comfortable and kind face, like someone you would want as a friend. This worked to her advantage when she was young, and older people wanted to ask her advice. You see Deborah was devoted to God and, in dreams, He told her where her father's livestock ought to graze, which goats to breed, and so forth. Naturally, her father's herds prospered. They grew bigger and fatter than anyone else's.

Neighbors noticed. People talked. When her father told them about his daughter, they began coming to her for advice for their herds and gradually asked her about other matters as well. Her reputation grew. And eventually the Lord made her a judge in Israel. Well, you get the picture."

I did!

In more ways than one.

A vision enveloped me. Mists swirled up around me, and tendrils of smoke from another time surrounded me. Through the haze, I saw Deborah as she must have been thousands of years ago, or as she was now, I don't know which. A creamy linen cloth flowed over dark hair. She raised her face from prayer, and on her brow rested a bright golden circlet—her eyes were unforgettable, dark chocolate, laughing with intelligence, dotted with fireflies of joy. She looked on me with such loving amusement I could not help but smile back.

I cannot explain the sense of peace emanating from her. She seemed completely at ease in the universe. Unafraid. It was as if she had not even an ounce of anxiety in her soul.

In that moment, I *changed.*

Enfolded in Deborah's gaze, I no longer feared following the path of the Wise Woman. Through her eyes, I saw life's road strewn with fertile experiences, that difficulties and conflict merely offered us depth and richness, challenge and interest. Each experience sowed seeds along our path, and those seeds eventually bloomed into fragrant flowers of bliss.

If Deborah were alive today, I would travel to the other side of the planet to sit at her feet, all for the simple hope of learning to smile with such pure contentment.

I reached out, trying to hold onto the vision, but Deborah's image faded. It left me sitting in glaring sunlight, no longer softened by the early morning haze.

Naomi was kneeling beside me, silent, waiting, watching me from the shadows under her wide brim. "You had a vision of her, didn't you?"

No need for me to answer.

"Remarkable, isn't she?" Naomi sat back smiling as if she, too, remembered Deborah's overwhelming serenity.

I searched my limited vocabulary for a word adequate enough to describe the encounter. "Radiant," I said. "Confident."

"Deborah was fearless." Naomi turned back to her garden, vigorously digging her spade into the soil, removing the scraggly roots of interloping weeds. "She and God were quite chummy. Hence, her certainty. No fear. Nothing to stand in the way of joy."

"And she's so full of love. It's difficult to believe *she* didn't want to be the Wise Woman."

Naomi's spade froze mid-air over the flowerbed, and she sat back. "Did any of us?"

That caught me out. "No, I suppose it isn't an easy thing. But your grandmother—didn't she?"

"No." She shook her head. "But *Shinálí* saw it as her calling and never looked back. She never dwelled on what her life might have been. For Deborah, though, it meant a great deal more than merely being the Wisdom-Keeper. She also served God as a prophetess *and* judge."

Deborah — illustrated by Sarah Beth Baca, Women of the Bible collection at: sarahbethart.com

"Wife, Wise Woman, prophet, mother, *and* a judge—" I counted her roles on my fingers. "How? How could anyone do all that?"

Naomi sighed with a sad smile. "With God's help, she accepted each day with her whole heart, and found joy in the small everyday things."

"Small things." I whispered, reiterating it to myself. How had the poem said it? Small things morphed into monstrous forces in our lives—for good or bad, I supposed. No, that wasn't quite it, but Naomi was telling me about Deborah and I didn't want to miss a word.

"Deborah could sing, but it was her storytelling that drew crowds. In the evenings, her kinsmen gathered around the fire. Orange sparks swirled up into the black night as Deborah related the cherished stories of her people. Lovely and mesmerizing, like softly played harp strings, her soothing voice penetrated their ears and hearts. Night after night, she sang to them and told stories. When she spoke of creation, they witnessed the stars dancing from God's fingertips and finding their places in the night sky.

When she told them the story of Moses's mother weaving a basket of bulrushes, they saw the young mother's hands tremble as she threaded the last reed into place. In the shadows of the campfire, farmers and shepherds did not smell the smoke curling up from the smoldering flames. It was the scent of the baby's hair that filled their nostrils. Smoke did not make those rugged men's eyes water; it was the milk-stained softness of that baby's cheek caressing theirs.

Deborah described the mighty river of Egypt turning to blood, and those sitting on rocks and stumps around her fire felt the thick red ooze flowing around their ankles. When she told them about the plagues of flies, they swatted at unseen insects.

Through her storytelling, her people gathered alongside their ancestors and witnessed the waters of the mighty Red Sea part. It felt as if they, too, took tentative steps onto the dry sea bed, pushing their handcarts, dragging their packs, and kicking sand out of their sandals. They watched their young children scampering along, eagerly grabbing up seashells as they all rushed to cross between the towering walls of water looming high above their heads. When the last of the Israelites finally reached the other side, Deborah's kinsmen gasped at the terrible roar when the massive waves crashed down upon their enemies. They saw war horses rearing in panic, soldiers screaming in terror, and chariots tossed about like flotsam. When Deborah fell silent, those listening lifted their faces in awe to the God who had saved them.

The Bermuda stalk I'd been twirling fell from my fingers. "Is that why the people were willing to follow her into battle."

Naomi murmured her agreement. "Her stories strengthened her generation. The people loved her. Trusted her. When they heard that God told her He would win the battle for them, they believed it."

I noticed a tinge of sadness coloring Naomi's tone and wondered what had caused her sorrow. Just then, a ladybug landed clumsily onto my arm.

Naomi stood up and dusted off her knees and the foam pad. "I should've been more like her. Deborah never missed a split second of delight." She pointed to the red-dotted guest climbing on my shoulder. "A brightly painted ladybug. The soft tickle of grass beneath your feet. A moment here, another there, they all gather together to become the sum and substance of your life."

Like the poem.

I remembered why I had come out in the first place. "Last night, I found a poem that said something similar about pain. Small wounds collect and become monstrous."

Naomi pulled off her gloves and dropped them and the trowel into her gardening basket. "And did you understand it?"

"I think so. It was tucked in with some beautiful drawings. And a story about two people fighting, creating a horrible Painbeast. The creature grew bigger and more awful every time they tried to run away. It described the agony of being swallowed up by the monster, and an overpowering grief that turns the world gray." I lowered my eyes and admitted, "I know that Painbeast."

She tilted her head, studying me. "We all do."

"Do you mean all Wisewomen experience this kind of pain?"

"No, my dear." The corner of her mouth quirked up. "It's a bit more universal than that. All women. All people."

I shook my head. "No, this is different. It's more than ordinary pain. Bigger." Whoever had written *Painbeast* understood me in a way no one ever has."

Naomi just didn't get it.

How could she—living her indulgent perfectly manicured life? I wanted to talk to that poet. "The drawings, they're primitive, yet remarkable. They're so..."

"Brutal? Honest?"

"Yes. Yes, exactly! And yet, they seem fairly new. The author might still be alive. Do you know her? Because, well, I thought, after you've taught me everything, perhaps I could go visit her."

Naomi nodded slowly and walked toward the house. I followed. "I realize we have a lot of training to do. But afterward..."

She didn't respond to my plea.

Halfway across the lawn, I grabbed her elbow, and she stopped. "Please. I must talk with the woman who wrote that poem."

Everything except her mouth was cast in shade from the hat. Her lips pressed a tiny bit too hard, betraying irritation. "The poem touched you. That should be enough. What difference does it make who wrote it?"

Then I knew. I let go of her arm and stared. "It was you!"

Naomi's mouth relaxed in a quirky half-grin. With a southern belle accent, she added, "Me? Now how could that be?" She chuckled and walked into the house, leaving me standing in the yard, with the harsh sun thumping me on the head.

Chapter 16
Flowers

I followed Naomi through the house and out to the front yard. Her white cotton dress fluttered around her calves in the slight breeze. With the gardening basket looped over one arm, and that floppy straw hat trailing broad gauzy ribbons, she looked like she'd stepped out of a 1940's movie, a white-haired Myrna Loy.

She turned to me and, out of the blue, presented me with a quiz. "What is the difference between men and women?"

That was easy. "Penises."

She paused, clippers poised before a hapless rose, and cast me a stern glare. "Do you think you might strive to be a trifle more serious?"

I might strive, but I wasn't very good at seriousness.

"I'll try." I stood all prim and student-like. "So, if the difference isn't mere body parts...hmm, let me see. Could it be that men are stubborn, thickheaded creatures who must have their way or they'll run over their opponent with a tank, or a tractor, or basically anything that's handy?"

She sighed. "Fine. If you don't want to discuss it, we won't."

I kicked half-heartedly at one of the small rocks comprising the yard's desert landscape. "I'm sorry. But honestly, both sexes seem equally stubborn, equally smart, equally driven..." I shrugged. "I don't know. What is the difference?"

"Design."

"Okaaay, but now we're back to body parts."

She clipped a rose off the bush and caught it in her basket.

"Why did you do that? That one was still pretty."

"Because I'm trying to behave more like a man." She moved on and clipped another rose. The guillotined stem beaded with a clear liquid and stood naked and useless in the sunlight. I tilted my head, watching her with one squinted eye, hoping to see her point.

"I don't get it."

"Isn't it obvious?" She tossed her head at my confusion. "Removing that faded rose makes the bush more productive. It will bear more blossoms because the plant won't be using its energy to sustain a dying flower."

"Are you saying men are more productive?"

"Heavens no!" She looked at me as if I'd just offered her a

raw turnip. "Productivity depends entirely upon the man or woman."

"I squinted again, mashing my eyebrows together, struggling to grasp her meaning. She made my brain hurt. I disliked these guessing games. "I give up! For pity's sake, just *tell me.*"

"Tell you *what*?" Naomi pursed her lips and plastered on an innocent old-lady face.

I wasn't buying her act. "Oh, I don't know. That men find more efficient ways to get what they want than we do. Or maybe that women are too sentimental, and they don't usually chop the heads off roses. Whatever it is, stop baiting me and explain your point!"

She chuckled. That was bad news, because it meant she was having too much fun toying with me. "Me? Baiting you?" she asked, eyebrows arched. "I haven't the foggiest idea what you're talking about."

I ignored her and turned back to the bush. "Here, let me help you with these roses." I snapped the head off of a bright red blossom. Immediately, I felt guilty, and brutal.

Naomi glared at me.

"What?" I attempted a nonchalant shrug. "Wasn't that one ready?" I wasn't as good at the innocent act as she was. For a minute, I thought she might whack me with her pruning shears.

"No! No, it was not ready." She lowered the shears and her face softened. "But I'm pleased to see you understand the point."

My shoulders sagged. *What point?* Apart from the fact that

I'd destroyed a perfectly good rose, I didn't understand anything. Maybe I was just too dense for this Wise Woman stuff. I wandered away and sat down on a concrete bench. It felt surprisingly cool on my legs despite the warm morning air.

Naomi followed me and stood in front of the bench holding the rose she'd clipped. Rotating it between her fingers, she held it out and asked, "What do you know about this flower?"

Glancing sideways, I took a deep cleansing breath and tried again to play the dutiful apprentice. "It's dying."

When she didn't answer, I leaned forward, peering more closely, a student staring at an equation on an algebra exam, worried the answer had come too easily. "Well... I suppose ...technically, it's dead now."

"Dying," she affirmed. "And this one?" She held up the perfect blossom I'd murdered.

"Not quite as dead."

"What makes you say that?"

Was this a botany lesson for dummies?

"The petals are brighter red and it isn't open as wide. If we put it in some water it might survive for a day or two."

She nodded and sat down beside me, dropping the newer blossom into her basket and exchanging it for the faded flower. Naomi reverently smoothed her fingers over the crusty brown edges of the outer petals. "This rose is me. And you..."

I sincerely hoped she wasn't going to point to the one with its head lopped off in the basket like Marie Antoinette. She didn't. She directed her index finger toward a rose on the bush just beginning to open. "Do you know why most women like flowers?"

"Flowers are pretty?" I said lamely.

"Yes!" She smiled brilliantly and cupped in her palm a tall orange daisy-like blossom nodding on a long gangly stem beside our bench. "Don't you just love all the colors and the fragrances?" The instructress in her voice disappeared. Suddenly we were friends and sisters, and I wasn't sure why.

I nodded.

"Men give us flowers on our birthdays, or when they want to make up after a fight. It's so odd that they do that. I doubt they understand why it's such an appropriate gift." She crossed her feet at the ankles and scrunched up her shoulders like a schoolgirl with a funny secret. "In a weird way they're giving us the gift of ourselves."

Why did this goofy statement make sense?

The old annoying adages comparing women to flowers zipped through my brain.

I am definitely not a flower.

"Except we aren't wimpy flowers," I insisted under my breath.

"No, decidedly not. Some of us are fierce warriors. History is full of brave heroines. Consider the Holy Spirit. True, she is beyond compare as a comforter, gentle as a dove, and yet in the Bible she is also likened to a mighty wind, rushing water, or fire. Gentleness and strength have nothing to do with why we love flowers."

"Alright, then why do we like them so much? It can't be because they smell good."

"No." She laughed—actually laughed—all friendly like—at something I'd said, and it wasn't even a smart-alecky joke. She twirled the blossom in her fingers. "We love flowers, Sophie, because we understand them."

"We do?"

"Yes. They are like us. Living according to cycles. Spring. Summer. Autumn. Winter. Dependent on biological rhythms. Sunshine. Rain. The seedling within them grows into budding plant. Flowering plant to fruit. Fruit to death. And then it starts all over again." She laid the rose I'd plucked too early in my lap. "We don't want them to come off before their time, because they are us."

The drooping petals grieved me.

She leaned forward and turned her too-serious gaze on me. "A man thinks of making the plant more efficient, more fruitful. This isn't a bad thing. A woman, deep in her soul, accepts the withered heads of her flowers. On some level, she grieves their passing, just as she knows she, herself, is changing with each season." She lifted the aged rose. "Wilting."

Such thoughts are not for the young. I set the sad rose back in her basket and glanced for reassurance at the newly opened bud on the bush, the one she had said represented me.

"Think about it, Sophie. Every month our wombs become fertile. And every month they wither. Our once fertile soil gets washed away. Our bodies' rhythms are as predictable as the seasons. And we reflect those seasons with storms and sunshine in our temperament. Women possess the delicacy and cyclical needs of a flowering plant. Yet we also share in their tremendous resilience. We bounce back. We take root and start again."

I remembered my mother bouncing back after her first bout with cancer. I'd felt it, too, that intense desire to rekindle my life after my dad's death. When we are torn down, or cut off, we send out shoots and bloom again.

Naomi clasped my hand. Her soft skin was parchment thin, yet she squeezed my palm with surprising strength and urgency. "This is an old truth, one ignored by women for centuries. Denying it robs us of our power. We have yielded our way of life to men. Culturally, women are out of balance."

Balance.

I had begun to hate that word. And here it was again, taunting me, as if I alone must press down mightily on some huge invisible fulcrum to restore balance. A fulcrum I didn't yet understand. "If we are like plants . . . what of men?"

"Ahhh, men." She let go of my hand and leaned back smiling. "Yin and yang, in a sense. They are our complimentary force. They're like horses, or oxen, or lions and wolves."

"Beasts." I chuckled softly.

"Yes. And when driven, come wind, rain, or snow, they keep going. Their needs are less cumbersome than ours." She ticked off on her fingers. "Food, sleep, shelter, and to breed. Survival and dominance." She ran her fingers over the handle of the basket. "Therein lies the problem. Out of necessity, or perhaps for practicality's sake, men structured the cultures of our world to suit their requirements, while the more complicated needs of females took a back seat."

A prickly pear growing in the yard caught my attention. The oblong pancake-shaped branches of the cacti had grown in a haphazard fashion—no discernible pattern.

Was that what happened to our world? One thing had led to another, until we had grown into a prickly tangled mess?

"Isn't there a way to make it different?" I asked.

"I doubt it. Cultures are structures. They have ironclad underpinnings as solid as any building. And like buildings, they are built one brick at a time, layer upon layer, one edifice atop another, until they form rambling cities. Men built their cities, nations, and cultures based on what worked for them. And society kept rolling forward, building on itself. Momentum is a powerful thing."

"We could change it." I ran my fingers over the rough fretwork on the edge on the bench, tracing the Greek egg and dart pattern. "It might be difficult, but it isn't impossible."

"Far more difficult than you think, Sophie. You still have the optimism of youth. Change seems to follow the path of least resistance. Eventually women stopped understanding their own needs and resigned themselves to male patterns of existence."

"Although," Naomi shuffled the gravel under the sole of her shoe. "I have to admit, sometimes I dream of what the world would be like if men had consulted God and built their societies and cultures with more loving consideration for women. Or perhaps if Godly women had exerted more influence on cultural development during the earlier ages." She shrugged and stared down at her basket of sad clipped flowers.

I grasped her arm. "Tell me what it would be like. *Please*, I want to know."

She glanced up at the sandstone rocks of Camelback Mountain, visualizing a world I wished I could see too. She answered with a slow drawl. "You're asking me to describe a culture that accepts seasons of dormancy. A culture that knows fallow soil encourages future growth. A society with time and space for quietness of mind. Where aging is valued and nurtured with the same attention given to budding toddlers."

I plucked the dying blossom back out of her basket, and when I stroked the petals they darkened like velvet rubbed against the grain. I joined in her dream. "A world where emotional intelligence would be respected and taught as zealously as mathematics or science."

"Yes," she said. "And genuine love would be prized over sexuality."

"Wouldn't that be something," I chuckled at the impossibility of it.

Naomi leaned forward drifting toward the possibilities of our utopia. "Just think, Sophie, how wonderful it would be if medicine studied our bodies as cyclical entities that depend on perfect balance, rather than viewing our complaints as a list of symptoms to suppress with drugs? Oh, my dear," she sighed.

"The possibilities are endless. Unfortunately, it's pointless to speculate. These things can never be."

"Why not? Maybe if we—"

"If we do what?" She snapped. "Turn back the clock?" She shook her head. "Fight centuries of momentum." She shook her head. "No, it's irreversible."

She might be right. In my heart, though, I clung to hope. We couldn't just give up. *Vision inspires change. There must be a way.*

She jumped up and shook out her dress. "Come along. I have two bushels of peaches to preserve. Besides, it's time I told you another fairy tale." She smiled mischievously, "And I know just the one."

Chapter 17
Beauty, Beasts, and Peaches

Naomi pulled a strainer of peaches from a large pot of boiling water. "Beauty and the Beast—"

I jumped in eagerly. "—is that a Wise Woman tale? But I thought the Brothers Grimm wrote it."

"Heavens no!" She fanned away my question with a hot pad and set to work pulling the skin off a blanched peach. "The Brothers Grimm were...well, to begin with, they were men, men who studied law. And I suspect their legal experiences may have skewed their commitment to the truth." She shook her head. "They distorted any number of perfectly useful tales. Aside from that, they lived in the nineteenth century." She tapped her paring knife against the cutting board, freeing it from fragrant juices and bits of peach skin. "Beauty is a much, much older tale. One of our earliest."

The smell, a soothing blend of tanginess unique to peaches, curled up around my nostrils. The warmth from the window and the cheery yellow of her kitchen bathed me in motherly bliss. "Cozy" was a word I normally disdained, but at that moment the word sidled up to my mind like a fat gray cat rubbing against my ankles, purring with contentment. I didn't care about the Grimm Brothers' stories, or Beauty and her nonexistent Beast. The smell of orchards, rich and pungent, lingering in magic sunny fruit, yellow striped curtains with lace, and plump geraniums—those things captivated my happy senses.

Naomi rambled on with her explanation, "Madame de Villeneuve wrote the modern version in 1740." She glanced up, gazing past my head as if Madame de Villeneuve's spectre floated behind me.

I turned to check, just in case.

"Sadly, even her version was tainted. Woefully watered down." Naomi split a peach and popped the pit out into a separate bowl. "For four hundred years the story has been told incorrectly, almost blasphemously. The important points have been entirely lost." Her slight shoulders rose and fell with a deep sigh.

Important points?

Really?

I doodled a giant invisible X with my finger on the counter.

Beauty meets Beast. Beast falls for beauty. He changes into a rich handsome prince. They live happily ever after, and a dancing teapot sings something to that effect.

Nothing new to see here, folks.

"Um, *what* important points?" The discarded peach pits in the bowl called to me, luring me to pick one up and suck off the tantalizing fronds of red and orange that remained.

"Well, for starters, in de Villeneuve's story Beauty tames the Beast. Ha! When has that ever happened in real life? Her version teaches a completely erroneous lesson to little girls—be sweet and beautiful and the big grouchy bad guy will turn good. Ugh! How wrong is that?"

"Let me count the ways," I said absently, still contemplating the peachy bits remaining on those pits.

"The real story is so much better. Much truer."

"Wait—how can something be *truer*?" Plucking up a dripping peach stone, I cocked my head. "A thing is either true or it isn't."

"Are you going to become frustrating again?" She tilted her head at me, irritation rearranging the wrinkles on her face, upsetting the delicate symmetry.

"No, I don't mean to be frustrating. It's just that words are important." I licked the juice running down my thumb. "They're our primary form of communication. If we can't agree on the meanings, how will we—"

Her pinched brow silenced my argument.

"All right, let's not argue semantics," I said. "Tell me the story."

"Hmm. I'm not sure I want to now."

"Oh, come on." I tried to cajole her while hiding a peach stone in my cheek. "I said I was sorry."

"You didn't."

"Well, I am. And these peaches are divine."

The lines on her face gradually relaxed as she deftly sliced a peach into a jar. "Well, I can tell you this much. The real story doesn't feature a demure Beauty reforming her Beast with syrupy goodness. None of that Hollywood hogwash. And he's no prince. This story has far too much truth for that nonsense. So, if you're hoping for that sort of tale—"

"No. That's all right." I half-grinned. "Give me the truer version." I replaced the peach pit in my mouth with one still dangling juicy morsels and let the sweetness loll on my tongue.

"Very well, Miss Smarty Pants. Prepare your mind to remember."

"What do you mean prepare?" I returned both peach pits to the bowl sans the luscious morsels of fruit that I'd removed from them.

She waved the paring knife like a wand. "Breathe slowly, deeply. Relax. Focus on the images. See the story—don't just hear it. Let your eyelids rest halfway. Yes, that's it. There." She pronounced approval on my breathing and posture. "Are you ready to remember?"

I nodded. "Ready to remember forever." I felt certain nothing about that morning would ever slip away from me. It would all be bound up together in the smell of peaches and the nurturing cocoon of her motherliness.

Beauty and the Beast

Long, long ago, during the dark days of swirling mists and fog, there lived a warrior known throughout the land for astonishing courage and strength. The fact that she was a beautiful woman made her no less extraordinary. Even in her youth, Dinah was a legend.

"Wait!" I blurted. "This Dinah person doesn't sound like much of a soft petaled flower-type girl. I thought you said—"

"No." Naomi winced at my intrusion into her story. "I told you, some of us are warriors. Women needn't be wimpy or weak. That's not our connection to flowers. Besides, Dinah was like a mother to her people. She loved them and wanted to protect them." Naomi shook her finger at me. "Now, stop interrupting."

When Dinah's people were afraid, they would cry out for her, and she came to their defense. Standing atop fortress walls her voice would ring out with the intoxicating power of strange music. Her words made courage swell and overflow in the hearts of her frightened clansmen.

Her fearless confidence made farmers and shepherds believe they had warrior strength throbbing through their veins.

And so they hefted their crude iron blades, their arrows and axes, and followed Dinah into battle.

Dinah had something they did not, a sword made especially for her by angels, fashioned of a metal like none found on earth. Unlike mortal blades, stiff and ungainly, her sword had the fluidity of molten lava. Sometimes it appeared long, nearly the length of a man's arm, other times short and deadly, suited for battles in close quarters. It knew what Dinah needed before she did. They worked together as one.

Thus, it came to be known as Dinah's Talon.

Talon shone as bright as sunlight, white fire, blinding the eyes of her enemies. It had the strength of seven blades, slicing through wooden shields as if they were mere butter.

A rumor spread far and wide, that during the great battle north of the river, Dinah's magic sword cut through her attacker's broadsword leaving him with nothing but an impotent stump. The same mighty stroke carried her blade through his leather breastplate, splitting his heart in twain. True or not, everyone believed the story.

Talon was not her only advantage. Dinah did not fear death. Some said, "With such a sword, why should she?" Except it wasn't her mystical weapon that kept her from being afraid. Dinah simply had no reason to rue death, no parents left to care for, no children depending upon her for sustenance. She was alone. Nothing bound her to Earth except the desire to protect her people.

Before each battle, she wondered if it might be her last

fight. In her heart, she believed she would triumph over her enemies, but if God deemed it time for her to die—so be it. She welcomed death as much as she did life, believing they were merely two sides of the same coin.

In those dark days, strange creatures roamed the earth, creatures from above and below. Dragons. Sea monsters. Giants with terrible strength. Some were thought to be the rampaging offspring of fallen angels and demons. More often, they were men whose cruelty rendered them almost inhuman.

And so it was when one afternoon a runner hailed Dinah from the road. Stooped and breathless, he described a terrible monster tearing apart his village, slaughtering their sheep, devouring their food, frightening the women and children. When the men tried to fight it, the creature's powerful tentacles coiled around them and flung them aside. His tail lashed out and knocked them from their feet. With his bare hands, he broke their swords and spears like dried twigs. He shoved their huts over as a child tumbles a stack of stones and left the people quaking in fear with nowhere to hide.

Dinah strapped on Talon and ran with the messenger to his village. Arriving late in the afternoon, she found a few men beating down the last flames of a scorched hut. Children cowered in the arms of their mothers, soot and dirt mixed with tears on their cheeks.

"Dinah! You came." The chieftainess rushed forward with her young son in her arms and her headdress drooping to one side as if it were as weary as the woman wearing it. "Praise be!"

Dinah pointed to the handful of men fighting the remnants of the fire. "Oanna, where are the rest of your men?"

"Injured. I sent three others, our bravest, into the forest to hunt the monster." Oanna cast a worried glance toward the trees. "He threatened to return on the morrow." Staring at the ground near Dinah's feet, she caught her bottom lip briefly before answering. "I thought perhaps if they caught him sleeping—"

"A creature like that does not sleep deeply. We must hurry."

The inhabitants of the village circled around Dinah. "Gather all who are still able to fight. We will find this monster tonight and put an end to his destruction."

The ragtag band of warriors, women, old men, and unseasoned youths followed Dinah, winding through the trees and undergrowth, tracking the first hunting party. At last they came upon the trio of warriors squatting in a circle scratching plans in the dirt.

A man wearing a chest protector of carved bone and an armband of beads rose to greet them, a finger to his lips warning them to be silent. "In there." The beads on his wrist clacked softly as he pointed toward a dark path leading into the underbrush.

The chieftainess scrutinized the uninviting passageway. "You're certain?"

"I saw him," the scout insisted, whispering as if their enemy might overhear. "But he's not asleep. That tail of his is twitching like a cat's."

Dinah stiffened. "Then he knows we're here."

The men shifted uncomfortably.

One of the elders standing near the chieftainess pulled absently on his long thin beard. "We could wait." He glanced hesitantly toward the mouth of the thicket. "He's bound to fall asleep sooner or later."

A tall gangly youth who had yet to grow into his large knobby joints stared at the newly sharpened point of his spear. "A beast like that may not need sleep." He spoke under his breath, but even so the others heard.

"We must fight him now." The chieftainess sighed deeply. "Or face him in the morning. We have no choice. You saw what he did today. Who knows what he might do next?"

Shoulders sagging, the younger men fidgeted with their weapons. Dinah watched them carefully, knowing fear was turning to bile in their mouths. She readied her hand on Talon. "Look up, men of the river! We are many. He is but one."

They responded with hope brightening their faces but fear written in their eyes.

"Come!" she said. "It is better that we face him now when he is sated and tired. Did you not tell me he ate almost an entire sheep not long ago? Even lions grow sluggish after such a meal." Dinah spoke softly, calling on the harp strings of heaven to turn her words into music for the soul. "Raise your weapons! We will march in together. *Together*, we will defeat this Beast. Never again will he cross the river. He will fall at our feet! And with his last breath, he will wish he had stayed far from your village."

She unsheathed her famous sword. The blade glittered before their eyes, a dazzling white blaze lighting the gloomy jungle. They murmured in awe. But as she held it up, Talon shrank. The molten blade pulled into itself, growing smaller and smaller until it became a wilted leaf of quivering blue metal.

The villagers drew in their breath. Their mouths gaped open, and they edged away from her.

Dinah shook off her surprise, grasped Talon firmly with both hands, and gave it a shake. "Come, sword. Rise up! We have a battle before us!"

The shining metal continued to pull down into itself until it was no more ferocious than a gleaming lump of quartz at the end of her hilt. She thumped it against her thigh, hoping she might jar it back into action. When nothing happened, she simply stared at it, waiting. Dinah had fought scores of battles with Talon. It had always known what she needed.

The bearded scout peered nervously at the nubbin in her hand. His fear became a shiver that rippled through the group.

"What's wrong with it?" the elder demanded.

Dinah shook her head in disbelief. Her lumpy blade would not even cut the scraggly hairs from the elder's chin. Talon shimmered a strange midnight blue and silver.

"Broken," the headwoman pronounced, shoving her turban into place and staring angrily at Dinah's offending weapon. "Give her another sword."

"No." Dinah lowered the useless nubbin. "It is an omen."

She guided the blade toward her belt and frowned as it changed shape to enter the sheath.

"What kind of omen is this?" The woman shook her spear at the opening in the trees. "Without your sword, how can we fight that creature?"

"You can't." Dinah straightened. "Leave. Go back to your village."

"But it will come out again tomorrow and—"

"Go home," Dinah ordered more firmly. "I must face him by myself. Without a sword."

"Have you gone mad?" The old elder limped forward. "Do you know what that monster in there has done? It nearly ripped off my leg. Tossed me aside as if I were no more than a bundle of sticks. He will tear you to pieces."

"Aye," the others agreed and thumped their spears against the ground in assent.

The headwoman held up her hand for silence. "Sol is right. This is our fight, Dinah. We cannot leave you to deal with that monster alone. If your sword has failed you, we will fight him without you."

The men nodded solemnly. Their little sparks of courage pleased Dinah, but she knew at the first counterattack they would run like frightened deer and some of them would be killed.

Dinah stood to her full height and inclined her head respectfully to the Chieftainess. "I sense this battle is mine and mine alone." Dinah laid her hand over her breast in the manner of one swearing to the truth. "A test. I have been lured here for this very purpose. The proof is this—if I needed a sword, I would have one."

The villagers stared at her and then backed away, all save the Headwoman. "Then we will wait here and stand watch until you return."

"No. Go home. Repair your huts. Tend to your families and to your wounded."

"We will wait."

Dinah lowered her eyes, humbled by the woman's steadfast concern. "Very well. Obey your conscience. Except I must ask that you do not wait for too long. For I make no promise about the outcome." And with that, Dinah turned and slipped into the deep undergrowth.

She crept through the vines and brambles, taking each step cautiously, watching for movement among the leaves. She had glimpsed her enemy reflected in her sword. Dark, he would easily meld into the shadows. Pungent with fertile decay and new growth, the forest opened slightly. High above her, a canopy of leaves blocked out the waning light, casting everything into muted greens and grays.

Dinah felt him watching as she moved stealthily through the maze of hanging branches. Countless insects crawled along the forest floor. Birds and animals peeped curiously at her as she wove through their tangled world. Although a thousand eyes watched her, never before had the fine hairs at the back of her neck prickled because of insects or bushy-tailed tree bats. Not even the great bears of the north or the roaring lions of the plains had caused a sensation such as this on her skin.

She could feel the Beast.

The deeper she went into the forest, the stronger her sense of him became. Images flashed into her mind. Dinah blinked as one did when blinded by bright light. She caught glimpses of him in all his terrible glory, tail and tentacles, fierce blue and black skin, a stripe of vibrating red slashed diagonally across his face. Muscles in his chest and arms were like those of a giant tiger.

More powerful than all of these fleeting images was his scent. Dinah tracked him by his aroma. In the past, she had hunted rogue lions by their musky smell, strong and unmistakable. The Beast's scent was nothing like that. It lured her with its subtleness. Perhaps there was no smell at all—for it did not seem to even have the strength of a flower blooming on the far side of a river. Yet, she followed the invisible fragrance as if it were a guide rope leading her through the darkness.

She puzzled over this. A monster such as this ought to reek of carnage and decay. He did not, and why was his scent so intoxicating?

The Beast stood in the clearing—a broadsword larger than any she had ever faced rested in his right hand. Arms muscular and taut like those of the giant northern men, except one of his arms glowed indigo blue, and the other was as black as a starless night. Behind him waved four wicked tentacles as long as bullwhips, undulating in the air above him like the skeletal remains of an angel's wings.

No angel, this Beast.

From behind his legs, his tail snaked toward her, rustling dead leaves as it came.

Dinah's breath caught in her throat, fear and awe choking her. Her hand went of its own accord to the hilt of her sword. When she slid it out of the sheath, it surprised her to see a long sharp blade glowing starlight into the gloam of the clearing. She took a battle stance.

He grinned.

Dinah shivered, waiting for him to raise his weapon. Talon grew heavy. Clasping it with both hands, she prepared to strike. The Beast's tail swayed calmly, just out of striking distance, unnerving her, as he leisurely appraised his opponent.

Enough!

She charged forward and slashed at him. A hasty decision.

Foolish.

She nearly tripped over a thick root hidden under the leaves. In the dimness, she scarcely glimpsed a blur of steel as he blocked her blade with his. Clanging metal echoed in her ears and jarred her arms. With all her might she pressed her blade against his, holding him in place, waiting for the telltale shift in weight that meant he would pull back and strike.

Locked thus, she looked into his eyes. Silver blue. She had thought they would be yellow like a tiger's or vicious green like a snake's. Instead, they called to her like the faraway cry of a wolf on a cold night, begging, hungry.

Dinah felt her arm strength ebbing. In one fluid movement, she pushed off from his broadsword and spun around to bring Talon full force against his unguarded side. But she struck metal once more.

How had he parried so quickly with so large a weapon? He leaned toward her. His nostrils widened, quivering almost imperceptibly as he breathed deep. If only her scent had the same unsettling effect on him as his tormenting male aroma did on her. She lowered her gaze from his too-perceptive eyes, following the slash of red that angled across his face, lower, to the deep blue that covered his lips and neck, sweeping down across the muscles of his left shoulder.

Edging her foot back, she readied herself for her next blow. The point of one of his tentacles brushed against the side of her arm. She flinched.

His chest rumbled as the Beast spoke. "I did not come to fight you, warrior."

The sound resonated inside her, exciting vibrations she did not comprehend, as if awakening to the voice of a long-lost friend.

It could not be.

This half-man half-beast was no friend of hers.

She swallowed the fear and confusion choking her. "Then you will die, for I came to kill you." Her words sounded thin, shallow, weak. Dinah forced herself to breathe evenly, to stop gasping for air like a frightened child.

His brow lifted slightly. "Perhaps," he whispered, staring

long into her face. "You are the one woman capable of it."

Some vague torment disturbed his features, a hint of pain. Perhaps one of the villagers had injured him, except Dinah spotted no wound. No. She saw only smooth skin, dark as blue moth wings, molded like polished leather over muscles that could all too easily destroy her.

"I must protect my people." She puffed up the words with as much fullness as her vocal cords would allow.

His gaze flickered to her sword. The hard lines of his jaw softened ever so slightly. His mouth curved into a soft, knowing smile. Talon had dwindled once more into a useless lump.

"No," Dinah implored under her breath. "No!" She panicked and dashed away from him, dodging behind a tree trunk, waiting for his deadly blow.

"Is that the best you can do, warrior? Hide?" He lowered his sword. "Do you not realize you hold a far more powerful weapon?"

Leaves rustled, crushing under his feet as he drew near the gnarled old tree trunk behind which Dinah hid. Closing her eyes, she inhaled sharply, searching the air for his scent.

Foolishness.

Death stalked her, and yet she savored its scent. Such madness would get her killed. "What weapon?" she murmured, with her hand on Talon's hilt.

A low rumble.

A *laugh?*

She hated him for laughing. Hated herself for hiding

powerlessly behind a tree. She glanced down at the small dagger secreted in a sheath on her calf. No magic there. Simple metal forged by human hands, sharpened on a stone wheel like all mortal knives. This one could not shrink of its own accord. She drew it and stepped out. Ready to kill or be killed.

They were too close. She lunged. He caught her fist and blade in one mighty hand. Jerking out of his grasp, she sliced across his palm. Tentacles splayed out in a sudden flash behind him, gigantic black spines. Just as quickly they softened, undulating, leaning in her direction as if he could scarcely restrain them from weaving toward her. "Do what you must. I will not fight you."

Dinah stepped back, gripping her knife. The Beast held his hand open wide, his slashed palm dripping crimson blood into the leaves at their feet, but not once did his gaze leave her face.

He bleeds.

He can be killed.

Yet, the thought of thrusting her knife into his heart sickened her, struck her stomach like a war hammer. She stumbled backward.

Why?

Why could she not kill this monster as she had hundreds of others? His blood trickled out in a stream, weeping into the bowels of the earth. She couldn't stand to watch. She felt an unbearable urge to make his pain stop, to bind up the ugly gash.

She shook her head and murmured to herself. "No, I am a warrior, not a healer."

Still, his wound called to her. His eyes beckoned. Those wretched spines of his lashed slowly to and fro, leaning toward her as if sensing her every thought and counting on her weakness.

"God help me." Dinah backed away until she collided with the thorny branches of the thicket. She dropped her dagger and turned, scrambling to find the slender opening in the undergrowth.

"No!" One of his tentacles coiled around her waist and pulled her back into the open. "Stay. Kill me if you must, but you cannot leave." He drew her close and pressed the dagger she had dropped in the leaves back into her hand.

"I can't," she whispered, bowing her head.

"Come, warrior." He brushed her cheek with the side of his finger. "I've heard the tales. You've dealt with dragons and demons. Why not me?"

She shook her head. "What weapon do I have against one such as you?"

"Can it be that you still do not understand?"

The only thing she understood was that even his coiled locks wisping against her shoulder drove her nearly senseless.

"Dinah, look at me."

She refused to glance up. Afraid of what she would see in his face. Not fearing hideousness. Not afraid of the deeper-than-night blackness of his skin, nor the frightening slash of scarlet blazing across his features, nor the changeling blue of his shoulders and chest, which glimmered different shades of indigo under each subtle shift of the light. No, Dinah feared seeing the one thing that would melt her very soul to water.

Yet, when she dared a glance, she did see it. In his eyes. Desire. Such deep want for her that she could not look away. Neither could she answer him.

She turned away, escaping his terrible need. Seeing his wounded hand, Dinah brushed her fingertips against the skin beside the gash. He did not move or breathe as she touched him. And suddenly she knew what she must do. Slicing away the bottom of her linen shirt, she took the strip of cloth and wrapped it around his bleeding palm. The Beast kept perfectly still as she ministered to him.

When she finished, his tentacle loosened from her waist and slid down to rest around her hips. "I have been waiting." He spoke in a hushed voice. The warmth of his words felt like feathers against her ear. They sluiced into her mind, and Dinah shivered. She might ask any number of foolish questions.

Waiting for what?

For whom?

Except she knew the answers, just as she seemed to know the Beast's soul, just as she knew they were somehow inextricably bound. She laid her palm lightly on his chest and bowed her head. "What do you expect of me?"

The now-familiar low rumble commenced again. She looked up to find his mouth cocked in a foolish grin, his tail and tentacles twitching like a self-satisfied tiger.

"We mate."

Naturally.

Only it wasn't natural. He was a...

And she was...

Being a male, he grabbed her wrist and started tugging. Being a woman, she resisted. "Wait!"

"I *have* been waiting." He stopped tugging, inhaled deeply, and let it out slowly. "A *very* long time."

"Then you will just have to wait some more." At last, she realized with triumph, her tone commanded the firmness she had so desperately wanted earlier.

He let go of her wrist. His tentacles arched. "You're going to make this difficult, aren't you?"

"Well..." She spread her hand in his direction. "Look at you. You have all those dangerous-looking colors. You're very large. And..." She pointed at his tentacles. "You have those spiny things."

"Spiny?" His whips curled in response. "They're not spiny. They're sleek as a lion's tail. Here, see for yourself."

"No, thank you." She cast his offer aside.

The beast folded his arms across his chest and stared silently down at her like an insulted child.

"And have you looked at me?" She tilted her shoulder so he had a clear view of her back. "No tentacles. More importantly, I'm not certain where all your extra parts might end up. I could die."

The corner of his mouth tilted up. "Are you afraid to find out, warrior?"

"No!" Dinah shook her head and took a step backward. "It's just that I prefer to die gloriously—in a battle."

"Glorious. Pfft." He growled. "You know perfectly well there's nothing glorious about dying, especially in battle. It's usually full of ugly gore and agony."

"I meant for a noble cause."

"Noble? Sooner or later all of us must die." He glanced down at her. "My people mate for life. Mating is considered noble." The spines in question, thrashed from side to side. His scarlet blaze glowed brighter.

Perhaps she would die in battle after all. It was a good thing she still had her knife. "Keep those things away from me."

"I won't hurt you."

Could she trust the word of a Beast? The way he was breathing and glowing red, he looked ready to rip one of the towering ancient trees out by the roots.

"I promise..." He moved slowly toward her until he held her shoulders in his hands. She felt the warmth of his blood seeping through the linen bandage onto her skin. "...I will never hurt you."

She shook her head. "You cannot promise such a thing. Pain is entwined with life."

He bowed his head for a moment and then slid his hand down her arm and laced his blue fingers into her pale ones. "What you say is true."

Chapter 18
Chemistry

Peach Pie

Place crust in pie pan. Mix 1 cup sugar and ½ teaspoon of cinnamon with 2 tablespoons cornstarch. Cover pie shell with ¾ of the mixture. Arrange peach slices close together. Sprinkle the remaining sugar mixture over the peaches. Pour 1 cup of cream over it all. Bake at 375° until custard turns clear, about 45 minutes.

Naomi stopped telling the story. Into each of the glass canning jars, brimming with peaches, she carefully poured a sugared brandy sauce. Setting the jars into a bath of hot water on the stove, she turned her attention to an empty pie shell. She spread the sugar mixture in the bottom, and carefully laid peach slices into the shell.

"Wait! You can't stop there. The story isn't over. What happened?"

Naomi glanced up briefly from the pie and her cheeks crinkled into a teasing grin.

"Well? Tell me what happened next," I asked sharply, feeling cheated and equally embarrassed, knowing I must sound like an over-eager child. So I straightened and pasted on a more scholarly attitude. "You can't begin a story and then leave out all the juicy bits."

Naomi grinned broadly, her teeth, a row of pale pearls, worn and polished with age, but still perfect. "Juicy bits?" One eyebrow flared up. "You're being a trifle voyeuristic, don't you think?"

"Tell me!" I demanded, losing patience with her baiting.

"Well," she shrugged. "Naturally, he led her through the woods to one of the ancient ponds, they waded in and—"

"No." I slapped my hand on the counter. "Don't just tell it. Make me see it."

She placed one last slice of peach, which completed a spiral of half-moons filling the pie crust. That soft, knowing smile of hers settled into place. "Have you ever tasted open-face peach pie? It's heavenly. Probably the most delicious thing—"

"The story," I begged in earnest.

"Very well..."

Beauty and The Beast, Part II

Dinah glanced down at her toes poised on the edge of the pond. A bright yellow and green lizard skittered away from the grass beside her feet. She'd heard stories about these old pools. People whispered that they had existed since before time, that they could swallow a man up and spit him out on the other side of the world. Some said the water would make you young again, or heal sickness. Despite all the stories, no one had ever mentioned the dark disks of colors pulsing and overlapping. These liquid orbs radiated emotions as well as color, charging the air with prickly energy, making each of her hairs stand on end, as if slices of the Earth's life force floated up, one after the other in a mesmerizing concentric dance of sensation, love, hate, pain, joy, anger.

Dinah clung to the Beast's hand, certain that if she stepped into the swirling depths it would swallow her up. Or would she become just another dark circle floating to the surface?

"Come." He stepped in. His black leg seemed like a natural extension of the mystical pond, but when the waters licked against the blue of the Beast's other side, sparks of light scattered across the surface. Dinah let go of his hand and held her breath as he moved deeper into the strange pool.

He waded out until he was submerged up to his waist, then turned and held out his hand for her. His tentacles snaked across the surface, gliding to her, winding over her toes and around her calves, leaving tracks of moisture as they climbed higher up her thighs.

"Dinah, come to me." The red slash that divided his face, blue skin from black, brightened like a stirred fire. His whips ventured toward the flesh under her linen kilt.

"Stop!" She grabbed a tentacle in each fist and yanked them away from her skin.

They coiled around her hands and urged her forward into the pool.

What madness is this?

She considered slicing his ruddy tentacles off, turning, and running away. Either that or summoning up a gilly-seed's worth of courage and stepping bravely toward her destiny. Dinah frowned, pondered her options, and plunged into the pond.

"It's warm." She had expected the water to be icy cold like a mountain lake or steaming hot like a sulfur spring, not warm and soothing. The thick water tickled her skin, and thousands of tiny bubbles rushed around her.

"You're smiling, warrior." But he was not. The muscles in his jaw remained taut, his eyes alert, luminous, like a man certain the battle had turned in his favor.

Dinah recognized the heat of certain triumph on his features. She had felt it herself in the midst of combat countless times.

Let him think he has won.

This battle is not over yet.

Her mouth settled into a calm knowing crescent. She

accepted his outstretched hand and let him pull her to him. The waters danced around them in vibrant circles, brighter now. Halos of sparkling light shot across the surface toward the shore.

The Beast clasped her shoulders. “Are you ready?”

“I’m here. That is all I can say. I doubt I shall ever be ready.”

“So be it.” The corner of his mouth curved up, smiling lopsidedly into his blue cheek, forming an iridescent dimple that both surprised and pleased Dinah. His fingers grazed the arc of her neck until he held her cheeks in his palms. He bent slowly toward Dinah, his dark mane, a mass of coiled black locks, fell forward, curtaining them off from the world.

She thought he meant to kiss her. Instead, he pressed his forehead against hers. Water splashed up, licking at their shoulders, nudging them deeper into the pond, bathing them in radiant warmth.

Suddenly, a blinding flash pierced Dinah’s mind. Startled, she tried to pull away, but the Beast held her firmly in place. Streams of light plunged into her cortex.

He heaved a deep breath, like a man desperate for air, and let it out in hesitant shudders. With each exhale, images flew into Dinah’s mind, a village in flames, the whiz of an axe blade, men fighting, strange food, towers of gleaming white stone, a land unlike any she’d ever seen, the soft touch of a mother’s soothing fingers, wind whipping atop tall cliffs, dark longings, and a deep yearning that stirred her like a promising dream from which one does not wish to awaken.

Dinah selfishly touched, smelled, and tasted his memories, until at last she heard groaning.

Deep guttural cries.

Her Beast shrieked in pain!

Yet, she could not let go, would not. Letting go seemed impossible. He struggled to free himself from their bond. Instinctively, she laced her fingers into his thick locks and clung to him.

Suddenly her own memories whirled up from the center of her being.

Dinah gasped, unable to catch her breath. They rushed past her mind's eye streaming toward him. Herself as a little girl in her mother's arms. Her mother's death. Angels. The day she received the sword. Monsters. Battles. Gardens. The rich smell of soil in her fingers. Climbing jagged rocks. And faces.

So many faces. Friends. Enemies. Those who had begged for help. Comrades she'd lost in battle. Foes she'd slain.

Worst of all, her own loneliness took form, rising out of her in a dark haunting body of its own. Yet, it did not rise alone. Bursting forth, like bright sparks in the deep of night, came hope.

Hope so exquisite, so beautiful, it made her hurt deep inside. Hope, so pitifully brave against the overwhelming sadness that Dinah began to weep. This thing, this yearning swelled inside her until she, too, cried out.

Dinah let go. The Beast fell back, splashing into the treacherous water, his arms spread wide. She feared he was dead. Her legs trembled. Weak and exhausted, she summoned the last of her ebbing strength and caught hold of his arm.

His weight nearly dragged her under as she struggled to pull him out. She trudged toward the bank, but before she reached it, she felt strength returning to his arm.

He surged up from the water and shook out his saturated mane, spraying her with droplets of moisture. In one vigorous motion he swooped his other arm around her and kissed her.

She wondered why he hadn't done that in the first place.

Triumph swelled his chest. "We survived."

"Nearly," she warned. The remains of his tentacles floated like debris against the edge of the pond. Her Beast no longer had whips weaving menacingly above his head.

Dinah glanced at their hands still entwined, a blue one and a pale one. It took her a moment before she realized that the pale one now belonged to him, and the butterfly blue hand was her own. She glimpsed her reflection in the now still pool; a red slash divided her features, pale from blue.

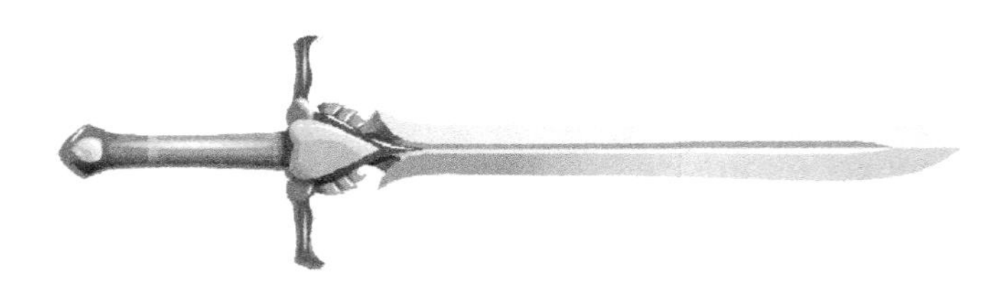

Naomi poured heavy cream over the peach pie and placed it in the oven.

"That's it? It's over?" I shivered even though the kitchen

was filled with steam from the boiling peaches.

"Yes." She set the oven timer and turned to me. "What did you learn?"

"Stay away from guys with tentacles."

Chapter 19
For the Love of Pi (π)

"I see through your little ploys, you know." Naomi wiped a dry cloth over the granite counter, scooting bits of flour into a neat little pile. "You hide your sensitivity and intelligence behind a façade of wisecracks and quips." After whisking remains of the flour into a trashcan, she smacked her hands on the counter and leaned toward me. "It won't do. We have too little time and too much to accomplish. If you continually refuse to be serious, how can I possibly teach you anything of value?"

No *more ploys*?

Could I do without them? I doubted it. I'd spent a lifetime perfecting those maneuvers she so glibly called ploys, training them up from baby dancing bears to tutu-wearing elephants. And now she wanted me to send them away. No more hiding behind alligators in clown suits?

"Tell me the point of that fairytale or no pie," Naomi said with the pleasantest of smiles, which made it all the more threatening.

"No pie?"

"Not one bite."

"Not even a teensy..." I pinched my fingers together suggesting a caterpillar-sized sliver.

She crossed her arms and shook her head.

"That's blackmail."

"Precisely." She opened the oven door to adjust her creamy golden-fringed hostage and with her hot pad strategically fanned the aroma in my direction. If God opened a bakery, it would smell like that. I clamped my lips tight to keep errant drool from embarrassing me.

She shut the oven, a smug smile tugging at her cheeks.

"Hmm." I tried to appear nonchalant and finally gave up. "Okay! But just so you know, you had me at '*I see through your little ploys*.'"

Naomi's eyebrow arched skeptically.

"You want secret codes deciphered? Fine!" *I can play the star pupil when I try.* "It turns out Beauty was just as changed by her relationship with the Beast as he was by her. I mean, *hello*—

she turned half blue. Ergo, the idea that a woman's love can transform a man is horsesh ...er, poppycock."

Naomi did her tilt-y-head thing, reminding me of a skinny owl.

"So, how'd I do?" I quizzed my ruthless blackmailer while salivating over lingering whiffs of peach pie.

"Not bad."

"But not great? What'd I miss?"

"Well, love isn't poppycock. Love does transform. A love relationship alters both the man and the woman. Which is why it's essential to choose our mates carefully. Inevitably, we adopt many of their traits—the good, the bad, and the disgusting. You can see why the modern version of the tale presents a problem. Supposedly, Beauty's love turns the Beast into a handsome prince, she redeems him, and he magically transforms. This is such a dangerous notion. No one except God can redeem a man or transform him. If a woman tries to do it, she's destined for frustration and failure. The modern story would also have you believe Beauty's big transformation was getting crowned princess and moving into a castle full of riches. Oh my, what a sacrifice for her." Naomi snorted sarcastically. "Complete and utter twaddle."

"Twaddle?" I muttered absently. For some reason, my thoughts had drifted to Ryder. Cataloging the few traits of his I knew about, I and wondered if I would be willing to turn half blue for him.

"He's still out there you know."

I glanced up sharply. "What do you mean?"

"Oh, don't act so surprised." Naomi chuckled at me. Her white hair glowed like a fuzzy halo as it caught the late afternoon sun streaming through the kitchen window. "You were a million miles away, or to be more accurate, about fifty yards away. In either case, your face got all gooey. What else could you have been thinking about?"

Am I that transparent? I pouted at my wise mind reader, and since Naomi had denied me the protective cover of dancing alligator clowns I failed to come up with a satisfactory quip.

She smiled, knowing she had stumped me. "Perhaps, when it comes out of the oven, you should take him a piece of pie."

"Are you suggesting I fraternize with my distraction?" It was my turn to arch a brow. The trouble was my stubborn eyebrows refused to operate independently. So, both brows popped up, and I probably looked more surprised than alarmed.

"Suit yourself." She shrugged and cocked a wry grin toward the dishcloth as if the two of them had a private joke going on.

I leaned in on my elbows. "Come to think of it, you never did mention who set him on my trail?"

Her face darkened, and she wouldn't look me in the eye.

Not a good sign.

Oh, she knew all right, but it looked like prying it out of her might take a crowbar and an electric winch. "So, who was it?"

Naomi mewed and um-ed and finally sputtered. "I can only speculate."

"Speculate away. I need to know."

“Now that you’re here, I don’t see that it really matters. Completely irrelevant.”

“Seems pretty relevant to me. There’s a man parked out in front of your house, watching us. Doesn’t that bother you?”

“Not in the least.” She swished her hand through the air swatting away my argument. “More importantly, we don’t have time for such distractions.”

“Oh. And yet, you think it’s perfectly all right for me to take him pie?”

She sighed deeply, the way only a seventy-something woman can, emphasizing her frailty, and making me feel like a complete bully. So, I abandoned the pursuit.

Sensing my surrender, Naomi’s spirits seemed to lift, and her Donna Reed pleasantness returned. “Let’s take a look at the bookcase, shall we? I can think of at least a dozen stories you’re ready to decode.”

And she did, too.

Dozens.

Later that night, after hearing how various civilizations approached storytelling, based on their era and culture, and how to distinguish a Phoenician legend from an Egyptian tale, and after calculating hidden messages and deciphering symbolism in tales from four different centuries, the decoder half of my brain collapsed. The Wise Woman toddled off to watch the news, and I slipped out to take Ryder a piece of pie.

I stood on the sloped drive astonished by the vast tapestry of lights in the valley. A welcome breeze had blown away the brown layer of smog that had been plaguing Phoenix. The city below sparkled so brightly it dimmed the stars. Lines and patterns of luminous dots stretched to the horizon and beyond, a streaming bustling universe of humans, rushing around, blinking, busily shining long into the night. While above us, the deep stillness of space oversaw it all with endless patience and peace.

Wind tousled my hair like a mother's fingers ruffling through her child's curls. *Hello, Mother.* Usually the night sky pulled me in, sucked me upward into the vast, lonely, hugeness of it all. No longer. Now my universe had changed forever. Standing there on that rocky slope, gazing at the enormity of the cosmos, I was no longer a lone traveler in space, no longer a tick on the dog's back. Me, Sophie, I was part of it all, the whole magnificent thing—every spiritual and physical inch of it. It belonged to me as much as I belonged to it.

I didn't have to worry about losing this kind of love, nor ever being parted from such perfect affection. I felt it inside of me, holding my very being together, spinning each subatomic particle in place, sustaining life. Warmth and peace shivered through me.

Ryder's white pickup was parked on the street, gleaming in the moonlight, reminding me, all too keenly, that I still walked with mortals. And that was okay, too.

I peeked inside. Sleeping, he looked so young and innocent. I rapped on the frame beside his open window. Ryder woke with a start, blinking, momentarily disoriented, stammering his garbled astonishment.

"Hey, buddy. Some stalker you are, sleeping on the job."

He raked back his dark wavy hair and opened the door, the cab light flashed on, blinding both of us, and the key alarm dinged loud enough to alert the entire neighborhood. He slid out and quickly shut the door. Ryder stood close, glancing up and down the street like maybe his boss was going to fire him for talking to me. "What are you doing out here?" he asked, hovering over me like a Secret Service agent.

"Pie." I presented him with the golden treasure. "And not just any pie. This is creamy-peach-little-slice-of-Heaven pie"

The fork rattled against the plate as he accepted it from my hands. "Thanks." He took a bite. "Whoa!"

I stood back as the hint of cinnamon flared his nostrils, and the smooth luxurious texture of the peaches and creamy custard turned his expression to pure bliss. Some men made a guttural rumble when they were eating, a truly wonderful sound—what was that? A moan? A groan? There should be a word. Anyway, he did that.

"Almost as good as kissing, isn't it?" I said.

Hard to tell in the gray shadows of night, but I was pretty sure Ryder turned red. He averted his eyes and admitted in a deep tough guy grumble. "It's good. Really good." He quickly took another bite. "You okay?" he asked, neatly changing the subject while chewing. "What are you working on in there?"

"We've been canning peaches and making pie. Oh, and trimming roses—"

"Yeah, I saw that much." He punctuated each of his questions by stabbing forkfuls of sweet quarter moons into his mouth. "Saw the roses, I mean. What about the other stuff?" He went after that pie as if he hadn't eaten in a week. "When are you gonna... I mean, isn't there something more important you're supposed to be doing?"

"What could be more important than making pie?" I sprinkled some of Naomi's Southern Belle charm into my northern accent and waited.

Ryder still seemed kind of groggy, he glanced sideways into his truck at a laptop lying on the passenger seat.

"Oh, now I remember." I batted my eyelashes, all innocent-like. "You're probably referring to that *saving the world* business?"

His attention riveted back to my face. "Yeah, that." His sleepy demeanor vanished, replaced by way too much alertness. "I'm pretty sure you didn't drive all the way from Minnesota to trim roses and make pie."

"Didn't I?" I relished his baffled expression. "Well," I shrugged. "She also tells me stories."

"Yeah, you mentioned that before. Is she going senile or something?" He cleaned up the last morsel of crust and sweet custard. "Is she one of those old people who tells the story over and over about what it was like when they were kids trudging through the snow and how they didn't even have mittens?"

I shook my head as innocently as possible. "She hasn't mentioned trudging anywhere, and I doubt there's much snow here in Arizona."

"You know what I mean."

I stopped teasing him. "No, she's definitely not senile," I confessed. "And I like her stories. Especially the way she tells them."

He set the empty plate on the hood of his truck and took my shoulders in his hands, staring at me eye-to-eye as if I was a slow twelve-year-old. "Listen to me, Sophie," he says in his way-to-serious voice. "That's all well and good, but you've got to get her to concentrate. There are things you have to do. Important things. And if you don't..." He paused, searching my face on his hunt for comprehension. "Well... you know."

I liked having the full force of his attention, even if it was in a bossy-big-brotherly way. I didn't even mind his day-old smell, nor those rings of... "Hey! You're all sweaty."

He let go and pulled back like he was embarrassed. "Yeah, I know. It gets kind of hot out here. The air-conditioning doesn't work so good in idle. Anyway, I don't like to leave the engine running. Bad for the environment."

"Hot?!" I put my hand on his chest, checking the dampness saturating his t-shirt. "It hasn't been hot, it's been boiling out here. You could die of heatstroke. Or dehydration."

"Nah. Don't worry. I've got plenty of water. I'm used to working outside. No big deal."

"You're right! This goes way past a big deal." I thumped his chest. "It's dangerous, that's what it is. You shouldn't be sitting out here all day."

He shifted uneasily, but then recovered too quickly—saved by his male bravado. Super-Ryder leaned against the truck, propping his elbows back, stretching his long legs out and crossing his boots at the ankles. I resisted the urge to yield to his languid posture. It didn't matter if I wanted to fold myself up alongside him, relax, and forget about everything. I couldn't. This was serious.

"It's not *all* day. I make a run to the gas station now and then. And like I said..." He took his time, looking me over as if he were remembering holding me close. "I'm used to the heat. Anyway, how else can I watch over you?"

"I don't know. Install a nanny cam. *Something*. This way isn't working."

"I told you, I'll be fine."

No, he wouldn't.

I refused to have his death on my conscience. The situation called for drastic measures.

"Heatstroke is a real thing, Ryder. A *killer* thing." I crossed my arms, refusing to give in to his enticing posture.

"Don't worry about me. I'll be fine."

Stubborn man.

I harumphed. "No, you won't."

He set his jaw and looked away.

"Alright mister, here's the deal. If you don't stop hanging around out here, I'm going to call the police and file one of those legal thingies, a court order, or an injunction, or whatever it's called." I waved my hand in the air threateningly. "Which means, if you show up within 600 feet of me again your sweaty, *albeit cute*, self will be spending the night in jail. And you know how those big hairy guys in jail like cowboys."

His eyes widened—not quite so relaxed anymore. "You wouldn't."

"Oh, yes, I would." I planted my hands on my hips. "If that's what it takes to keep you from roasting yourself out here in the street." And just so he didn't get the idea I was soft on him or anything, I sniffed haughtily and added, "Naomi and I don't want your over-baked carcass messing up the front yard. It would be too traumatic for the roses."

"I can take the heat," he argued in his man-sized, grizzly bear voice.

"No one can take *this* kind of heat day in and day out, night in or night out—*or whatever*. You can't!"

"Fine." He caught my hand and pulled me close. "Sophie, sweetheart, if you don't lower your voice, we'll both be spending the night with hairy cellmates." He actually, almost, grinned. Playful sparks in his eyes melted my frustration and he bent so close, for one foolish moment, I thought he might kiss me. Instead, he brushed my hair back. "The last thing I want is to upset you. If it worries you that much, I'll stop parking out here all the time."

What?

Wait.

"All the time?" What did that mean? My stomach thudded down to my ankles. He was going to leave. I didn't want him to go away—*not entirely*. On the other hand, I didn't want him sitting out here suffering in the heat. The thought of not seeing him again made me queasy. "Um, so, where will you go?"

Oh no!

That came out sounding way too clingy.

I don't do clingy.

The trouble was I liked him being around, but I didn't want him to roast to death. What could I do? I would've invited him in except it wasn't my house. Frustrated, I reached past him to retrieve Naomi's plate and fork. He'd won—he had all the cards in his hand. I had nothing left, no pride, no dignity, only an empty plate with not even a crumb left on it.

His palm slid down my ribs, lingering for a moment on my waist before he let go. "I won't be far and if you need me—"

"I don't *need* you." And I meant that. I took a deep big girl breath. "Ryder, listen to me. You may as well go home—back to Kansas or wherever. I could be here a very long time. Weeks. Months. Maybe even years."

"Not years. We know it won't be years. I told you about—"

"You did. And I don't want to hear any more about that apocalyptic video. That awful stuff isn't going to happen because I'm here now, and even if it means just listening to stories half the time, I'm doing my job."

"Right. You're doing your job and you can't seriously expect me to do anything less."

"I expect you to stay alive and have a life." I bit the corner of my lip.

"You can count on that." He leaned down and kissed me goodbye. It wasn't great. Part of my bottom lip was still stuck between my teeth.

I pushed away from him, feeling as if I was already changing color. If I'd been born with tentacles they'd probably be shriveling up and getting ready to fall off and it looked I was the only one changing. He would be riding off into the sunset unaltered.

Gravel crunched under my sandals and echoed off the rock mountain, amplifying each grinding step and shattering my self-confidence. It took forever to hike up that drive to the house. When I finally grabbed the front door handle, I glanced back. Ryder was still standing beside his truck, watching.

I hurried in, latched the door, and leaned my forehead against the thick oak barrier.

"So how did it go?" Naomi stood in the dark entry behind me Obviously, she'd been spying on me, so she already knew.

"Not the way I wanted."

"I'm sorry," she said and rested her hand on my shoulder.

That sounded suspiciously like genuine concern.

I swallowed my frustration and spouted a stupid question. "Instead of being sorry, why don't you tell me about those powers you said women supposedly have. Because right now, I feel like a donkey trying to run in a horse race."

She chuckled and patted my back. "Poor thing, I watched you through the window. Arguing rarely works. Persuasion, though, that is a different matter—very effective. It's one of our gifts."

"Finally!" I rubbed my palms together with overblown glee. "It's about time you gave me one of our superpowers."

She sighed. "Are you never serious?"

"Sorry," I said, instantly sobered. "I *am* serious. Very serious. I want to know about persuasion. I *need* to know."

"Hmm." She sniffed and squinted at me, no doubt checking for sincerity.

"I really do want to know," I urged.

"Persuasion is not a gift to be taken lightly." She was still scrutinizing me. "Too many women use it for their own selfish purposes, and that generally ends in misery for her and the people around her. A wise woman uses it solely to benefit those she loves."

"And a foolish woman?"

"Doesn't use it at all."

"And a bullheaded woman?"

"Just make jokes."

"Persuasion, huh?" I grimaced and shook my head. "I always figured a reasoned debate was the way to go. That's what they taught us in school."

"Yes, I noticed how well that worked out for you." She smiled that all-knowing half-smile of hers. "And the threats, where did you learn that technique?"

I shrugged and looked away. "I don't know. TV, I suppose."

"Debate and threats are tools lawyers and gangsters tend to use." She peeked out at the street through the blinds.

I rushed to her side. "Did he leave?"

"No. He's just sitting there staring at his steering wheel."

I edged away and flopped back against the wall. "See!" I gestured at the blinds. "He didn't listen to me anyway. Then I got mad and said things I didn't mean. And yes, all right, I made threats. Now, he'll either sit there and cook himself to death or go away forever. That's what I would do if I were him. Go away, I mean." I blew out a big *angry-at-myself* raspberry. "Obviously the persuasion gene skipped right on over me."

She leaned against the wall beside me, and waited for a moment or two before quietly saying, "Don't be silly, persuasion is part of being female. Even baby girls practice persuasion until they learn that throwing a tantrum works quicker."

"Well, obviously, I lost it somewhere along the line. My persuasion score is a big fat F minus." I sketched my failing grade in the air with the fork.

"Nonesense. It's simply a matter of remembering how it works and practicing. Do you know the story of Esther?"

"Yeah, I think so. Isn't she the girl back in Bible days who won the Miss Persia beauty pageant, got picked to be queen, and saved her people by wooing the king at a candlelight dinner."

Naomi groaned. "Wooing? Hardly. More to the point, that is *not* how I taught you to tell a story."

I ducked my head, not in the mood for a scolding.

When silence got thicker than an oatmeal bath and just as uncomfortable, she sighed. "Okay. I'll tell you what, let's discuss it your way, using your lingo."

"Lingo?" I glanced up and even in the dark I could see that tricky eyebrow of hers was arched pretty high.

She dove in with a fairly good imitation of my Minnesota twang. "Ya see, what Queen Esther didn't do was march into the throne room and say, 'Hey, Kingy! We have a big problemo.' And Esther, *I'm-so-pretty-I-could-be-a-movie-star*, did not point her finger at his evil sidekick, Haman, and say, 'Your good buddy over there—that beady-eyed snaggle-toothed chief advisor of yours—has tricked you into signing a law to have me killed in three days, along with my uncle Morty, the trusted servant who saved your life, and all of our kinfolk. Whatcha gonna do about that, huh?'"

I tried hard not to smile at her parody of my voice, I fiddled with the fork and plate still in my hand. "I'm pretty sure I wouldn't have called him *Kingy*."

That eyebrow of hers shot up again. "You think not?"

Maybe.

Oh, alright, I probably would've.

I shrugged. "Snaggle-toothed, that was good though. I might catalog that for future use." I let go of critiquing her impression of me and jumped back to the issue. "So, are you saying we should do what Esther did, and use our seductive powers to get what we want?"

"No!" Hands on her hips, Naomi blinked repeatedly at me—probably Morse code for "you are frustrating me." "That is not what I'm saying at all. What Esther did was miles above seduction. *Miles!* Light years. She did a far more difficult thing."

"And that was...?"

"She invited Haman and the king to a banquet and treated both the king and her enemy with unparalleled respect and honor. Knowing that a man craves honor and respect as much as he does food, Ester prepared King Xerxes's favorite recipes and served him the best wine. While he dined, she gave him her attentive respectful company, and then when he asked what he could do for her, she invited him to return for dinner again the following night. Esther patiently waited until the exact right moment, when she knew his heart was strongly inclined toward hers and then cautiously made her grave predicament known to him."

I air-wrote a note to myself. "Food and respect—got it."

"Not just that. The path of persuasion is through the heart. Not only with men, the way you truly persuade *anyone* is through the heart. Tonight, out there with your young man, did you sincerely and respectfully try to reach his emotions?"

No.

Although now I wished I had.

Suddenly, I could envision an entirely different outcome to our little exchange. I had softened him up with pie. *Half of the equation.* Except then I'd resisted the instinct to nestle up beside him and missed the perfect opportunity to draw him in deeper emotionally. Not to mention the fact that persuading would've been way more fun. But I didn't even try that. No, instead, I tried to badger and force him.

Trumpets and Alligators!

Why hadn't I simply told Ryder the truth? That he was important to me, that it worried me to think of him sitting out there roasting to death in the heat, and that despite the danger, I still wanted him nearby, *somehow*. Together we could've figured something out. Instead, I threatened him and ordered him back to Kansas.

Maybe it wasn't too late.

I turned to the door and flung it open just in time to see him drive away. The fork slid off the pie plate and clattered to the floor.

Chapter 20
Poison

The next morning, despite my gloomy mood, we went back to working on novice business. Naomi gave me orders before the next exercise. "For this to succeed, you must relax. Close your eyes. Breathe slowly and deeply." It was a mantra I knew well by now, one that eased me into a semi-hypnotic state, so I could fully experience her stories. That way the stories became part of me.

This time, something different happened.

This time, *I became part of the story.*

At first, colors and images flowed into my mind as she talked. "Twelve people, all perfect strangers, suddenly appeared in a cage. Trapped like wild rabbits. The cage was black and white, a little larger than a child's ball pit, the kind filled with red, blue, green, and yellow balls. Only there were no bright colors in this enclosure. Tall metal poles rose up from a short concrete wall. Between the poles stretched a taut black mesh. Outside the structure everything looked hazy gray, like a vast smoke-filled studio."

The Wise Woman's voice continued, except it sounded further and further away. Until it faded into a distant whisper, and then it disappeared altogether.

Suddenly, I was plunked down in the midst of those trapped souls. I found myself sitting on the cold concrete floor, hugging my knees.

Startled.

Watchful.

One guy, younger than me, maybe eighteen or nineteen, a gold ring through his nostril and patches of hair sprouting on his chin. In a heavy British accent, he insisted we hunt for a hidden camera. "Don't ya see? It's gotta be one of them Yank reality shows. Ya know, like *Punked*, or maybe a new one." He inspected the tall posts rising at each hexagonal juncture in our prison. "Gotta be." When the poles proved barren of electronic equipment, he slapped his hand against the last one. The metallic chime twanged everyone's nerves. "Betcha it's that *Boiling Point* series, because I'm gettin' roaring mad." He spun around searching for another place that might be hiding a camera.

"Smile, Junior. You're on The Twilight Zone." This cynical comment came from an older man standing next to me, a man built like a has been weight-lifter, with striking features and curly dark hair. He folded his arms across his chest and leaned against the fencing as if our predicament didn't bother him in the least—a tough guy. I tried to place the accent, Brooklyn or maybe Jersey.

"Shut it!" The kid with the nose ring snarled at him. "Stow it, unless you got a better idea?"

Jersey shrugged and cracked his knuckles.

I jumped up to get out of their way in case they started punching one another.

A pediatric nurse wearing brightly colored scrubs decorated with giraffes and elephants, grabbed hold of the mesh and shouted. "Hellooo! Hey! Anybody here?"

"Quiet!" ordered a policeman. "We don't know who these people might be." He straightened to his full height. "We don't want to alert whoever put us in this cage. First, we need to figure out how to escape." With a shaky air of authority, he held up his hand to draw our attention. Only he didn't get past point one before he bit the inside of his cheek in what looked like a failed effort to silence the quiver in his voice. He swallowed hard. "They could be aliens or..."

"Or maybe all of us are dead," Jersey remarked with a raspy accent like some hoodlum from a bygone era.

"And what? This is purgatory?" The kid with the nose ring scoffed. "I don't think so."

"Yeah, I don't feel dead." The police officer took out a pocketknife and began examining the construction of the mesh.

"Hey!" nose-ring boy shouted. "He's got a knife."

"Stay calm, kid," the cop warned.

"And a gun," the nurse murmured.

The kid shoved through everyone else until he stood right beside the policeman. "Go on then, cut a hole in it."

The cop ignored the boy's impatience and sawed vigorously at the black mesh material. We all watched. Hopeful. After a few moments, he held his knife up to the light, illuminating multiple dents and scars on the blade. The webbing hadn't given way at all. He closed the knife with a snap and pocketed it. "Can't get through it—too strong."

Like a herd of panicked cows, they all pushed forward, bawling suggestions all at once. "Try a different spot." "Let me try." "Maybe you didn't push hard enough."

He held up his hands. "Don't worry, folks. Just stay calm. We'll figure another way outta here."

Fine words, considering his worried expression.

"Let's stop and think this through. Remain calm..." Then his bravado failed altogether. His hands dropped to his side, and he rubbed absently at his thigh until his fingers came to rest reassuringly on his holster. Shaking his head, he muttered, "I was driving my car. Lights on. Siren. Then, bam!" He slugged his palm. "I'm here." He glanced at us for confirmation.

The nurse touched his elbow compassionately. "Is it possible you crashed?" She cast an anxious glance at Jersey. "He might be right. Maybe we're all dead."

A blonde in the corner snorted and strutted toward them. "Oh, honey, you're not dead. Not yet. And neither am I." She could've doubled for Marilyn Monroe except for the wig and thirty years of wrinkles she couldn't quite disguise under heavy pancake make-up. Old Marilyn waved her fake fingernails dismissively through the air. "But you..." She sauntered up to a man standing in the middle of the cage. "You know something, don't you?"

He ignored her. *Odd*, I hadn't noticed him before—a man so tall and dark, his skin shone like varnished mahogany against his navy-blue shirt. He stood out from the rest of us because he lacked the slightest hint of worry. In fact, he appeared completely absorbed in observing us. I thought Marilyn might be right. He seemed to be a guard or a sentinel of some kind.

She prodded his chest with her polished-pink pointer finger. "I asked you— What. Is. Going. On?" She poked him again, but he didn't flinch. "You'd better let me out of here, Mister. I have important things to do." She jabbed him again. "Do you have any idea who I am?"

"I know exactly who you are." The sentinel leveled her with a hard stare. "Do you?"

That got her. Phony Marilyn stepped back, bristling, way more nervous than before. Her hand shook so much I thought the heavy rings might go flying off. She flipped her hair back, thrust her chin in the air, and let him have it. "Listen to me. If this is some kind of sick practical joke, I'm going to sue you six ways to Sunday." Muscling up her courage, she closed in on him, ready to poke his chest again.

"Step back." He ordered in a quiet but firm voice. "You're not first."

Marilyn got a scared look in her eyes. "First?"

"You." He pointed at a middle-aged man standing silently behind the others, colorless, almost invisible. "You're first."

His subject stood motionless, shocked. The poor bland fellow pulled his faded polyester sweater tight and attempted to sink into the shadows.

First?

To do what?

We shrank away from Mr. Bland. Pale, balding, with thick glasses, he looked like a guy who tallied numbers all day and didn't mind doing it. He could have been anyone, an IRS agent, the owner of a dry cleaners, anyone.

"What do you want?" Mr. Bland's voice squeaked, yet he managed to ask the question we all wanted answered.

"Tell the truth." The dark sentinel's voice resonated like the low notes on a guitar, and set strings shivering inside our hearts.

Bland's shoulders pinched up defensively. "What do you mean? I always tell the truth." He made a noble effort to steady his wobbling voice, struggling to keep it from pitching upward like a frightened little girl's.

"Good. Then speak it."

"F-fine," he stuttered. "B-but you need to be more sp-specific." Sweat beaded on his forehead. He fidgeted, adjusting his glasses.

The sentinel said nothing. His gaze moved to the wall where a large black spider crawled through the mesh near Mr. Bland.

We all shuffled away from it, except Jersey. He stayed put, still lounging as if he hadn't a care in the world. The spider crawled down the wall onto the floor.

Mr. Bland cowered, squeezed past us, and ran to the other side of the hexagon in an effort to escape the marching insect. Except it changed course and followed him.

With a disgusted snort, Mr. tough-guy Jersey pushed away from the wall, walked over to the spider, and stomped on it. Just like that, he tried to grind it under his sole.

Punctuated snaps echoed through our prison. The staccato crunch sounded like cracking open a particularly tough crab leg at a seafood dinner.

It startled us. So did the fact that a man as muscular and large as Jersey had to lean into the effort of smashing a spider, big though it was.

Finally, he raised his foot.

We drifted closer to inspect the remains. Weird. There was no goo or juice of any kind oozing out of the flattened black body. A segment at the end of a thin leg twitched in final surrender.

Nose-ring kid chuckled with delight. "Now *that's* what dead looks like."

Behind him, Marilyn shrieked and pointed at two new

spiders. We all backed away as the macabre pair neared the body of their fallen comrade. A split second later, they changed direction and pattered across the floor toward Mr. Bland.

"*Non ci credo!*" the guy from Jersey swore and backed away as the crushed spider slowly un-crushed itself.

I inhaled sharply and so did the nurse.

Each segment re-inflated like a tiny balloon filling with air, until at last the body puffed up. Good as new, the ghastly thing headed toward its prey, armored legs tapping noisily against the concrete.

Like hail beating on a tin roof, the cage filled with the sound of metallic clattering. Jersey stumbled, scrambling out of the way, as an unstoppable army of tiny-clawed spiders poured in through the mesh. *Thousands!* The black tide spilled noisily into our cage, spreading across the concrete.

They clicked and clacked, marching straight for Mr. Bland. He backed up as far as he could go, pressing his back against the mesh, edging away from them. But they were fast. Too fast. It seemed unfair, all those venomous creatures ticking and hissing, marching relentlessly toward the skinniest, weakest guy in the group.

Why him? Why poor helpless Mr. Bland?

Even Marilyn Monroe stood a better chance against the spiders than that guy. I guessed the policeman thought it was unfair too. He pulled a gun on the sentinel. "Make it stop."

Bland screamed as spiders crawled up his leg. I had to do something, had to help him somehow. I tried knocking them off.

As soon as I did another one leapt onto his pant leg. When I turned back hoping the cop had been able to convince our sentinel to make this cruel torture stop, his Smith & Wesson was pointed at nothing but air.

The sentinel had vanished.

Angry and desperate, the cop pointed his pistol at the spiders. "Everyone stand back." He motioned for us to get behind him, aimed, and pulled the trigger.

The nurse held her hands over her ears. She needn't have. There was no deafening explosion. The hammer snapped in place with a hollow clunk. The cop checked the chamber and tried again, and again, with the same results.

Spiders crawled onto Bland's shoulders. "Get 'em off me!" He screamed and swatted futilely at them. As soon as he knocked one spider away two more took its place.

"Tell the truth." At the sound of his voice, I spun around. The sentinel stood right behind me, calmly reissuing his order.

"What truth?!" Mr. Bland wasn't so bland anymore. He was angry, furious, scrubbing spiders away with the hysterical madness of Lady Macbeth scrubbing at the guilty blood spot she could never wash away. "What do you want? Trade secrets? I don't have any! I'm an accountant, for pity's sake. Ichenbach makes shoes. And they don't doctor the books. There's nothing to tell!"

"Not their secrets," The sentinel said calmly. "*Your* secrets."

A spider found its mark and sank poisonous fangs into the

tender skin of Mr. Bland's neck. He cried out, a surprisingly manly cry, not the girlish scream I'd expected.

"Help him," urged the nurse, grasping the sentinel's arm. "I beg you."

The sentinel remained unmoved. "He must help himself."

"Please." She used a honeyed tone, one that must have mollified hundreds of patients in her past. "Don't you see? The poor man doesn't know what you want."

The sentinel turned his attention to her. "He knows. In his heart, he knows."

Mr. Bland charged frantically into the center of the hexagon, scraping off spiders as he went. He swore. Another spider bit him near his ear. "Alright! Alright! I'll tell you."

The spiders froze in place, *waiting*, their bodies flexing up and down in a strange holding pattern.

"You want the truth? Fine! I hate them. I hate my stepchildren. Even my own children." He rubbed the red welt on his ear. "Oh, I pretend to care. I pay the mortgage and for everything else. Only they all make me sick. *She* makes me sick, my wife, with her mindless arrogance. Her holier than thou attitude. Every night I come home and go straight to my study. I lock the door, turn on my music, and hope they'll all leave me alone. Except they don't, do they? It's all '*Daddy, daddy, do something, mommy is mad.*'" He raked through the wispy strands of his balding hair. "Mad?! The woman isn't just *angry* mad, she's insane—certifiable. I can't stand my wife. Is that what you wanted to hear?" His face contorted in such disgust, I worried he might vomit. "Twenty years I've pretended. To myself. To them. Tried to do the right thing. Every year it gets worse."

He brushed a spider from the top of his balding head and stared at our guardian, our captor. The insect struck the floor with a hollow clunk and righted itself.

We all watched Mr. Bland in amazement. It was strange to see color rising in his pale cheeks and his shoulders resting square, rather than the rounded humps they had been. He looked like a man now.

Spiders fell off of him and fluttered to the floor like dead leaves.

"Very well." The sentinel nodded. "You may go."

"That's it?" Bland squinted, staring at the guardian, completely bewildered.

"Yes. You confessed your poison. Now, you are free to make a decision. Will you face your trouble and find a solution or continue to let it fester, making yourself and everyone around you ill." The guardian pointed across our prison. "Go."

Mr. Bland walked away from us, and a door swung open in front of him. As soon as he passed through the opening disappeared.

Nose-ring kid ran to where the portal had been and searched uselessly for a seam. Failing that he looped his fingers into the mesh and hung on, watching Mr. Bland trek across the gray void. "So, where's he off to? Heaven? Hell?"

"Home," the sentinel answered softly. "To face the truth and, hopefully, to help his children."

"That's it?" Nose-ring kid took a deep breath. "Alright then, I'll have a go. Me, next. Let's get this over with." He rubbed his hands together. "Let's see...where to start? Got my girlfriend preggers. Stole money from my Gran. And just last week, I—"

"No. These are not secrets. Merely symptoms." The dark guardian said flatly. "And it's not your turn."

"Hey! Give over, man. I want to go home. Got places to go." He waved at the spiders, tapping his shoulders, inviting them to start for him. "Bring 'em on."

"Not your turn."

"Why not, eh? You let that mousy bloke go first. Why him?"

"He had suffered the most. The poison was killing him." The sentinel turned away from the kid.

I knew who was next.

Without question, I knew.

Panic welled up inside me. I didn't have any idea what I should say. I didn't hate anybody. I went to the guardian and stood in front of him, head bowed. "Please," I implored, and risked looking up into his eyes. "Help me know what to say."

It was eerie standing so near to him. He seemed solid enough, yet he also seemed to shimmer and radiated a kind of heat that warmed me to my marrow. Despite that, I dreaded the test coming. The ominous clicking and clattering of the spiders crawling toward me made my insides quake. I didn't look at them. Couldn't. I kept my gaze fixed on his face. Hoping for mercy. "Help me," I begged.

"Tell the truth, little one." He looked down at me with such kindness, I felt miraculously safe. Only, I wasn't. They were coming. Clicking closer with every ragged breath I took. He rested his hand on my shoulder and fear melted away.

"Wake up, Sophie."

I did.

No more prison.

No more cage.

It was Naomi shaking my shoulder. I was seated at the Wise Woman's kitchen counter, and one large spider tapped slowly toward me.

Click.

Click.

Click.

Tell the truth.

"I killed my father."

Chapter 21
Stains

Bitter tears
Blood of the mind
Stains first
The soul inside
—from The Wise Woman Chronicles

The spider disappeared.

My confession, on the other hand, hung in the air between us like a dead possum—smelly, and with really sharp teeth.

"Come with me." The Wise Woman stood to leave the kitchen.

"Wait!" I jumped up, stumbled, and grabbed my stool to

keep it from toppling over. "Don't you want to know what happened?"

She turned back to me. "Not particularly."

"But...?"

Naomi breathed in and out heavily, the way she does when I've perturbed her. "The important thing is that now you know what keeps you from loving completely. You know your poison."

"Whoa! Wait just one minute. I love plenty of people. There's my brother, Danny. I'd do anything for him. His wife. And—"

"Does he know you killed your father?"

"Danny?" I drew back at the question. "Yeah. Well...*probably*. It's complicated."

"It always is."

I followed her down the hall. "Slow down. Give me a chance to explain. I don't want you to worry I might slit your throat in the middle of the night or anything like that."

She stopped, her shoulders stiff, then she spun around and grabbed my arms. "Sophie, darlin', I doubt you could cut the head off a chicken, even if it meant that otherwise you'd starve to death."

"That's not true." I shook my head. "Seriously, if it came down to me or the chicken, I could do it." I whisked my hands together in a slicing motion that ended up being more of a sideways clap.

She scoffed and turned away.

"I could!" Underneath, I worried she might be right. Maybe

I didn't have the stomach to do the brutal necessities. It didn't matter. I killed my father just the same as if I'd taken an ax to him.

We're, all of us, capable of evil.

It all comes down to choices. Sometimes we choose the noble thing. Other times, we sidle over to the murky side and do something so ugly we regret it the rest of our lives.

That is what happened to me.

Naomi waited for me, like always, studying my face while I mulled it over. "Time is short, child. Don't be hanging onto your regrets."

I swear, that woman could read my mind.

And that's disturbing.

"All right," she sighed. "Go on then, tell me what you did."

My conscience held up Daddy's gray lifeless corpse as a testament against me. *I killed him.*

"What did you do?" she asked again, as if I'd forgotten the awful question.

Tell the truth.

I began cautiously, almost in a whisper. Afraid that if I spoke too loud maybe the earth would crack open and swallow me up as a punishment. God knows I deserved it. "It was my fault." I admitted, not the Wise Woman, to some unseen tribunal.

She bowed her head slightly, attending me with a sideways ear, a priest's ear, hearing the words, but listening for the soul's voice.

"After Mamma died, I couldn't bear my father's grief. Or

mine. It filled our house like a vapor, at first. But then it became a thick sad soup. A sour heavy sludge suffocating both of us."

Drowning me.

That familiar panic made my throat tighten. I paused to stomp down old fears.

Naomi remained silent.

"Danny was in college at the time. So, after the funeral it was just me and Dad out on the farm. I'd taken over Mom's chores when she got too sick, cooking, cleaning, and that stuff. Dad's diabetes was out of control. I tried to make him eat his meals on time. Only, he'd forget. I'd find him out in the barn, sitting on a stool, puttering with machinery or staring into space."

I crossed my arms squeezing them tight against the memories. "He kept pretending her cancer would just go away. Disappear. Until she died. Then..."

I shook my head, still angry that he hadn't faced it sooner. "He was lost. Too grieved to function. A zombie, going through the motions. As time passed, the silence between us grew. It was..."

Worse than her death.

I shrugged as if it had been no big deal.

That was a lie.

Tell the truth.

"Truth is, I couldn't wait to get out of there." *To breathe.*

I slumped against Naomi's wall, the texture grated against my bare shoulder, a reminder that I wasn't back there, watching my father stumble around without hope, without purpose. "I won a scholarship to U of M that fall. Dad insisted he was fine. He promised to remember meals, check his blood sugar, and take his insulin. But I knew better. I shouldn't have gone."

She nodded, priestly disappointment in the sinner.

In clipped sterile tones I recited the litany of those awful events. "On the tenth of October, at two o'clock in the morning, I woke up in the dorm. My head throbbed as if it was going to explode. I had a feeling..."

No. Not a feeling...

I knew.

The same way I'd known when Jace was drowning.

I didn't need to tell her about that. "I threw on clothes and drove home as fast as I could, but an early winter storm slowed me down. I finally pulled into the yard sometime after five. It was still pitch-black outside. Sleeting. Blue light from the TV flickered in the front window. For a moment, I thought maybe that luminous motion meant there was life inside."

Traitorous hope.

"I opened the door. The smell..."

My stomach roiled. *I mustn't think of the smell.*

"He sat in his chair, looking straight at me, as if he'd known I would come through that door. His jaw hung open, and..."

I'd thought I heard him calling me, an anguished scream, "Sophie!" Except, he made no sound. The shriek was mine.

Regret.

And it would be mine forever.

"He was dead." Naomi pronounced, as if that was a detail I'd missed.

"Yeah." I didn't tell her I'd fainted. Didn't tell her that before I was able to phone for help, I'd crawled out on the front porch, vomited, and collapsed. I'd awakened to sleet battering me, a thousand cold needles stinging me back to life.

Afterward, the corpse in my father's chair haunted me. I no longer recalled images of the man who taught me to ride a horse or carried me onto his shoulders after a long day. Where was the man who used to lift my chin and called me his sweet pea?

I'd let him die.

"Two months." I raised my voice, daring the earth to swallow me up, wishing it would. Sinking against the wall when it didn't. "He only lasted two months without me. I never should have left him."

I felt like screaming, moaning, thrashing my head against the wall. Instead, I bowed my head and let shame beat my shoulders. "I shouldn't have left him. Why? Why? Why didn't I stay?"

Naomi didn't answer. How could she? There was no answer except one.

I chose evil. I killed him.

Scalding acid boiled up, searing my throat, curdling behind my clenched jaw muscles, scorching my tear ducts. I pressed fists against it, hating my weakness.

The Wise Woman gently pulled my hands away from my face. She didn't say, *oh, sweetheart, it wasn't your fault*, like everyone else had.

"Sophie," she whispered. "He forgives you."

She couldn't know that. I couldn't meet her eyes. The hallway seemed to shrink around us like a suffocating straight jacket.

"Think," she said. "Search your soul. Does your father still blame you?"

There was nowhere to run. Nowhere to hide. I turned to her, words tearing out of my throat in a hoarse pleading screech. "I left him to die."

She nodded matter-of-factly. "You did." Her voice held a motherly tenderness, and yet it bore the cold edge of a judge demanding facts. "Does he still blame you?"

Yes. Yes. Yes.

His corpse still haunts me.

I heard tapping and the spider click-click-clicking down the hall toward me. The sentinel's warning reverberated through me. *Tell the truth.*

Truth can be so hard to find sometimes. It's a cruel irony that we often run from things that might set us free. Could it be because we think we don't deserve freedom?

What was the truth?

I closed my eyes tight and considered what I remembered of my father. If he knew the guilt poisoning my veins, he would come racing back to me, he would lift me in the air with his strong arms and hold me in a tight bear hug.

My father would never blame me.

I knew it as surely as if he was standing right there telling me. I had tormented myself. Every lash my guilty conscience whipped across my back kept me from grieving for him, kept me from facing the terrifying fact that I'd lost the most important person in my life.

The judge's hammer fell, and Naomi's lips delivered the verdict. "It's over, Sophie."

Over?

Could it ever be?

"Over." I whispered, testing my absolution out loud. The throbbing in my temples changed to a steady beat—soft, like cleansing rain. The world blurred behind my watery eyes.

My father's face glimmered into memory, no longer gray, but ruddy and warm, smiling and bright. I'm ten years-old,running to bring him his lunch. Fresh cut hay fills the air with a thousand swirling sunbeams and a sweet green fragrance as he tosses the alfalfa onto the hay truck. I grab hold of his strong shoulders and he hoists me up to sit on the end of the flatbed. Swinging my legs back and forth, I watch as Daddy peers into the lunch sack. "Hey there, Sweet Pea, what did you bring me today?"

Tears.

Chapter 22
Superstitions

We sat in the hallway on the floor, leaning against each other like two drunks on Skid Row. I swiped at the salty residue of tears on my cheeks, embarrassed because I had a pretty good idea of how red and swollen my face must have looked after crying for so long. Until now, Naomi sat silently beside me, not one word aimed at damming up my emotional flood, making no solicitous attempts to soothe away my grief. Her quiet presence had gifted me with eloquent compassion, comforting me while at the same time respecting my need to mourn.

Naomi patted my knee. “We need a field trip. And I know just the place.”

When I tried to speak, my voice cracked and grated. "Field trip?"

"Yes. It'll be just the thing." Naomi hopped up with the elastic energy of a twelve-year-old. I remained on the hard floor, my butt had gone numb, and I wondered if my entire left leg was asleep. She reached out to help me up.

It's humbling to require the assistance of so elderly a woman. But the truth was—I needed it. She waited, extending her hand, waxed paper pale, pleated with wrinkles, yet unexpectedly soft. That was the way it was with her, always a surprise. Her small sinewy muscles and delicate bones surged with strength as she pulled me to my feet.

I stood there, holding her hand, unwilling to let go. There were things I wished to say, needed to say, but couldn't. I finally let go, unable to collect all my emotions into a cohesive statement. Naomi gave my shoulder a motherly squeeze. And then, just as if I hadn't spilled my affection for her all over her Spanish tile, she sprang into action.

"You'll need to change clothes," she instructed. "Put on hiking gear. We're going to the Superstitions!" She rushed down the hallway issuing directives in her wake. "Wear something cool. Lucky for us it's hot outside. We'll have the entire place to ourselves." She disappeared into her bedroom and whisked the door shut.

"Superstitions?" I was still hazy from my crying jag and didn't have a clue what she meant. If I had, I might have stopped the whole thing right then and there. It was another of those catalytic moments, the innocent pivotal nanosecond, when you had an opportunity to change destiny, but ignorance cheated you out of the chance.

"Something cool," I repeated like a dumb automaton and toddled off to rummage through my clothing.

When I emerged, Naomi stood in the middle of the family room beneath a voluminous white Greta Garbo hat. This time, though, instead of a movie star she looked more like Teddy Roosevelt on safari, only skinny. She'd cinched up blousy white walking shorts and a bleached cotton camp shirt with a green army belt. A canteen hung from it, a hunting knife, a clip-on compass, and who knew what else in all the various pouches. To complete this remarkable ensemble, she sported a pair of clunky hiking boots suitable for Mount Everest.

I fully expected her to produce a riding crop, slap it against her thigh, and shout, "Tally ho!" Instead, she stared at my cut-offs and Nikes as if I'd committed some sort of fashion *faux pas*, and said, "Are those the sturdiest shoes you can come up with?"

"Yep," I nodded. "On such short notice." Turnabout was fair play, so I puckered up my forehead and said, "About your hat..." *We aren't going to a garden party in Newport.* "Won't it make you hotter?"

"Not at all. The right chapeau keeps one cooler." She smoothed her fingers over the broad upturned brim and cocked her chin the same way a runway model might. "*This* is a Panama grass sunhat, custom-made in Ecuador to my exact specifications—it's the perfect thing."

Maybe Arizona hikers preferred to tromp around the desert in haute couture. What did I know? I'm not the fashion-dictator type. I shrugged.

"You'll need this." Naomi tossed me a canvas belt, fully loaded with two water bottles strapped into Velcro slings. "You don't mind driving, do you, dear?" She glanced out the living room window to the driveway. "That jeep of yours will get us much farther up the trail than my Mercedes. Besides," she turned to me, her eyes sparkling with eagerness. "I've never ridden in one quite like yours before."

"Oh?" I pictured my dusty torn-vinyl seats, duct-taped roof, and floorboards coated with a layer of sandstorm grit. "Well, in that case, you're in for a treat."

"Splendid! I'll grab my walking stick and we'll be off."

I had to admire the way Naomi didn't complain about the grimy interior of the jeep. Although, before climbing in there was an awkward moment until she found something to wipe off the seat. Naturally, Naomi had a small packet of wipes stowed in one of those many compartments on her belt.

Impressive woman. I didn't even have to help her climb in. Finally aboard and buckled in, Madame Roosevelt and I took off for our expedition to the Superstition Wilderness Area.

Superstition Mountain juts up out of the desert like a can of petrified dog food dumped out on a plate. Once upon a time it must've been a volcano. It looked like part of the caldera still stood, but after thousands of years of meteors and earthquakes rearranging Earth's furniture, the caldera must've reshaped itself into a scattered series of small mesas, chunky boulder piles, and numerous small canyons and gorges.

Not long after passing a place called Tortilla Flats, our paved road ended and turned into a smooth well-traveled dirt road. After winding through endless rock formations and sage brush and leaving a plume of dust in our wake, Naomi leaned forward and pointed, “There! That’s it. Turn there.”

I wheeled the jeep onto a much bumpier dirt road. I had no idea where we were, what trail we had just taken, or what “it” she referred to, I simply followed her instructions. “Turn right. Take that fork,” she shouted above the engine noise as we bounced over ruts on terrain that was looking less and less like a road and more like a suggestion. “After that next rise watch for a sharp left. Cross that dry wash and...”

Gears clunked into place. The transmission groaned as the jeep strained to climb gravel-covered ridges and boulder-ridden ravines. When we finally came to a stop and I switched the engine off, my ears still rattled.

“Beautiful, isn’t it?” She swung her hand as if unveiling the vista.

I tilted up my sunglasses. A blast of white desert light shocked my pupils, forcing me to drop the smoky lenses back onto my nose. I didn’t know what to say. In Minnesota we called it “beautiful” when maple leaves turned brilliant red and gold in the autumn, or when we came across a waterfall splashing over mossy stones.

This was way different.

Dagger-like rock formations pierced the bumpy terrain. Skeletal plants waved gray appendages like monstrous upside-down spiders. A yellow Cholla jumping-cactus loomed a few feet in front of the jeep, each hairy segment loaded with a billion hypodermic needles poised to lodge in my skin. This was not what I would call beautiful. Impressive, yes. But it also looked dangerous, harsh, unforgiving, and even a little terrifying.

"Um, interesting," I muttered.

"It'll grow on you." She opened her door and with a stone crunching thump she thrust down her mage's staff, thus announcing her arrival to the scorpions and cacti. In retrospect, I think they already knew she was coming.

I reluctantly left the shade of the jeep. The minute I set foot on the gravel, although insulated by two layers of high-density rubber and compression-molded vinyl, my soles began to melt.

I've heard people say, "Arizona heat is like walking into an oven." Not true. In an oven, you know you're going to die. Out in that desert, there was just enough untoasted oxygen to keep breathing. You probably wouldn't die. Maybe you'd wish you could, but you wouldn't, especially if you had ten pounds of water strapped to your belt like I did.

Naomi pointed out a narrow trail with her staff. "I brought you here for a purpose."

I didn't respond. My lips were shriveling from the heat, so I opted to preserve the small amount of moisture remaining in my mouth.

"We're here to escape all the stories." She broke into a

steady pace over the rocky path.

"Wait, what?" I hurried to catch up. "Escape? But I thought stories were the point."

"In part." The trail took a drastic angle upward. She secured a handhold on a boulder and mounted it with the sureness of an old mountain goat. "Over the past few days, we've feasted on stories from The Wise Woman Chronicles. You know what it's like at Thanksgiving, don't you? Feasts can overwhelm the senses. It's hard to remember how the turkey tasted because you're too busy licking pumpkin pie off your teeth. We needed to take a break. Refresh the soul." She nodded her floppy sunbonnet in the direction of a tall old Saguaro whose fat arms curved up in dubious greeting. Its prickly green flesh was riddled with holes for wrens. "We must rest our minds." She spread her arms. "Cleanse the palate."

Cleanse the palate? Or scorch it off?

Naomi took a deep breath as if inhaling cool crisp mountain air. "It's therapy."

If I took a breath like that, the tiny air sacks in my lungs would swell up and burst like popcorn. "I'm perfectly okay with taking a break back at your house in the air-conditioning."

"No, that won't do." The Greta Garbo hat shook from side to side as Naomi stabbed her staff into the rocks and leveraged herself up onto the next small rise. "Cities are crammed with stories. Everywhere you look there are stories vying for your attention, movies, billboards, advertisements—"

"Even ads?" I asked.

"Yes. Well written ads pull you into a story. Now, as I was saying, in the city we are surrounded by video games, the news, music, radio—that reminds me, did I ever explain to you that music is story, too?"

"You did not." I slid sideways on some loose rocks and muttered, "Can't say I heard much of a story in Prokofiev's tunes."

"It's there." She argued without turning around. "Think of the notes as impressionistic words that stir an emotion. Sneaky stuff, music. The important point is that all these stories solicit your emotions and compete for space in your mind."

I was just about to make a smart comment about brain space, except my foot slipped again. This time I clutched a granite boulder to keep from falling. An instant later, I jerked my hand back and glared at a trio of sneaky, cactus-buttons growing out of a crevice in the boulder. They'd plunged several dozen elfin arrows into my palm—*vicious sharp barbs laden with their own brand of poison.*

I stumbled along behind Naomi, trying to listen while tugging, without much success, at the hair-thin fishhooks stuck in my palm, already making it swell.

"Our culture is inundated with stories," she said. "Each one packed with ideologies and instruction. And mind you, they aren't always constructive lessons. Too often they breed fear." She glanced back at me, frowning, because I was lagging behind. "What's wrong?"

"Oh, nothing much. Just cleansing my palm with a little cactus therapy."

"Oh dear. Come here. Let me see it." Naomi took hold of my hand and set to work unsnapping pouches on her superhero belt like a bleached-out Batwoman. She produced a mini-can of topical analgesic, sprayed my hand until it was numb, whipped out a pair of broad tip tweezers and away she went, plucking at the speed of light.

"You've done this before."

"Hold still."

I obeyed, grateful to share the shade of her garden hat while she worked. It was amazing how good it felt to have the needles pulled out. Even so, my palm still itched like mad, but each removal brought an immediate sense of relief, almost euphoric.

She finished yanking out cactus barbs, sprayed my hand again, and presented me with a quiz. "Have you heard *anything* I've said?"

"Yep."

"Don't say, *yep*. Yes or no will do nicely."

"Very well, m'lady. Yes. I heard you. Stories everywhere. Too many teach fear."

"Hmm." She seemed surprised that I'd actually been listening. "Right. Well, they teach a number of other things, too. Greed, for one. Lust. Vanity. Name a vice and today's stories teach it."

"Not all of them." I argued, although not too vehemently, because the examples that popped into my head weren't terribly current. "What about *Charlotte's Web* or *Enola Holmes*? And I've seen some Korean dramas that are—"

"Of course, not *all*. The problem is the preponderance of damaging stories." She picked up her staff. "Come along. Let's get going." She trudged ahead on the "trail," which was becoming more and more obscure. "Keep in mind," she said, switching back into teaching mode. "Even silly movies like *Dumb and Dumber* have messages. There's always a moral. It's unavoidable. Our minds need a rest from all that. A chance to sort through all the input—a little silence in which to decide what to believe."

I paused to sip from the camel's hump strapped to my hip. "And why, exactly, do you think *this* is so restful?" I held out my arms to the endless miles of crumbling stone and saw-toothed cliffs.

"The desert purifies. Keep walking."

Yeah, purifies by fire.

I'm a Minnesota girl, Nordic stock, thick blood and pale skin. My winter-loving body temp was rapidly approaching the boiling mark. I flipped my skimpy baseball cap backward to keep the sun off my neck and squinted with envy at Naomi. She looked amazingly sweat free.

The slope got steeper, and it baffled me how a woman her age could move with such ease over gullies and table-sized ridges. *Shouldn't she be worried about breaking a hip?*

"Where are we going?" I demanded between ragged, dusty breaths.

"Ah, young padawan, it is not the destination but the

journey that is important." Naomi laughed, a soft self-conscious giggle at her own joke. Who knew she was a *Star Wars* fan? Not only that, it was the first time I'd ever heard her attempt humor.

I chuckled, not because her quip was funny, but because it was so weird to see her try to make a joke. "You can't distract me with your *little ploys*," I countered. "Fess up, oh mighty Queen of the Desert. Where are we going?"

The heat must have been getting to her, because she didn't usually laugh at my smart-mouth remarks, and this time she did. "Well, since you insist on spoiling the surprise—we're going to a hidden spring."

"Water?" I glanced around at the sparse clumps of dried grass. "Out here?" Heat shimmered up from the reddish cliffs in the distance. "If you wanted to see some water, why didn't we drive up to those forests to the east? I saw miles and miles of pine trees coming down the mountain. It would be so much cooler and—"

"Because!" She stopped, thrust her royal staff into the ground, and rested both hands atop the gnarl that formed the handle. "This place is the perfect metaphor for life. Yes, we could've gone to the White Mountains or Flagstaff and hiked through nice cushy pine forests. You'd expect a babbling brook there, wouldn't you?" She stepped out of the way of a procession of black ants crossing her path. "Here, we must trek through thorns, dust, and miles of jagged rocks. When we finally come to a tiny grotto hidden among those cliffs, it will be completely unexpected."

She had me there.

"Think of how happy you'll be to find shade and a trickle of cool water whispering down those dark stone walls," she said, pointing her staff at the cliffs in the distance. "In that moment, you will think it's the most beautiful thing in all the world."

I pictured a shadowy crevice in those distant cliffs. I imagined exposed roots straining to catch a droplet of the precious moisture seeping out of the rock wall, dripping into this ravenous heat, granting life before being consumed into vapor. Then I remembered Deborah's source of joy, and whispered, "Small things."

"Precisely!" She nodded and turned to climb the next rise. Rocks gave way under her foot, and she slipped onto her side. I rushed to help her.

"I'm fine," she insisted, brushing sand off her white capris. She'd scraped her arm. "It's nothing." She briskly wiped away the droplets of blood.

I followed Naomi up the sandstone incline and noticed traces of her blood remained on the rough surface, telegraphing her presence to the inhabitants of the desert.

Sharks smell blood from miles away. Out here, where moisture and food are a premium, who knows how far predators might come...

Stop!

Those were silly thoughts. I shivered, but it didn't dispel the unwarranted paranoia crackling up my spine.

"Okay." I cleared my throat to get her attention. "The

desert is a metaphor. I get it. Maybe we should go home now."

She ignored me.

Since we weren't turning around, I tried a different tactic. "Aren't there times when life is more like a lush cool meadow, than it is like *this*?" We walked side by side now, on the stony surface of an ancient lava flow. "So barren and dry?"

"*This* isn't barren." She poked her staff at a tiny scrub oak surviving in a rocky fissure and beside it a horned lizard scampered away. "That's the point."

"Yeah, but *sometimes* life is full of joy—like a nice shady park. And frankly, a whole lot safer than this place."

"Would you really want a life like that? Soft, safe, and secure?"

Yea-ah!

Safety ranked pretty high on my wish list.

When I hesitated to answer, she harumphed at me and marched forward. "Perhaps you haven't noticed—" Naomi thumped her stick against the fractured rock beneath our feet. "We live in a dangerous world. And it's getting more dangerous every day. Do you really believe the objective of our existence is to be safe? To live pain free? No troubles?" She glanced sideways at me, that imperious eyebrow of hers at full mast. "Look around you, Sophie! The world wasn't designed to be safe."

I frowned at all the sharp, rugged, pointy, poisonous proof. *Why did God make it so hostile?* I didn't like it, yet in the pit of my stomach I knew she was right. I opened a defense anyway. "It doesn't make sense. I mean, obviously, we're also designed to *want* safety?"

Want it badly.

"Oh yes." She patted my shoulder. "Women especially tend to want guarantees. In reality, life is meant to be a daring adventure. When trouble slams into us—that's the real test of who we are. That's when we 'safety-craving' humans must set our fragile mortality aside and behave with extraordinary courage." She grinned. "Or not."

I needed to sit down and think, only Naomi kept walking.

She swung that stupid staff at the sky as if pointing at something. "How does it make you feel when you hear about a thirteen-year-old girl donating her kidney to save her little sister? Or when a soldier throws himself on a grenade to protect the rest of his platoon?"

"I don't know exactly . . . proud maybe? Amazed." I thought harder. "Sometimes, those kinds of stories make me cry. I feel overwhelmed in a good way that someone would do something so selfless."

"Exactly." Naomi stopped and studied the toes of her boots for a moment. "Most of the time our courageous moments don't make the nightly news or even Twitter. Thousands of those moments happen every day in the privacy of quiet lonely rooms. A little boy lies in his hospital bed after cancer has stripped his frail body of the ability to fight even a simple cold. Each click of the oxygen tank signals another painful rasping breath. He struggles, fighting not to cry—just so his mother won't be sad." Naomi glanced off into the distance. "And his mother..." Her voice broke off for a moment. "Her son's brave face twists her heart into a tight throbbing knot. She wants to scream for him. Howl her fear. Collapse in grief."

Naomi's arms closed around her as if chilled under the blazing sun. "She doesn't, though. Instead, she stays and sits quietly beside him, smiling for his sake, trying to read his favorite book to him without choking on every word." Naomi hid under the shadow of her big hat, a furtive tear catching a glimmer of sunlight as it slid from her cheek.

"Your son." I whispered.

She nodded, clamping her lips together and shaking her head to escape the remembered agony. We continued uphill, Naomi's steps less spry than before—shuffling against stones instead of stepping over them. "He was so brave," she whispered. "So noble. Only seven years old."

The trail disappeared completely. Talus from the eroding cliffs crunched under our feet, while grief seared us on the inside.

"Nobility of character," she paused and leaned heavily on her stick. "It makes our lives beautiful. The alternative is..." Her lips pressed tight as she searched for the right word.

"Ugly," I said.

"Yes."

Sun beat on my shoulders, french-frying them, but at that moment there was nowhere else I would rather be. I felt the universe unlocking its dimensions like a magic cube. *Beauty. Purpose.* The matrix dissolved, and I glimpsed it all. Angels watching us intently. Demons playing their part. Fear no longer existed as the enemy, but as a device to expose man's soul.

Naomi touched my shoulder, yanking me from my vision. "You're too young to remember, but after 9/11 for days and days afterward people seemed awakened to what was truly important in life. No one cared about political differences or skin color or any of that. I remember going to the supermarket and seeing a group of junior high cheerleaders standing outside the entrance, holding out firemen's boots, collecting money for the families of the heroes who had died in the Towers. Those normally perky little girls instead of shopping for make-up or clothes felt a fierce determination to do something good for the fallen. We were all broken-hearted together."

Naomi nodded as if she could still see those cheerleaders. "At times like those I believe God weeps, moved by our compassion, touched by our love, rejoicing in our nobility of character. Armies of angels shout in triumph over the heroic spirit of mortals. In those moments, we feel the rush of God's love."

Naomi and I walked on in single-file silence. I lagged behind, lost in remembered nobility.

Purified.

Naomi yelped.

I glanced at her—uncomprehending. The ground ahead seemed to be moving.

She cried out again and jumped back against a broad pillar of granite. Her hat fell off, fluttering to the dirt next to a creosote bush, leaving her white hair matted and sticking out.

Then it all came into focus. The ground wasn't moving. Something gyrated on it. Snakes. Nothing like the brightly banded garter snakes of Minnesota. These blended perfectly with the desert—until they moved. Then they became frightening warrior spears wrapped in diamond plated armor. Their heads—deadly, fanged triangles. Dark slitted eyes filled with eternal night. Eyes, so many eyes, with narrow focused apertures. All of them focused on Naomi.

"Stay back!" she warned. Her words quivered through the air, stabbing me with fear.

I froze, uncertain whether she was shouting at me or the serpents writhing in front of her. Pressing against the granite boulder, she glanced over. "Sophie! Don't move!"

Beside me, I heard dry hollow clicking. Faster now. An angry buzz. I peeked sideways. Slick eyes. A warty heart-shaped arrow. Aimed at me.

"Don't move!" Naomi ordered again, her voice shaking.

I jumped.

I couldn't help it. Basketball muscles took over. No thought. No calculation. I leapt backward! And the snake sprang forward, striking air.

I fought to keep my balance. The rattlesnake regrouped, blocking my path. I edged back, out of striking distance.

Naomi whispered, "Go for help." Blood streamed out of the vampire punctures on her leg. Her eyes bulged wide, darting every which way. Her face had blanched white as dry bones.

"I can't leave you!"

She held remarkably still in front of that horrid army of coiled vipers. Even when she spoke, she barely moved a muscle. "Go get help."

"I'm not leaving you!" The angry snake in front of me rattled another warning.

"Sophie, go! People don't die of snakebites unless they don't get help." She issued each word with clipped eerie control, except it held an unmistakable tremor and her suppressed panic seemed to pulsate through the ground.

"You have a cell phone." She stood very, very, very still. "Get. Away. And. Use. It."

"Left it in the jeep."

She grimaced. I must've moved. My rattler puffed up, stretching taller. Like a Māori dancer, his black-spiked tongue flicked out a warning. We were caught between a rock and, well, a very bad place. Kind of like being trapped between a flimsy jeep door and a cougar.

Yeah, just like that.

And suddenly I knew what to do.

Only this time I knew understood where that kind of power came from. Prayers don't always have words. That one didn't. And the wind of the Holy Spirit instantly filled my being. It lifted my heart with fearlessness and certainty that only comes from above.

"Get back!" I ordered, speaking with a voice that was more Spirit than mine.

The rattler tipped its head sideways, eyeing me warily with one narrowed black oval.

The air was hot and still as death, yet a cooling wind rushed through me. Enveloped in an incredible peace that banished all fear, I commanded, "Go away."

With watchful reluctance, the snake dipped its head, morphed into an S, and zipped away into the dry grass and rocks.

"What are you doing?" Naomi asked through clenched teeth, her frantic pitch an octave higher than before.

"Telling that snake to go away."

"Well stop!" she gasped. "They're moving closer to me."

It was true. The swarm of rattlers were edging away from me and slithering nearer to her. I backed away, giving them space, and tried to approach Naomi by sneaking around the side of the granite outcropping. Except they had her cornered.

"Naomi, you do it." I urged. "Speak to them from the deep place. Follow that cord of light running through you. The one that binds you to God. Let the Spirit flow through you.

For the briefest moment, she forgot the snakes and tilted her gaze to me.

"Focus on that place inside you where God is. And tell the snakes to go."

She turned back to her captors. Their tails rattled with erratic threats. Shallow breaths made Naomi's chest tremble. Her palms were pressed hard against the granite wall pinning her in. Her fingertips dug into the rock, gripping the earth for support.

At last, she exhaled. Her hands relaxed and she straightened to her full height, “Leave.” It wasn’t loud, but the force of that one word rippled through her tormentors. Several of the larger snakes reared back, arching their heads higher. For an instant, I thought they might lash forward and strike.

“You are done here.” Her voice was level, calm, devoid of fear, and yet it seemed to shake the ground. “Go!”

They drew back. With her staff, Naomi etched an arc in the hard earth in front of her. The warriors flattened their scales and backed away, surrendering in reluctant zigzags.

Naomi sank against the granite, watching them go. “So, this is how it’s to be,” she muttered. “Six thousand years...and this is the best you can come up with?”

I got the feeling she wasn’t talking to me or the retreating snakes.

Chapter 23
The Opposite Side of the Universe

Naomi's leg was rapidly turning into a very swollen grisly ham hock.

I squared my shoulders ready to do what must be done. "Sit here." I dusted off a boulder. "Hand me your knife. I'll cut it and suck out the venom."

"They don't do that anymore." Naomi pulled a roll of gauze out of a compartment on her belt.

"A tourniquet? I know for sure those are out."

"Not a tourniquet. A soft pressure bandage." She handed

the gauze to me and flinched as she stuck out her leg. "Wrap above the wound. There. Right below my knee. Not too tight." Pain peppered her voice with a slight tremble. "Don't restrict the blood flow, just slow it down."

I did as she asked and then with a tuft of excess gauze blotted the blood oozing from the fang marks. Her quick intake of breath warned me not to touch the wound.

Naomi draped her arm over my shoulder, and we hobbled down the return path. "We need to move a bit faster," she sounded so unruffled, as if we'd been doing nothing more than playing bridge on Sunday afternoon. "I'm not feeling quite up to par."

She winced with every step. At that pace we'd never get to a hospital in time. "How about I carry you piggyback?"

"Don't be ridiculous." Despite her protest, she surveyed me speculatively. "You can't. We're nearly the same size."

"Not even close. Besides, I was a lifeguard—I'm super strong." I tossed her a cheesy grin and flexed my free arm.

She responded with a scolding sideways glare, but instead of intimidating me Naomi appeared helpless and frighteningly fragile. Too bad we'd left her hat behind. Both of us might've felt better if she had it to hide under.

"It's like this," I threatened. "If you won't ride piggyback, I'll use a fireman's carry on you. You won't like that—it means I'll have to sling you over my shoulders and—"

"I know what it is," she snapped, and gingerly touched her lips. "Are my lips swollen?"

"No."

"They feel funny."

"Funny how?"

"Like I've been to the dentist."

"Okay then, piggyback it is."

Naomi exhaled noisily. "Oh, very well."

I squatted down while she suffered the indignity of climbing onto my back and being carried like a child. Blood dripped steadily from her calf. Her other leg was bleeding too but not as much, maybe it was a scrape. Or another bite? So far she'd stayed amazingly calm, and I didn't want to upset her by asking scary questions. As we rushed down the trail, I hoped she'd stay conscious long enough to keep pointing out which way to go.

The late afternoon sun burned hotter than ever. It baked my insides to powdered ash. Clearly, I wasn't as strong as I had boasted. It didn't matter. No time for any of that. Adrenalin had me darting around stones and obstacles like a scared rabbit. I nearly fell twice going downhill on the talus. Finally, I discovered the rockslide would carry us to the bottom almost like an escalator if I positioned our weight just right. When we hit the hard surface of the lava flow, I took off again.

"Stop running," Naomi ordered. "You'll kill us both."

"I'm not running."

"You are." She cuffed my shouldered for lying. "There's no need. People don't die of snakebites anymore. Less than one percent."

One percent was one too many. I kept going.

"Slow down!"

The ride must've been getting too rough for her, but what was I supposed to do? She needed anti-venom. Every second ticking by decreased her chances of survival. I did a quick calculation of how long it would take to get back to the jeep and to my phone. My chest tightened. No time to think like that. Run!

We hit a drop off. Instead of stopping so Naomi could disembark while we climbed down the small descent, I jumped. We tipped sideways on the landing. I stumbled forward and caught my balance on a low ridge. Unfortunately, I had to let go of one of her legs. Naomi groaned as we slid apart. That was when I heard someone charging up the path.

He rounded the bend at a full gallop and skidded to a halt when he saw us tangled up like a pair of kindergarten gymnasts.

"Ryder," I murmured. "Thank goodness!"

"That's him?" Naomi whispered.

"Yeah."

"Not bad."

I smiled in agreement.

"I vote we let him carry me."

"If you insist." I pretended reluctance. "But just you watch where you put your hands."

She chuckled, and I took that as a good sign.

"I heard you screaming." Ryder stooped over, panting like a steam engine. "What happened?"

Naomi and I exchanged glances. "We didn't scream," I said.

"Earlier." He squinted at Naomi's bloody leg. "I heard you."

"No." I shook my head. "We were trying to be quiet. There were rattlesnakes, LOTS of rattlesnakes. They bit Naomi."

He swore softly. "Diamondbacks?"

"I believe so." Naomi poked oddly at her cheek. I guessed she was testing for numbness.

Ryder didn't wait for introductions. "Don't worry, ma'am." He scooped her up and cradled her to his chest. "We'll get you to the ER right away."

"Thank you." The pinched up wrinkles in Naomi's forehead relaxed a little.

Ryder strode down the trail, shaking his head. "It's weird, Sophie. I'd have sworn I heard you yelling for someone to go away, to leave you alone. I ran because I thought..." He shrugged.

Somehow, he must've heard the "voice." It was the only possible explanation. I trotted to keep pace with his long strides, glad he'd shown up no matter what the reason. "I'm guessing you didn't hear us shouting all the way from Phoenix?"

"Of course not." He smirked at me as if I was a complete ditz. "I followed you."

"How? I didn't see you. Not even on the dirt road."

He made a low grumbly noise in his throat. "The same way I found you in the dust storm." He picked up his pace. "That first night in New Mexico, I put a GPS signal on your jeep."

I caught up, gasping like an asthmatic. "Oh! Well. That explains it." If I sounded slightly miffed, it was because I was. I appreciated him showing up. On the other hand, I wasn't fond of having my privacy invaded. "You two haven't been formally introduced, have you?" Even breathless, I managed a biting tone. "Naomi, meet my stalker, Ryder."

"Not a stalker." His face turned all stony. He managed to

crack it long enough to flash Naomi a quick smile. "Pleased to meet you."

She crinkled up in return. "Sorry about getting blood on your shirt."

He ignored that and asked, "How're you feeling?"

Petite and delicate, she rested in his arms like an elderly pixie. Her mouth curved up with quick courage. "Not my best, thank you."

"Any shortness of breath?"

"No. My leg burns a bit."

A *bit*? Her calf had swollen to double its normal size, and big maroon-colored blisters bulged out. Her leg had to be burning like the fires of Mount Doom.

"Tingly lips." Naomi wiggled her fingers. "A bit prickly everywhere."

He nodded. "Sounds about normal." Regardless of his optimistic appraisal, the muscles in his jaw tensed. "Sophie," he ordered quietly. "There's a cell phone in my right pocket. See if you can get service."

He paused, just long enough for me to grab it out of his jeans pocket. As soon as I had it, he marched off down the slope. I stayed on the hill checking for a signal and punching in 9-1-1. The signal bars wobbled between one and nothing. Every time I tried to dial, the call dropped. I growled in frustration and jogged to Ryder's side. "It's not working," I shouted.

"Keep trying."

I stumbled along behind them turning in different directions searching for a signal, holding the phone higher, and pressing redial. Finally, it rang. I hollered out to reassure Ryder and Naomi, "I got through! They're answering."

"Request a police escort," he shouted back. "Describe the truck. F-150. Kansas plates." He kept on moving.

The operator asked our location. "Superstitions..." I fumbled trying to describe the entrance we'd taken into the park. If only I'd paid better attention. I couldn't ask Ryder and Naomi. They were a good hundred yards ahead and out of earshot. I gave up and impressed the critical facts upon the dispatcher. I explained that Naomi was an elderly woman with multiple snakebites. Static crackled our flimsy connection. I wanted to cry out that "*she's most important woman in the world and her life is at stake here! Do something!*" Except if I did that, the dispatcher would probably write me off as a crank call and hang up. In between bouts of static, the woman remained irritatingly calm, asking more questions, telling me to share our location, and giving me strict instructions not to apply a tourniquet and not to cut and suck the wounds.

"Okay, okay. Just send help."

Ryder and Naomi disappeared from view. I hurried to the top of the next rise and spotted my jeep and Ryder's truck in the distance. "They're almost to the truck. We're gonna make it!" I hollered to my impassive 911 operator. Despite nausea and sweat rolling off my back, I felt like jumping up and down and cheering. "I've got to run and catch up. That means I'll probably lose the signal," I explained. She assured me we weren't far from a hospital, that an officer would rendezvous with us on Highway 88, and that an ambulance was on their way. I clicked the phone off and sprinted for our vehicles.

We loaded Naomi into the Ford and I squeezed beside her. We took off, and Ryder floored it. I kept my arm around Naomi to steady her as we raced across the desert, scraping bottom, bouncing like jackrabbits over the bumpy road.

"Are you alright?" Ryder asked. He was talking to Naomi, but his eyes landed on me for a half second.

I nodded and leaned toward the vent blowing beautiful miraculous cool air.

He exhaled softly.

"I'll be fine, dear." Naomi's hand shook as she tried to sip water from her canteen. The simple act seemed to drain her strength.

We had to do something quick. "Do you have any ice in your cooler?" I gestured at the orange container behind the seat. "We could use it to slow the poison down. Reduce swelling."

Ryder kept his eyes on the rugged terrain. "The manuals say not to do that."

"Manuals?"

"Yeah."

I tipped my head quizzically. "*What* manuals?"

He sighed. His jaw muscles bunched and un-bunched before answering at a barely audible level. "Boy Scout manuals."

I couldn't repress a loud, unladylike, half-gasp, half-laugh. "My stalker is a Boy Scout? Go figure. The universe conspires against me, and I don't even rate a bona fide bad boy?"

"Obviously you never went to scout camp." He pressed harder on the gas, swerving to miss a boulder, sending a wave of dirt arcing behind us. "Plenty of scouts are bad boys."

Naomi patted his leg. "I'm certain you're sufficiently bad, young man."

"Yeah." I tried not to sputter. "Why don't you tell us just how bad you are, Ryder? Start with why you stuck a tracking signal on my jeep."

He glanced over, and I swore I've never seen anyone look so penitent. "I had to. You know why."

"It's perfectly understandable," Naomi crooned, patting him again. "You can tell her about him now."

At least the conversation was diverting Naomi's attention, which was good. Not so good that it also diverted Ryder's. He gawked at her in amazement.

"Careful!" I pointed. *Too late.* He mowed down a sprawling Prickly Pear. We bounced over it and sent cactus guts flying every which way. No telling what one of those thorns might do to his tires.

Ryder fixed his eyes back on the almost nonexistent road. "Him? You know the guy in the suit?"

"Oh yes. I know him. Well, to be fair, I don't know what sort of suit he's wearing these days." Naomi chuckled. I sighed with relief at the sound. Her quick wit meant she could still think clearly. Except I wished she didn't look so scary pale.

Ryder shook his head. "Who is he?"

"I'll be happy to tell you. But first, tell me what you know about him."

His shoulders tensed and finally he drew a deep breath and started in. "Thing is, I don't know much at all. The guy comes into my office. Stark white hair. Military cut. You know, Rutger Hauer in general-mode. Only he's wearing a dark gray suit that looked like it was handmade in Italy and flashed a government badge with acronyms I'd never even heard of before. Then, he flipped open a laptop like nothing you've ever seen before. Wafer thin. A hologram 3-D screen. Lightning fast. He pulled up a dossier on Sophie, photos, name, weight, place of birth—"

"Wait, what?" I gasped. "He told you my weight?" I cringed and sat back trying to make myself look thinner.

"Yeah." Ryder acted like that horrid breach of my privacy was no big deal. "Then he explains that she's some sort of key component to the future. Without her, he says, everything will crash and burn. He showed me all kinds of gruesome stuff that's going to happen if she doesn't..." Ryder rubbed the side of his face like he was trying to get clean by smearing in the dust. "That video." He shook his head and grimaced. "I still can't forget it."

"Tell Naomi about the video." I couldn't keep the jitters out of my voice. "This guy had footage from the future."

"Yeah, some kind of live feed from a different time zone—as in *a different a year*." Ryder gunned the truck up a ravine. "Impossible, I know. I don't expect you to believe me."

"I believe you," Naomi winced as the truck angled upward, but she gritted her teeth and explained, "It's a sad irony that he always uses truth to his advantage, twists it for his nefarious purposes."

Ryder and I both turned to Naomi. "Nefarious?" I asked. "That means bad, right? And you didn't warn me?"

Naomi ignored my high-pitched worried tone. She leaned

her head back and closed her eyes. "Sophie, have you told Ryder about llama girl?"

"Llama girl?" Ryder muttered, as if both of his passengers had suddenly broken out in purple polka-dots. "You mentioned llamas before, but what's a llama girl?"

I shrugged and stared out the side window avoiding both of their scrutiny. The road had gotten more substantial.

"That's what I thought," Naomi chided me. "Haven't I taught you about balance?"

Of course, she had. Everyone had been harping at me about balance, even the short-order cook at Esperanza's—but I still didn't see what that had to do with Ryder's super-spy from the world beyond. I sank my chin deeper into my hand and frowned at my faint reflection in the window.

"Don't you see?" she continued to lecture as if I was a kid who'd failed a simple math test. "Llama-girl has an opponent," she trailed off wearily and leaned her head back. "An opposite."

I sat up straight. "So, this guy from the future represents..."

"Right!" Her eyes lit up. "The opposite of peace, balance, and wisdom."

"War?" I shivered.

"Not war alone. Chaos, certainly. Confusion, always. And destruction. Misery. Corruption. He's a front-row fan of the world having knowledge without wisdom."

"What!" Ryder stiffened and thumped the steering wheel. "You mean like the devil or something? No! No, that can't be it. That would mean, what I'm doing is..." He glanced at me, anguish twisting his features, then he shook his head and stared at the terrain ahead. "That's impossible. This guy was clean-cut, organized, intense. There was nothing chaotic about him. He wanted me to save the world from those things."

"Is that what he told you?" Even weak as she was, Naomi used her *laying-a-trap* teaching voice.

"He—" Ryder paused, and for a second or two I doubted he was seeing the road. "Not exactly. He just showed me what would happen if Sophie didn't do what she was meant to do."

"And what did he want you to do?"

"Protect her. Make sure she—"

"Protect her? Clever of him." Naomi rubbed her thigh.as if trying to sooth the burning that must be searing her veins. "Did he happen to mention against what?" she asked quietly. "Or why he was sending you?"

"Exactly what I asked," I interrupted. "This guy from the future comes and why didn't he send a Blackhawk full of Navy SEALs? Or the CIA? Or Robocop for pity's sake!"

"Sophie," Naomi rested her hand on my arm. "Let the man think, dear."

"It's a good question." Ryder rubbed the back of his neck and then gripped the steering wheel with both hands. "I did ask him, why me?"

"And?" I leaned forward, smiling, gently trying to employ some of that persuasive tone Naomi had tried to teach me.

Naomi leaned her head back again, saying nothing.

Ryder shrugged as if the answer wasn't all that important. More telling was the fact that he refused to even peek in my direction. "According to the guy..."

I did my best to continue smiling semi-persuasively at Ryder and to keep my foot from tapping a hole in the floorboards.

He glanced at me guiltily. "It's like this, Sophie..."

"Like...?" I kept my tone pleasant and non-confrontive.

"Well," he squirmed, his angular cheeks blushing as red as a schoolgirl's. "According to the guy with the laptop, I possess a distinct set of attributes to which you are likely to respond positively."

Naomi started to chuckle but stopped short, grimacing with what must have been a blast of pain.

"Don't laugh." Ryder glanced at her, worry pinching his brow. "It speeds up your heart."

With a soft moan Naomi hunched forward, took a breath, and turned to me. "Distraction, remember? But, Sophie, what others intend for evil, God can use for good. It's quite possible Ryder might be ideal for you and not merely a distraction."

I put my arm around her again and eased her back against the seat. It was my turn to blush. *Lucky me*, I had a matchmaker from hell. Though to be perfectly honest, Mr. Chaos had done a darned good job. Ryder had definitely distracted me.

We skidded from the dirt road onto the glorious paved highway. Shortly thereafter, we were met with the welcome wail of sirens. Not only a police escort, but also an ambulance met us.

The ambulance ride to the hospital lives in my memory as a noisy blur, rattling gurney, wheezing BP cuff, IV lines, and questions about my relationship to the patient, to which Naomi volunteered, "She's my sister." I thought it odd that she didn't call me her daughter. In the space of a few short days, she'd become a mother to me in so many ways.

Since I was family, they let me ride with her. Naomi looked totally different from the day we'd met. No longer the poised white-haired movie star lounging beside a pool, she was just a woman. A woman holding onto the thin cord of life that bound her to those she loved, to those she had nurtured. Strong and yet also helpless, just like the rest of us, her sisters.

Sisters. Yes, I could see it then. The two of us were born for the same purpose. Ultimately, of the same mother.

Sirens continued to scream, a whirling nauseating shriek—amidst all that skull-piercing noise. There was no way to explain the silence I felt. We felt. I held Naomi's hand until they rolled her into the ER, and I hurried in their wake.

Hospital nurses wear special shoes that rush without noise. They carry needles that poke without warning and remove blood without worrying that most of the precious supply has already dripped out.

They are a colony of benevolent ants.

I sat beside Naomi's elevated bed waiting for the ants to scurry off. They gave her a tetanus shot, then two more injections to see if she was allergic to antivenom, wired her chest to a heart monitor, hung a bag of antibiotics, a bag of blood, and finally—finally!—they administered the first vial of antivenom into the IV line.

We all watched as it dripped in. Holding our breath. Even the ants stopped bustling. Blue-clad interns and lab-coated physicians stared at the old school-style clock on the wall. Waiting. Counting. The second hand ticked with altered slowness.

One minute.

Two.

The intern checked the numbers on the machine beside her bed. Three minutes. "Blood pressure is low, but she's not rejecting the serum." The doctor jotted notes on his clipboard and spoke quietly to the nurse. "It may take several bags of antivenom." Just then the speaker in the ER called a code blue, and he and the nurses rushed away.

Naomi had not rejected the serum.

This is good!

I remembered to breathe. That meant she was going to make it, didn't it? Except she looked way too pale, and her legs were still grotesquely swollen. When the intern stepped out and we were finally alone for a half a second, I reached for Naomi's hand and asked softly, "They've notified Ashley. She'll get here as soon as she can. I could go meet her in the lobby and bring her straight back."

"No. Stay." She smiled weakly. "I've had years with her. Only moments with you."

"But we'll have more moments." I argued too loud. "Lots more. The anti-venom is working. You're going to be fine."

She looked at me with that expression, the one that said, *Nonsense. You know the truth.*

My breath caught. I winced as if I'd been snake bit. My stomach dropped out like we'd just driven over a cliff.

"No." I choked, my pulse crashing against my skull.

She looked at me placidly. Her head moved, almost infinitesimally, from side to side.

"No," I moaned. "Naomi, you can't." I pleaded. I hated the truth throbbing through me, drumming against my temples. "Please. This can't be it."

My protests only made it more real.

On the opposite side of the bed, her palm lay open unresisting. From somewhere came the annoying sound of soft bleating, and an animal-like hum.

No, no, not here.

Not now.

That furry-necked llama poked her head through the drapery surrounding Naomi's bed. She trotted in and nuzzled her aristocratic nose against Naomi's cheek. She pressed up against the mattress and Naomi caught some of the llama's white dreadlocks in her palm. Her fingers twitched and curled weakly around the llama's hair. The big animal moaned again, a soft sound like the plaintive mew of a kitten.

Llama girl stood beside me. I gripped her cloak in my fist and begged. "Not yet. Don't let her go yet. Please."

Llama girl patted my shoulder.

"Not yet," I said with more force.

"Sophie." Naomi's voice wafted over me in a faraway whisper. "No regrets."

"It can't be time." My words quivered.

"It is." She whispered hoarsely. "Your time."

No! *I'm not ready!*

I wanted to beg her to stay, but my throat constricted into a useless lump.

Naomi looked so shadowed and gray, but then her face suddenly brightened. "Ah, there you are..." She murmured with fondness, a faraway look glazing her eyes. I supposed she must have been seeing her dead husband or her little boy.

"Wait." I choked, trying to call her back. "Don't go. I don't know what to do. I can't do this without you."

Llama girl placed a restraining hand on my shoulder. "You are not alone."

I looked up from Naomi's ashen face and thought I must be having another vision. Then I realized, there in the twilight between life and death, I was finally seeing reality.

I wasn't alone.

The room was crowded, overflowing with women. No vague white shadows, these. Each of them shimmered with power and had far more substance than the brick walls of the ER. What was more, I knew them—recognized each one as if we had known and loved each other forever. Closest to the bed stood Naomi's grandmother. And there was Deborah, Esther, and Elizabeth. Hundreds of others, a massive, joyous crowd that extended far beyond the hospital walls.

Naomi rose up out of the bed, unfettered by I.V. tubes and wires, and walked into the open arms of her sisters.

Our sisters.

"Never alone," Llama girl murmured and disappeared.

The machine beside Naomi's bed set off an ear-splitting alarm. Hospital staff rushed in, unknowingly crossing paths with Wise Women from long forgotten centuries.

Human hands grasped my shoulders and guided me out of the room and into the waiting area. Ryder looked up from where he sat, head in hands, and rushed to me.

I leaned my forehead against his blood-streaked t-shirt. "She's gone." I whispered.

He wrapped his arms around me.

Ever so softly I added, "But not far."

Epilogue
A New Wise Woman

I swim in the sanctity of a warm dark cave.

Muscles stronger than a man's arm shove me out of the dark waters of my cocoon, squeezing my head until I am afraid it will press all of my mother's experiences out of my memory. I cling to them, clawing at my slippery world, fighting to hold on. I cannot lose the stories of my grandmothers and my mother. Without them, how will I remember my place in eternity? How would I face the uncertainties ahead? I'm not sure I even exist without these histories that are wound so tightly around my galloping heart.

My mother screams.

Or is that me?

The sound curdles my courage. I shrink back to the place

of gray comfort. Solitude. Although it's cramped, I'll stay here and hide from the terrifying force threatening to crush me.

More screaming.

My mother's womb collapses, tightening around me. Life-waters slip through the too-narrow opening, flowing around my mouth, gushing past my nose, escaping. There is no going back. Only forward.

As the new world pulls on me, all I have left is a slender tether to my mother. One thin cord connects me to the everlasting. Oh, why had I yearned for change? It hurts. Pressure on my head blots out everything. Only pain remains, scorching new pathways on my cortex.

We scream.

Mine is silent, pure fear. Even in the suffocating grip of this endless birth canal, my body quakes as the noiseless shriek jolts through me. Placid dreams are erased.

Suddenly there is light.

Suction tubes shoved into my mouth. Something burns my throat. Air. My first breath. Or is it?

Am I the mother? Or the child?

We do not know.

And it no longer matters.

I am born.

There are days we never forget.
Days that change the course of our lives forever.
Sometimes they feel like joy,
other times like muddy terror.

Days pass,
the sun polishes them
Against the tender cloth of our souls.
Treasures hidden in the folds our heart.

Today, I kiss my baby's wrinkled brow as the nurse places her on my chest. Touching my lips against her forehead, breathing in her newness, I hear the tinkling bell atop llama girl's hat. Out of the corner of my eye, I see her tilt her head and smile as she slips quietly out of our delivery room.

In the hallway stands another figure, surprisingly familiar, Ryder's Agent of Destruction, the man in the slick gray suit. I realize then that I've seen that guy before, sulking in shadows, staring out through other faces, watching from corners with his slitted snake eyes, always on the hunt for a chance to steal hope.

The llama growls at him, a low throaty rumble and stomps a threatening two-toed hoof in his direction. One of the geese honks and flaps at him.

Mr. Destruction doesn't even flinch. He smirks at their ineffectual gesture.

Llama girl restrains her protective little flock with a gentle touch of her hand. She and her opponent exchange curt nods and head in opposite directions.

He disappears through a slippery gray mirror, no doubt off to get his next havoc-wreaking assignment from his boss, because this guy can't be more than a high-ranking underling, a senior provocateur of rack and ruin. Not Mr. Evil himself. Just as my beloved llama girl is merely a servant of the one true

Shepherd.

Llama girl, with her mangy herd in tow, climbs a grassy sunlit knoll dotted with blue asters and lupine. Most of the llamas gallop up ahead of her, nudging each other playfully. The tallest one strides with dignity and stays close to the shepherdess's side, while the geese waddle happily behind. The hill vanishes in a shimmering haze, replaced by bustling nurses, hospital intercoms, and interns checking the clock.

It's true, I do sometimes see a few unusual things, but in the end I'm just an ordinary woman. If you search for me, you won't find me sitting in the desert under a palm tree or meditating in a Himalayan monastery. You'll find me next door or down the street. You'll know me. I'm your sister, your friend, and like Deborah I no longer walk in fear.

By now, you must surely realize that I married my distraction. Except Team Evil underestimated how much God loves Ryder, and they seriously overlooked how much this guy cares about goodness and truth. Instead of a distraction, he has proved to be the perfect companion on this journey. *Love.*

Ryder stands beside me now, holding my hand, touching our daughter's puffy bruised face, telling us both how beautiful we are. And, although my hair strings down in sweat-soaked strands, we foolishly believe him. I'm fairly certain beauty is measured differently in moments like these.

Are you wondering if wisdom will remain on the earth?

Do you look around you and see trouble rising faster than floodwaters and wisdom fading like a lost dream? Balance seems to be tipping near the breaking point. Until the One who makes all things new returns, you might wonder how wisdom will survive this turmoil?

Our time grows short, and knowing my weaknesses, knowing how easily I get pulled in by distractions, I wrote all these things down for you. For me. For all of us. The question is, will the daughters of Eve read stories to their children—stories that make them wise? Will they tell them of God's astonishing love for us?

Will you whisper in your daughter's ear the truth about who she is?

Sometimes, it's the simple things we do that change the world.

36 Years in the Making

My dear Reader,

Thank you for bravely following me into a completely different kind of story!

I hope *The Last Wise Woman* brought you encouragement, joy, and the assurance that women hold a valued and sacred position with God.

The Last Wise Woman began its journey in 1986 with *Painbeast*, the short story mentioned in Chapter 15. *Painbeast* is an illustrated short story I plan to make available for anyone who bought *The Last Wise Woman*. Please email me if you would like a copy of it, and as soon as it is available I'll send you a link.

In 1998 I wrote the first full draft of *Wise Woman*. I felt hesitant about sharing these sacred concepts surrounding the Holy Spirit with the general population. And because this book was so different from what I usually write, I sent the manuscript to my agent for her opinion. I also contacted a prominent book reviewer to see if she would be willing to give me her thoughts.

The reviewer reluctantly agreed but said she'd only look at the first three chapters. I sent her the whole thing anyway.

My agent called to say she hated it. "I don't like philosophy in my fiction." I was crushed!

To my surprise, the book reviewer called and said, "I read your whole book! Couldn't put it down. When I finished reading early this morning, I sat in my garden holding the manuscript on my lap and wept. It changed my life."

These extreme responses startled me. Uncertain how to proceed, I asked God what to do. The answer I received was, "Nothing yet."

Nothing? I ached to share these ideas with my readers and other women. Even so, I trusted God and waited. Twenty-four years passed. I wrote more books, acquired a new agent, and contracted with a major publisher for the Stranje House novels. Then, on April 5, 2022, while working on *Sanctuary for Seers*, the fifth Stranje House novel, I felt God tap me on the shoulder. "Time has come to publish Wise Woman." So, I went to work updating the now 24-year-old manuscript.

I realize *The Last Wise Woman* is controversial. Beta readers' reactions have been intense and polarized. They seem to hate it or love it. No matter your reaction, my deepest desire is that *The Last Wise Woman* will be a blessing to you and that your life will be filled with love and peace. Like Deborah, may you find joy in the small moments.

If you enjoyed this book, please lend it to others.

All my best,

Kathleen Baldwin

PS: To explore these ideas further, I'm creating a companion journal/devotional for you. It will include references and topics for discussion. *The Wisdom Keeper's Daily Inspirational Journal* will be available soon at all booksellers.

Readers' discussion guides, videos, blogs, and other curiosities are available for you at:
KathleenBaldwin.com

While you're there, join Kathleen's Tea Time Newsletter!

New subscribers receive a gift eBook in the welcome note. In addition, you'll get exclusive short stories, insider info, sneak peeks, contest scoops, free eBooks, and other scrumptious tidbits.

Note: Kathleen's newsletter only comes out a few times a year. Be sure to add her email address to your contacts so you don't miss out. Kathleen@KathleenBaldwin.com

WHAT CRITICS SAY ABOUT THE STRANJE HOUSE NOVELS

"Sign me up for Kathleen Baldwin's *School for Unusual Girls*. It sucked me in from the first few pages and kept me reading until late into the night."

—**Meg Cabot**, #1 NYT-USA *Today* bestselling author

"A *School for Unusual Girls* by Kathleen Baldwin is enticing from the first sentence . . . Baldwin has an ear for period dialogue as she draws us into this world of sharp, smart young ladies who are actually being trained and deployed for the British war effort by the mysterious headmistress, Miss Stranje. It's speculative historical fiction, with a trace of steampunk inventiveness."

— ***New York Times Sunday Book Review***

"I enjoyed this story immensely and I closed my kindle with a satisfied sigh." —**YA *Insider***

"Spellbinding! A *School for Unusual Girls* is a beautifully written tale that will appeal to every girl who has ever felt different . . . a true page-turner!"

-**Lorraine Heath**, NYT-USA *Today* bestselling author

"Baldwin has a winning series here: her characters are intriguing and fully rendered." —***Booklist***

"Refuge for Masterminds moves at a fast pace from the first page and doesn't stop. Although it is written with a young adult audience in mind, it is a fun and enjoyable novel and will also appeal to adult readers." —***Historical Novel Society***

"I am in love with the Stranje House novels. Seriously, in love."

—***Book Briefs***

The Stranje House Novels

"Enticing from the first sentence"–*New York Times Sunday Book Review*

A girl's spy school set amidst Jane Austen's High Society

Printed in Great Britain
by Amazon